X

INDIAN SUMMER

When her husband's affair with artist Francesca Delgado threatens to become headline news, Caroline Fraser rents a cottage on the north-east coast of Yorkshire, which local legend says is haunted by a woman in white. Intent on restoring the cottage to its former glory—despite attempts by the enigmatic owner, Cameron McCauley to prevent her—Caroline regains a sense of purpose and identity. Just as her resentment of McCauley turns more to understanding, her husband Felix reappears, desperate to save their marriage. Caroline must decide whether to rebuild the past, or hold on to her new future.

INDIAN SUMMER

INDIAN SUMMER

by
Louise Brindley

Magna Large Print Books
Long Preston, North Yorkshire,
England.

British Library Cataloguing in Publication Data.

Brindley, Louise
  Indian summer.

  A catalogue record for this book is
  available from the British Library

  ISBN 0-7505-1306-3

First published in Great Britain by Severn House Publishers
Ltd., 1997

Copyright © 1997 by Louise Brindley

Cover illustration © Hancock by arrangement with P.W.A.
International Ltd.

The moral right of the author has been asserted

Published in Large Print 1999 by arrangement with Severn
House Publishers Ltd.

Magna Large Print is an imprint of
Library Magna Books Ltd.
Printed and bound in Great Britain by
T.J. International Ltd., Cornwall, PL28 8RW.

For my friend, Julia Mann,
who made even rainy days
seem sunny.

Part One

Chapter One

From where she was standing, the cottage looked like a miniature Noah's Ark washed up by the sea and stranded on a ledge of rock out of reach of the incoming tide. The path leading down to it was edged with gorse bushes, briars and the ruins of a grey stone wall embedded with clumps of sea-pinks and willowherb. The sea curling in on the sand resembled watered silk in green and blue.

The estate agent had warned her that 'Driftwood' was isolated, and he was right. There was no living person in sight, no sound except the ceaseless wash of the tide coming in on the shore and the crying of the seagulls overhead.

He had done his best to fob her off with a smaller, less isolated cottage near the coble landing and seemed surprised when she told him that solitude was what she wanted.

Entering his office she had given her name, Caroline Fraser, and her London address, saying that she wanted to rent a cottage near the sea for a month, possibly two.

'You've come at the right time,' the agent said. 'We've plenty of accommodation on offer now the season's over.'

Sizing her up as she leafed through the brochures he had given her, she was definitely not an artist, he thought. The painting fraternity who came in droves during the summer were a scruffily dressed lot on the whole, gregarious by nature, cheerfully uninhibited; the men bearded, the women as brown as gypsies, with flyaway hair.

A writer? Possibly, but he doubted it. A successful authoress—and this woman was obviously not short of money—would be more likely to spend the autumn in Italy that a rented cottage in Yorkshire.

Sensing a mystery, he noticed her clothes were well cut, clearly expensive but unimaginative, worn without flair, as if she couldn't care less about style. Or perhaps she had dressed in a hurry?

She would be in her mid-forties, he reckoned; attractive in a faded kind of way, as if she had been ill recently. Slenderness was fashionable, but this woman was painfully thin, and there was a puffiness about her eyes, as if she'd been crying. Her hair, though well cut, lacked lustre. Somehow, she reminded him of a garden sparrow in her lightweight brown skirt and matching cashmere sweater. She wore no jewellery apart from a wedding ring, but her car, parked on the forecourt, was a recently registered Mercedes with personalised number plates.

It seemed decidedly odd that a woman rolling in money had come to a seaside village on the northeast coast of Yorkshire on the off chance of finding rented accommodation. So why was she here? And what had prompted her to choose Driftwood of all places?

Not that the house lacked charm and character, but with the nights beginning to draw in more quickly, she'd be far better off in a cottage near the slipway, with shops, pubs and cafès close at hand. Even so, he could scarcely argue with a woman who knew what she wanted and was prepared to pay two months' rent in advance.

Finding her cheque-book and pen, 'Is anything the matter?' Caroline asked. 'I'm sorry, I didn't catch your name.'

'Rossiter,' he said. 'Reg Rossiter. But please don't make the cheque payable to me personally; to "The McCauley Accommodation Agency" if you don't mind.'

'Thanks, but you haven't answered my question. Is there something wrong with Driftwood? Something you're not telling me?'

'No, of course not. It's just that it is more of a family residence. Rather too big for just one person.'

Caroline smiled faintly, 'I'm in need of space right now, Mr Rossiter.'

Reg wondered if he should tell her about that child, two summers ago, who had run indoors screaming to tell his parents he'd seen a ghost; a woman in white who had been there one minute, gone the next. No, of course not! The kid had probably eaten too many hamburgers and ice-cream cornets. Besides which, if he really had seen a woman in white, she'd probably been a trespasser on a private beach who had hurried towards the breakwater to escape detection.

Breaking into his reverie, Caroline said quietly, handing him the cheque and her credit card, 'Now, may I have the keys, please?'

'The keys? Yes, of course.' Reg turned to the pigeon-holes behind the counter, found what he was looking for and handed them to her; adding pleasantly, 'If you'll hold on just a sec, I'll hang the "Closed" notice on the door; show you the way and lend a hand with your luggage and groceries.'

'That won't be necessary, Mr Rossiter,' Caroline said coolly. 'I am perfectly capable of finding my own way. Besides which, I have only one suitcase, and no groceries.'

14

'No groceries?' Rossiter's eyebrows shot up in surprise. 'But you'll need bread, milk and so on, not to mention tinned stuff, frozen food and the like. As I said before, Driftwood is very isolated. I'm sorry, Mrs Fraser, but no way can you live on fresh air!'

'Of course, you are quite right,' she responded gratefully. 'I'm just a little tired after my journey. Is there a supermarket handy?'

'Yes, there's one just round the corner from here.'

'Thanks, Mr Rossiter, you have been most helpful.'

Tucking the keys into her shoulder-bag, Caroline smiled vaguely and walked out of the office, on her way to the supermarket, Reg presumed. This had been a curious encounter, one he was unlikely to forget in a hurry, to do with the woman herself—a sad and lonely person he suspected, despite her wealth, her veneer of independence. To his credit, he'd done his best to steer her away from Driftwood. Short of telling her the place might be haunted, what more could he have done?

Leaving her belongings in the car, she walked down the cliff path unimpeded feeling curiously drained, numb almost, the way one feels after a bereavement—except that betrayal was, in a sense, worse than the death of a loved one.

She'd suspected her husband and Francesca Delgado were having an affair. The brutal newspaper headline, *'Felix and Francesca in American Love Nest Scandal'* confirmed it.

Escape seemed the only option open to her, and she had taken that option on a tide of anger at odds with her usually compliant nature, before Felix returned from his American trip and the media laid siege to the house.

He had committed minor indiscretions before, to which she had turned a blind eye, but nothing as blatant and spectacular as this, and with the media in full cry, her own privacy and peace of mind shattered beyond repair.

Packing a few belongings, she had left London in the early hours of the morning with no clear idea where she was going, not much caring where to as long as she was well clear of London when Felix came home, jet-lagged and boorish, demanding attention, pretending that nothing untoward had happened in America, refusing to even discuss his affair with Francesca. She knew him so well ...

Well, goodbye to all that, Caroline thought grimly, walking down the cliff path towards Driftwood. This had been a long, fraught day. Now she would remain here, in blessed seclusion, until she had come to terms with the past and decided what to do about the future.

Approaching the cottage, she noticed there was a sea-facing verandah with an octagonal turret room above. Entranced, she saw that the verandah steps led to a narrow path edged with oddly shaped pieces of driftwood, then down to a fan shaped wedge of sand protected by breakwaters and landslides of rock.

Pausing a while, her mind painted pictures of Edwardian children hauling those convoluted driftwood sculptures up the beach to the path—little girls in white needlecord dresses and straw boaters, ribbons streaming behind them as they played with small knickerbockered boys, yelling their delight as the waves creamed about their ankles and they dragged ashore other items of jetsam to add to their collection.

Why the Edwardian image arose, Caroline had no clear idea except that Driftwood, no ordinary seaside cottage, seemed to belong to a bygone era out of step with present day lifestyles.

Entering the house, she found herself in a spacious hall facing a charmingly proportioned staircase, with rooms to right and left and a passage leading to the kitchen quarters.

To her disappointment the passage, stairs and rooms were carpeted with a fibrous matting out of keeping with the character of the cottage. Her dismay deepened when she saw its fireplaces were boarded up and the furniture resembled the contents of a DIY warehouse.

So what had she expected? This, after all, was a holiday home not a five star hotel. Even so, could she bear to live with all those scratch-resistant tables, vinyl-covered dining chairs, vases of artificial flowers, brightly coloured chintz curtains and cottage-suites with wafter-thin cushions?

The kitchen at least retained a touch of individuality in the shape of a built-in dresser, although its shelves displayed the usual clutter of earthenware available in chain stores the length and breadth of the British Isles.

Coming to grips with the situation, Caroline realised that parents with young children would not want the worry of expensive china or carpets spoilt with sand and sea water; that every young mother in her right senses would thank heaven for a fridge-freezer, a washing-machine and a microwave oven. It just seemed a shame that the Edwardian character of Driftwood had been ruined in the modernisation process.

Then something very strange happened. Walking slowly upstairs, her hand resting on the satinwood banister rail, aware of a strange affinity with the house, Caroline sensed that she had been there before, and in that moment of *déjà-vu*, she felt carpet not fibre-matting beneath her feet, saw gilt-framed seascapes on the walls, a polished satinwood table in the hall below, caught the scent of beeswax polish, and heard voices in the kitchen. Then, equally suddenly, the sensation faded. A short-lived illusion to do with tiredness, she thought to herself, and walked slowly to the top of the stairs.

Two sizeable bedrooms and a smaller room furnished with bunk-beds, mobiles, and with brightly patterned wallpaper, opened on to the landing, plus a modernised bathroom with a shower unit. A short flight of stairs led to the turret room, octagonal in shape, with french windows leading to a wooden balcony.

Stepping on to the balcony, Caroline saw spread before her a vast expanse of blue-green water, wave-flecked and dappled with sunlight. Standing there, her hands on the rail, it felt like being on the deck of a sailing ship at anchor, with the sea so close and seagulls wheeling in the blue

19

sky above. She stayed there for some time, weighing up the pros and cons; deciding what to do next. Her mind made up, she returned to the car and drove back to the estate agent's office.

Reg Rossiter looked up from his desk, startled to see her again so soon. Had she seen something to upset her? His heart sank.

'I'm sorry,' she said, 'Driftwood is not for me, I'm afraid.'

Swallowing hard, 'Of course, I understand! It *is* very isolated.'

'No, you don't understand at all, Mr Rossiter. I love the cottage, its situation, everything about it apart from the furniture. The place is totally lacking in comfort and warmth. No way can I envisage spending the next few weeks sitting on wafer-thin cushions, near a one bar electric fire. This is, after all, September, with a few warm days and increasingly chilly nights.' She smiled ruefully. 'I'd feel like Ebenezer Scrooge huddled in a blanket to keep warm.'

'I see.' Relief flooded through Reg like strong wine, making him feel suddenly reckless, otherwise he might have thought twice about saying what he did. 'I know exactly what you mean, and you're absolutely right! Now, let me think.'

Exploring his chin with his hand, he wished he hadn't shaved off his beard. It hadn't amounted to much, but he missed the feel of it. Somehow he'd felt much stronger, far more resolute with it than without it.

'Of course!' The idea came to him in perfect clarity. He said eagerly, 'When Driftwood was modernised five years ago, the old furniture was put into storage. My business partner wanted to hang on to it pro tem. So how would it be if we moved some of it back? If I unboarded the sitting room fireplace and arranged for the delivery of logs, that should take care of the heating problem. Well, what do you think?'

Catching his enthusiasm, 'That sounds marvellous,' Caroline said gratefully, 'if you are sure it wouldn't be too much trouble?'

'Not at all!' Reg liked this woman and wanted to help her. Her frailty and vulnerability had made him feel strangely protective towards her. Picking up the phone, he said, 'I'll ring the repository right away.'

They went in her car. Sam Cooper, the repository owner, was in his office when they arrived.

A small, elderly, somewhat wizened man

21

whose looks belied his strength, he greeted Reg with a smile and a nod of his head saying in a broad Yorkshire accent, 'So my lady 'ere wants to tek a look at the Driftwood furniture? About time someone took notice of it, in my opinion! Good stuff like that left to gather dust! The poor ould lady would hev a fit if she knew!' Picking up a set of keys from his desk, he led the way across an asphalted area to the repository. 'Just a sec,' he said over his shoulder, 'while I switch on the lights. An' you tek care, my lady, it's main dusty in 'ere.'

It was a large building, curiously still, like a graveyard at sunset. In this case a graveyard of unwanted furniture stacked neatly in bays beneath the harsh overhead lighting.

Entering the Driftwood bay, again came that feeling of *déjà-vu* Caroline had experienced so strongly before, as if she had entered a time-warp.

'Take your time, my lady,' Sam Cooper said kindly. 'Choose what you want an' I'll see it's delivered the first thing tomorrow morning.'

Moving forward slowly, she ran her fingers lightly over the surface of a satinwood table; caressed lovingly the faded velvet of a high-backed armchair. Looking about her, she caught the gleam of

22

brass bedsteads and mirrored overmantles, and noticed, amid the wealth of Edwardian furniture, a simply fashioned oak rocking-chair similar to the one that had belonged to Grandma Heritage when she, Caroline, was just a child. She had never forgotten that rocking-chair, or its owner.

There were blue velvet curtains in polythene bags, rolled up rugs and carpets, tea chests of household china, canteens of cutlery, crystal-lustred oil lamps, water-colours, in gilded frames, wardrobes and dressing tables, washstands and whatnots, footstools and firescreens.

Common sense warned her not to take too much, just enough to furnish the drawing room and the turret room. She would close the doors on the other rooms, none of which she would need—apart from the bathroom and kitchen. Above all, she wanted to see the kitchen dresser filled with the kind of china which had once taken pride of place there: gold bordered dinner plates and meat dishes, tureens and side plates, delicately fashioned teacups and saucers.

And when the drawing room fireplace was unboarded, she would need a brass fender and fire-tongs, a log-basket, and an overmantle to replace the cheap print of a green-faced woman.

She went about the task of selection

conscientiously and quietly, knowing instinctively what to choose and what to reject.

Her final choice included the blue velvet armchair and matching curtains, a richly patterned Axminster carpet, a brass fender and fire-tongs, a log basket, two gilt-framed seascapes, a chiffonier and a whatnot for the drawing room, a single brass bedstead, a small dressing table and wardrobe, two Oriental rugs, red velvet curtains and a carved oak chest for the turret room, a chest of household china and a canteen of cutlery for the kitchen, the satinwood table for the hall, and the oak rocking-chair for the verandah.

'Quite sure you've got enough to make yourself comfortable?' Reg enquired anxiously, peering in through the car window when she dropped him off outside his office.

'Perfectly sure, thank you.'

Tugging at his non-existent beard, thinking the sooner he started growing it again, the better, he blurted anxiously, 'And you are quite sure you'll be all right on your own until morning?'

'Yes of course I shall. Why ever not?'

'Well, I haven't explained about the electricity meters,' he said feebly, wondering if he had done the right thing in

24

encouraging his client to stay on at Driftwood. 'They're in the cupboard under the stairs.'

'Most electricity meters are,' she said patiently. 'Now, Mr Rossiter, if you don't mind, it's been a long day and I *am* rather tired.' Physically exhausted, emotionally drained, needing desperately to put this long, fraught day behind her, Caroline nosed the bonnet of the Mercedes away from the pavement.

Too tired to bathe, almost too tired to undress, not even bothering to eat or drink, she went upstairs to the turret room and got into bed.

On the verge of sleep, she heard the lullaby of the sea on the shore, and something else besides—what sounded like the creak of a rocking-chair on the verandah—to and fro, to and fro, to and fro ...

A trick of the wind, perhaps? But there was no wind, and there was no rocking-chair on the verandah.

Chapter Two

Waking early, Caroline felt that she was drifting weightlessly on warm air currents, like a seabird in flight, aware of a soft ebbing and flowing, the wash of the sea on the shore, a sound vaguely familiar and soothing, reminiscent of seaside holidays with her parents a long time ago.

She had slept dreamlessly, like a child after play and, in the first moments of wakefulness had not clearly recalled where she was; the sound of the sea in the distance, the white wood furniture, her clothes in a heap on the floor. It was then that memory came flooding back to her. Memories she had pushed to the back of her mind the day before, and with them the pain, bitterness and anger she'd experienced when she'd known for certain that her husband's affair with Francesca Delgado had reached the point of no return.

Getting up, she crossed to the french windows, stepped on to the balcony and stood there, the sun warm on her face, looking out to sea, remembering her first meeting with Felix at an acquaintance's flat-warming party, twenty years ago.

He'd been a struggling freelance journalist at the time, untidy, moody, imbued with a restless vitality, undeniably attractive and good looking; something of a social misfit at that gathering of young sophisticates—as she herself had been—a plain, somewhat shy young woman invited, she'd suspected at the time, to even up the numbers. So, apparently, had he. And they had gravitated towards one another as if by mutual consent: two misfits in a roomful of strangers.

He'd confessed that evening to wanting to leave the rat-race of journalism and write books for a living. Asked what kind of books, thrillers, he told her. Nothing too mind bending. He was no Hemingway. He enjoyed detective fiction, and there was money to be made. Lots of money. He'd made no secret of the fact that he wanted the good things in life that money could buy: fast cars, designer clothes, foreign travel. She'd had the feeling he'd get what he wanted, and she was right.

Writing under the pen-name Felix Felton, his brilliantly-crafted crime novels had netted him a fortune in royalties, film and TV contracts. But fame and fortune had emphasised not softened the inherent harshness of his nature, nor had

27

it appeased his appetite for other women. She couldn't help wondering how he would fare in an intense physical relationship with a woman as famous, dominant and ambitious as himself.

Of course she was jealous of Francesca. 'The Madonna of the Paintbrush', as one besotted journalist had dubbed her. Six months ago they had been invited to a preview of the Francesca Delgado exhibition at the Purcell Galleries in Bond Street; one of those prestigious champagne affairs where one rubbed shoulders with the *crème de la crème* of the theatre, literary and art worlds, as well as the inevitable pressgang of TV and newspaper reporters, none of whom Caroline knew—apart from Felix's agent, Alec Porteous, who had waxed lyrical about Francesca.

'Now *that's* what I call a beautiful woman,' he'd said, feasting his eyes on the centre of attention. 'My God, just look at that bone structure, the way she moves. I'll wager there isn't a man in this room who wouldn't want to—'

'Sleep with her, you mean?' Caroline had always disliked Alec intensely.

'Well, yes. To be brutally frank, that's exactly what I meant.'

Francesca *was* beautiful. Tall and slender with a cloud of dark shoulder length hair, smouldering eyes and a tantalising Mona Lisa smile, faintly mocking, rather cruel, whose self-portrait, *'The Shadow of Francesca'* dominated the exhibition.

Painted on a terrace in the sun, against a background of blue Mediterranean sea, the central figure bestrode the canvas like a colossus; proudly arrogant, wearing jodhpurs, riding boots, her breasts and nipples clearly defined against the fabric of a white silk shirt.

The critics had gone mad about the portrait. The brushwork was impeccable, the roses and bougainvillaea trailing the balustrade were so vibrant that one could almost scent their fragrance. As for the central figure, here was a force to be reckoned with, a leading art critic enthused in next morning's reviews: a warning to every woman to beware *'The Shadow of Francesca'*—the potential 'other woman' in all their lives.

Reading that review, Caroline had thrown down the paper in disgust. Obviously the man was more entranced with the artist than her brushwork—as Felix had been.

Despite the oppressive heat of the room, a cold feeling had swept over Caroline when she'd noticed Felix and Francesca standing close together near the buffet, drinking champagne, looking into each other's eyes, apparently oblivious of the cameramen surrounding them, recording for posterity that certain look, certain smile of Francesca's as she gazed into the eyes of another woman's husband.

And that had been the beginning of the affair ...

'Just a minute, I'm coming!' Someone was beating a tattoo on the front door.

God, was that the time? Almost eight o'clock! She had forgotten Sam Cooper's promise to deliver the furniture first thing in the morning. Serve her right! She'd spent far too long on the balcony conjuring up memories of the past—and to what purpose?

If only she hadn't forgotten to pack her toilet bag containing her moisturiser and bits and pieces of makeup in her headlong flight from home yesterday morning, she thought, hurrying downstairs to answer the door.

Two fair haired young giants were on the verandah, smiling broadly, one of whom was holding a rolled up carpet, the other a whatnot.

'I'm Jake Cooper,' said the taller of the two, 'he's my brother Zach. Dad and Reg Rossiter are on their way with the armchair.'

'Please come in!' Warmed by their friendliness, Caroline forgot about her somewhat dishevelled appearance and smiled back at them. 'I'll put the kettle on for a cuppa. Just dump that stuff anywhere for the time being and come through to the kitchen.' Over her shoulder, 'Would you like some toast, by the way?'

'We've just nicely had us breakfasts,' Jake explained. 'Oh, go on then. I dare say we could manage a couple of slices.'

When Sam Cooper, his two sons and Reg Rossiter were seated at the kitchen table, a plan of campaign emerged.

'You two lads,' Sam decreed, 'had best start shifting the stuff the lady won't be wanting from the front parlour an' that there turret room, then we can start laying the carpets.'

'On top of the existing floor covering, you mean?' Jake asked, lavishly buttering his third slice of toast.

'Of course. No way can we rive up that coconut matting. In any case there's no need. It'll keep out the draughts. Then you, Reg, had best start unboarding the fireplace.'

'Where shall we put all the surplus furniture, Pa?' Zach delved into the marmalade.

'Gawd's truth, lad,' Sam exploded, 'put it in the dining room or one of the spare bedrooms. Put it anywhere just as long as the lady don't keep tripping over it every time she turns round!'

'Yes, Pa. Sorry, Pa!'

Sam said, looking worried, 'About that there fireplace. Happen the chimney'll need sweeping first. The last thing the lady needs is a fall of soot.'

'Not to worry,' Reg said cheerfully, unearthing a screwdriver from his anorak pocket, 'Cam had the chimneys swept before the fireplaces were boarded up.'

'That's all right then.' Sam nodded his approval. 'When's he due back, by the way?'

'Cam? Any day now. He didn't say exactly when.'

'Nice for some,' Sam commented drily. 'I could do with a month in Jamaica myself right now, come to think of it.'

Intrigued, 'Who is—Cam?' Caroline asked, clearing away the plates and mugs from the kitchen table as her guests rose to their feet.

'Cameron McCauley's my business partner, the owner of Driftwood,' Reg explained. 'The one who had the furniture put into store until he'd decided what to do with it.'

'I see. And do you think he'll approve of what is being done with it now?'

Reg rubbed his chin ruefully, 'Well, that I can't say for certain. If not, he'll soon get over it. Cam's bark is much worse than his bite!'

'So it was Mr McCauley who modernised Driftwood?' Caroline asked conversationally, thinking that if ever she met the man she'd give him a piece of her mind for his ruination of an Edwardian gem of a house. 'And am I right in thinking he'll eventually sell this furniture and the rest of it to the highest bidder?'

'Well yes and no,' Reg confided uneasily. 'You see he intends to open an antiques shop in due course—when he gets around to it.'

'Does he, indeed?' Anger welled up in Caroline. This Cameron McCauley must be a man totally lacking in sensitivity to have even contemplated separating Driftwood from its original furnishings in favour of modern day junk. And that was putting it mildly. And *why?* For money, of course. *Money,* the root of all evil so far as she was concerned. The reason why Felix had married her in the first place, she knew now—not because he was in love with her, simply because she'd inherited money from her grandmother, and stood to inherit a great deal more when her father died.

As Sam Cooper and his sons heaved and hefted items of furniture down the path from the removal van parked on the

33

clifftop, Caroline experienced a mounting sense of excitement watching the items she had chosen restored to their original setting.

Reg had returned to the office after unboarding the drawing room fireplace, revealing a wealth of hand-painted tiles.

Soon, what she thought of as the DIY junk had been removed to the dining room, the carpet had been laid over the matting, the velvet curtains hung, and the overmantle restored to its rightful place.

Later, she would find ornaments for the overmantle and the whatnot; buy fresh flowers and plants for the windowsills to make the room look lived in.

Sam Cooper said apologetically, 'I hope I ain't done wrong, my lady, but I've taken the liberty of bringing a few extra bits an' pieces you didn't ask for, if that's all right?'

'What—bits and pieces?'

'A few extra occasional tables an' a sofa to match the armchair—so you could lie down near the fire if you felt like it, to read or watch television.'

'How thoughtful of you, but I shan't be watching television, just reading or listening to the radio.'

'Hev I done wrong, then?' Sam's face wrinkled in concern.

'No, Mr Cooper, you haven't. I'll adore

the sofa; the sheer luxury of lying down on it.'

'That's all right then,' he breathed a sigh of relief. 'My word, what a difference eh? The ould lady would be real chuffed to see that fender back in place, her fire-tongs an' that log basket.'

'Forgive my asking, but which old lady do you mean?'

'Danged if I can remember her name.' Sam pushed back his cap to scratch his forehead. 'I dain't remember her me'self, but my grandmother used to clean up for her once a week. She'd scrub the kitchen floor, polish the brass an' silver an' so on. A real nice lady she was by all accounts.'

He went on reflectively, 'Two of 'em, there was, Grandma told me, the one she called "madame" an' her companion who did the cooking. They didn't live here 'cept in the summertime of course. They came here in May and stayed till September, then they'd pack up an' go back to Scarborough for the winter.'

He sighed deeply, 'Funny how things change, ain't it? An' not always for the better, if you ask me. It ain't everyone who has a feeling for the past, but I can see that you have, my lady, an' you don't know the good it's done me to clap eyes on that brass fender an' those fire-tongs—the ones my grandmother used to polish.'

Jake and Zach appeared at that moment, straining beneath the weight of the carved oak chest destined for the turret room. 'This 'ere must be filled with bricks or summat by the feel of it,' Jake complained good-naturedly, 'Talk about a ton weight!'

'Then why in tarnation didn't you empty it first?' Sam demanded.

'We would've done, Pa,' Zach explained, 'only there ain't no key.'

'I'll make some coffee,' Caroline said placatingly, going through to the kitchen where Sam had already deposited the tea chest of household china and other boxes containing cutlery, vases and ornaments.

'By 'eck, Miss,' Jake said admiringly, nursing his coffee mug, 'I wouldn't have believed the difference a few bits and bobs of furniture would make to the place if I hadn't seen it with my own eyes. That turret room looks a treat now, I must say, with the old brass bedstead in place, an' them red velvet curtains. Now there's only that rocking-chair to bring down from the van, then the bedroom will be complete.'

'Oh no,' Caroline said decisively, 'the rocking-chair belongs on the verandah. Don't ask me how I know, I just do, that's all.'

Zach laughed. 'It'll be the "Woman in

36

White" tipping you the wink, I shouldn't wonder.'

Caroline frowned. 'What—Woman in White?'

'Oh, tek no notice of him,' Jake snorted derisively, 'he reads too many James Herbert novels if you ask me!'

Sam said quickly—a shade too quickly perhaps—'About that car of yours, my lady. I'd think twice about leaving it on the clifftop if I were you, things being what they are nowadays, an' that vehicle being what it is.'

'Yes, I had thought about that,' Caroline admitted. 'The truth is I've decided to get rid of it.'

'Get rid of a brand new Mercedes? That's a bit drastic, ain't it?' Jake demurred. 'You mean—sell it?'

'Well, yes. It's far too big for me anyway. I much preferred my old Mini.' How could she explain that the Mercedes had been given to her as a status symbol by an uncaring husband who set great store by material trophies: Omega and Rolex watches, Italian silk shirts, Gucci shoes, Veuve Clicquot champagne, Napoleon brandy, Givenchy aftershave and the rest? She couldn't. Nor had she any intention of doing so. She said brightly, 'I thought I might hire a Mini for the time being. Do you know of a reliable garage?'

Zach said obligingly, 'You could try Pitman's Garage in Whitby. They'd take the Merc off your hands in a flash, though I doubt they're into the car hire game; they're far too posh for that. But if it's a "banger" you're after, I could give you the address of a friend of mine if you like?'

Alone in the kitchen when her guests had departed, Caroline started to unpack the contents of the tea chest. A dinner service, gold bordered, decorated with hand-painted flowers, complete with meat dishes, soup plates and tureens, emerged from the packaging, then a tea set comprising rose-embellished cups, saucers, plates, sugar basin and milk jug, all in need of a good wash in warm soapy water.

In other containers, Caroline discovered a wealth of Goss china ornaments, cut glass vases, a Georgian silver teapot, the canteen of cutlery she had set her heart on, silver sugar tongs, mustard and jam spoons, pearl-handled pastry forks, and two silver napkin rings, all in need of cleaning. With *what* precisely? She had neither washing-up liquid nor silver polish in her store cupboard.

Sitting at the kitchen table, she began making a shopping list. She would need more bread and milk to begin with. The

Cooper brothers, Sam and Reg Rossiter had polished off the sliced loaf and pint of milk she'd bought yesterday. Not that she minded. Their presence, kindness and laughter had made possible her brave new beginning.

Writing rapidly, she added to the list all the things she'd forgotten to bring from London. The list included a radio, plus batteries. She could live without a television set but not without a radio for the music, the plays, the late night shipping forecast.

And what about clothes? This after all was Yorkshire, not London, and the few items of clothing she'd thrown hurriedly into her suitcase the day before yesterday were in no way suitable for beachcombing. Completing the list, she stood up and folded it into her shoulder-bag.

At that moment there came a knock on the front door. 'Just a minute,' she called out, wondering who it could be. The Cooper brothers perhaps, in search of something they'd left behind?

The man on the verandah said quietly, 'I've brought you the logs you ordered. My name is Peter Augustine. Reg Rossiter sent me.'

'Yes, of course. How silly of me, I'd forgotten all about them. I'm Caroline

Fraser, by the way.'

Peter Augustine was a tall young man with black curly hair and a charming smile, his eyes as dark as his skin.

Chapter Three

They discovered a small yard with a fuel store to the rear of the cottage.

Peter Augustine had brought the wood in sacks which he hefted as easily as Jake Cooper had done the rolled up Axminster carpet. 'I've brought you some kindling and old newspapers as well as the logs,' he said simply.

'Thanks very much. How thoughtful of you.' Her curiosity getting the better of her, 'Tell me, Mr Augustine, where are you from?'

'Jamaica. A place called Ocho Rios. And please call me Peter. Everyone else does.'

'So you're a friend of Reg Rossiter?'

'Yes, he and his mother have been very kind to me,' stacking wood as he spoke, 'but it was Cam McCauley who sponsored my visit to England and found me a job.'

'I see.' He had long slender hands, Caroline noticed, and his forearms were seamed with whipcord veins. 'What, if you don't mind my asking, are you doing here?'

'Learning the hotel trade. Working at

41

the New Moon Hotel in Whitby as a waiter; studying economics and catering in my spare time.' Straightening his back, 'If you have a basket for the wood,' he said, 'I'll take some indoors for you; lay the fire for you if you like?' He added charmingly, 'Reg said you'd be glad of a helping hand.'

'Did he indeed? Why? Does he see me as some kind of imbecile incapable of taking care of myself?'

'Lord, ma'am, I'm sure that thought never entered his head!' Peter looked stricken. 'Me and my big mouth! I guess I still have a lot to learn!'

Deeply ashamed of her outburst, 'No, *you* haven't, *I* have. I'm sorry, I'm trying hard to be independent, you see. Not making a very good job of it apparently.'

'That's not for me to say. All I know is, everyone needs a helping hand now and then. I know I do.'

'You're right. The log basket's in the drawing room. I'll show you the way.' Wanting to make amends for her churlishness, 'Perhaps you'll give me a lesson in firelighting? It's something I've never tackled before. Then I'll make some coffee.'

She watched as Peter rolled up and knotted newspapers from the pile of old tabloids he had brought with him and carefully arranged the kindling in a small pyramid. She would need this fire tonight, when the September day had faded and darkness came.

Carrying the coffee, she returned to the drawing room. Peter was sitting on his heels, skilfully arranging a pile of logs for the flames to catch hold of.

Smiling, he rose to his feet when she came into the room, dusting his hands on the seat of his jeans as he did so, and it struck her as odd that he seemed completely at ease in the drawing room, so that she, not he, appeared the stranger; the one lacking in grace and dignity.

Pouring the coffee, she asked him about his home, his family, and listened intently, conjuring up pictures in her mind as he explained that he was the oldest child of Rosa and Salvatore Augustine, that his father worked on a banana plantation and his mother cooked and cleaned for Cameron McCauley during his frequent visits to the island to ensure that the restoration work on his property was proceeding according to plan.

'What—property?' Caroline asked.

'Cam bought an old plantation house about a year ago,' Peter explained, 'very big and rambling and run down, which he's opening as a hotel when the workmen have finished with it. That's why he sponsored my trip to England to learn hotel management. He's putting me in charge of it when I've finished my training.'

'I see. So he doesn't intend living there himself?'

Peter laughed. 'I don't know for sure. Maybe sometime in the future. It's what he calls an investment for his old age.'

'Investment!' Caroline uttered the word sarcastically. Everything she'd heard about Cameron McCauley so far had fed her belief that all he cared about was money. His insensitive modernisation of Driftwood convinced her she was right in that respect. She couldn't help wondering if, in his declining years, he would end up amid a welter of scratch-resistant furniture with a print of a green-faced woman over the mantelpiece. Or were such dubious delights meant for others, not himself?

Finishing his coffee, Peter thanked her and said he'd better be going. 'I'll just clear away these old newspapers first,' he said. Then, frowning slightly, he noticed that she was trembling, staring at the pile of newspapers, ashen-faced. 'What is it?' he asked, 'What's wrong?'

Following her eyes, he saw she was looking at an old Sunday tabloid, a press photograph of a tall woman, wearing dark glasses, presumably caught offguard on her arrival at Heathrow Airport. The headline read: *'Francesca's Mystery Flight to America'*.

There was no getting away from her, Caroline thought bleakly. Wherever she went, whatever she did from now on, the shadow of Francesca would always be there, hovering over her like a dark cloud blotting out the sun. The photograph must have been taken a month ago when she had flown to the US to meet up with Felix in New York. Uttering a low cry of distress, Caroline covered her face with her hands.

Suddenly Peter Augustine's arms were about her, and she was sobbing against his shoulder, deriving comfort from his presence; aware of a strong undercurrent of physical attraction passing between them.

Pulling herself together, withdrawing from his arms, she said hoarsely, 'I'm sorry. Please forgive me. I don't usually behave so badly.'

He said simply, 'There's nothing to forgive.'

'It's just that I ...'

'Please, there's no need to explain. I was here when you needed help. That's all that matters to me: being here for you when you needed someone.'

'Thanks, Peter.'

When he had gone, Caroline, still shaken by the encounter, relived every detail. Until Peter Augustine had held her in his arms, she hadn't realised how much she needed the warm physical presence of a loving man in her life. It had been a long time since anyone had held her so tenderly or cared enough to notice her distress.

But as for the attraction she'd sensed so strongly between them, this had surely been a figment of her imagination? She was old enough to be his mother, for heaven's sake! Even so, his nearness, the feel of his arms about her, the warmth of his body close to hers, had stirred half forgotten memories of what it felt like to be young, in love, and to be loved—the way she had believed herself to be with Felix all those years ago ...

Abruptly shaking herself back to reality, Caroline saw it was almost past time to do her shopping. This was Saturday so the banks would be closed. Her cash in hand was dwindling, but she had her cheque-book and credit card with her. Thankfully, she had her own bank account, her own source of income. Her father had seen to that. She had inherited after his death five years ago, the bulk of his estate—a considerable sum of money, plus the accrued interest of his investments which, on the advice of her business consultant, she had reinvested according to her father's wishes.

Her father, John Heritage, the only man who had ever really loved her. She knew that now.

She had never visited Whitby before. Driving along the coast road Caroline was enchanted by the scenery. When she had settled down in her new environment, she would take pleasure in exploring this area of Yorkshire more fully.

Felix, of course, had preferred more exotic locations—the Greek Islands, Hawaii, Bermuda, Italy, Paris and New York—and had never understood her reluctance to trail in his wake like excess baggage.

Frankly she'd hated his penchant for snapping his fingers at waiters, kicking up a fuss if the food and wine was not to his liking, demanding the best of everything; making his presence felt in the most demeaning way possible. A far cry from the one-time struggling journalist who, devouring steak pie and chips in some seedy pub or other round the corner from Fleet Street, had not even cared that the pie he wolfed was as stale as yesterday's news.

Whitby was crowded with shoppers on this warm September afternoon. Mingling

47

amongs them, Caroline recalled Bram Stoker's *Dracula,* and paused awhile on the bridge over the estuary to catch sight of the ruined abbey, the parish church and the graveyard on the hill overlooking the town on the opposite bank; remembering at the same time that she had Driftwood to look forward to when her shopping spree was over: blue velvet curtains to draw against the darkness when evening came, a fire in the grate, a sofa to lie on, books to read and a play to listen to on Radio Four.

Throwing caution to the wind, she treated herself to moisturising lotion, tinted foundation, two lipsticks, vitamin pills, soap, bath essence, talcum-powder and an expensive bottle of perfume.

In a bookshop she bought two Agatha Christie paperbacks, a couple of other classic novels, and a copy of *The Radio Times.* She also purchased a small portable radio plus batteries; several sweaters, two thigh-length cardigans, a couple of pairs of trousers and a button-through dressing gown with a mandarin collar.

Finally, in the supermarket, she filled her shopping trolley with bread, pasta, cheeses, dusters, silver polish, washing-up liquid, fruit and vegetables—savouring the freedom of choosing for herself, not having to worry about Felix's likes and dislikes or the necessity of discussing the weekend menus with their cook, Mrs Gordon, beforehand; useless in any case if Felix had taken it into his head to invite extra people for Sunday lunch or dinner at the drop of a hat and wanted everything on the menu changed at the last minute.

On her way to the car park, Caroline stopped at a florist's to buy bunches of flame coloured dahlias and yellow and white chrysanthemums.

Driving back to Driftwood, her thoughts centred on her London home—another status symbol so far as she was concerned—in which she had never felt entirely comfortable. It was far too big for one thing, a showpiece more than a home.

In vain she'd begged Felix to settle for a much smaller house, worried as she had been at the time about the initial outlay and the cost of furnishing, maintaining and staffing a ten bedroom house in central London. He was a writer, for heaven's sake, not a Texan oil baron!

He had called her eccentric.

'*Eccentric?* Why? Because I hate the thought of living above our means?'

'The trouble with you, Caroline, is you think small. You always have. A throwback to your upbringing, I imagine. Take your father for example: a comparatively rich man who never made full use of his money, who preferred to squirrel it away against the proverbial rainy day. What a waste!'

'How dare you criticise my father! He at least knew the value of money; that once spent, squandered, thrown away, it is gone forever!'

Quarrels over money had sprung up endlessly between herself and Felix. Her heart had sank, for instance, the day he gave her the Mercedes, not understanding that she had much preferred her old Mini, which Felix had regarded as an affront to his role as a bestselling author.

'Have you no pride, no self-respect?' he'd flung at her, 'Driving round London in that bloody old banger!'

'It happened to suit me, that's all.'

'Really? Well all I can say is you have strange ideas about suitability! Look at your clothes, your *hair!* For Christ's sake, woman, you look and act more like a maiden aunt than the wife of a successful author!'

And that was the nub and kernel of the matter, Caroline thought, gripping the steering wheel tightly. Never had she been the kind of woman he really wanted —exciting, glamorous, desirable. Even on their wedding night she had failed to arouse his ardour. He had simply robbed her of her virginity and fallen asleep afterwards, having done his duty as a bridegroom who had married for money—not love.

Now Francesca Delgado had come between them, and Caroline realised she was powerless to prevent the final break-up of her marriage. And did it really matter any more? Did she really *need* Felix so much that she was prepared, at any price, to cling to the embers of a burnt out marriage?

No. This time there could be no turning a blind eye, no compromise. In the fullness of time, when she had come to terms with this latest blow to her pride and self-respect, she would visit her London solicitor and instruct him to begin divorce proceedings as quickly as possible.

Entering Driftwood with her packages, flowers and plastic carriers, she experienced a sense of homecoming. Caroline felt that the house was pleased to see her, as though a warm presence awaited her arrival; the way she had felt when her mother was alive.

Glancing in the drawing room she saw that the fire Peter had lit for her had not gone out. Tentatively, she fed fresh logs on the glowing embers, taking care to prop them up in a pyramid formation as he had done.

The fire rekindled, she went through to the kitchen to unpack her groceries and place the flowers in a bucket of water. This had been an eventful day—feeding and cosseting the Coopers and Reg Rossiter; standing in the arms of Peter Augustine ... Would they ever meet again? she wondered, going upstairs to unpack the rest of her purchases.

Steppping on to the balcony, she saw that daylight was fading to a translucent twilight with a scattering of stars. She recalled her confrontation with Alec Porteous when she'd gone to his office to find out if the newspaper reports about Felix and Francesca were true, if he had known about the affair all along; and whether Francesca had flown out to America to be with Felix on his promotional tour of the USA.

Porteous had said impatiently, 'I'm Felix's agent, for God's sake, not his keeper! Look, Caroline, these things happen. Women fall for him like a ton of bricks—you know that as well as I do!'

'And that's your answer, is it *These things happen!* What sticks in my throat is that you *allowed* it to happen!'

'Now look here, Caroline—' Porteous blustered.

'No! *You* look! Take a long, hard look! Felix would have listened to you had you warned him about the repercussions, the muck-raking, the scandal involved when the affair was discovered. Or perhaps that's what you wanted! A nice juicy scandal to sell more books!' Turning at the door of his office, 'Frankly, Alec, you disgust me. Hopefully I shall never have the misfortune to set eyes on you again!'

'What do you mean?' Seriously worried, he scarcely recognised the angry woman confronting him as Felix's normally quiet and compliant wife. 'All this will soon blow over when Felix gets back from America. All you have to do is tell the media that he and Francesca met in America with your full knowledge and approval.'

'That might prove difficult,' she'd said grimly. 'You see, Alec, I have no intention of being here when Felix comes home tomorrow.'

'You mean you're leaving him? But you *can't!*'

'Can't I! Watch me!'

Her tears had come later, along with the pain of rejection, and the realisation that her old way of life was finally over and done with. This time there could be no picking up the pieces of a broken marriage glued together despite the lies, deceit and betrayal.

All she wanted now was peace of mind. Time and space in which to draw together the shattered fragments of her life. And, when the time came, she wanted to give Felix his freedom without bitterness or regret; he had married the wrong woman, at the wrong time, for the wrong reasons and now she wanted her life back.

Going downstairs to the kitchen in her new dressing gown with her radio and the paperback novels she'd bought earlier, she set about preparing a simple meal of scrambled eggs on toast, planning the evening ahead; looking forward to drawing the curtains against the night, watching firelight dancing on the walls and ceiling, relaxing on the blue velvet sofa, listening to the Saturday night play on Radio Four; re-reading *Rebecca*.

Too late now to begin washing china and polishing silver, or arranging flowers, she realised. She would derive infinite pleasure from getting up early next morning to perform these tasks; breaking off perhaps to take a walk along the beach to gather driftwood, to sit in the rocking chair on the verandah with a mid-morning mug of coffee, to savour the sound of the sea washing in on the shore and watch the wheeling seabirds overhead.

Keeping an eye on the time, having finished her supper and done the washing-up, on an impulse Caroline picked up the two silver napkin rings on the dresser, thinking that come tomorrow, they'd be clean and shining once more.

Balancing them in the palms of her hands, she wondered idly who had they belonged to? Then, examining them more closely, she noticed that one of the rings was engraved with the initials S.S.J., the other with the initials E.R., and the Prince of Wales' feathers.

Chapter Four

Cameron McCauley arrived home the following week. A spare man, deeply suntanned, he listened with mounting displeasure to Reg Rossiter's account of the Driftwood saga.

'You mean to tell me that you authorised the removal of furniture from Sam Cooper's repository at the request of some silly, hysterical woman you didn't know from Adam? I'm surprised at you, Reg. You should have known better.'

'It wasn't like that,' Reg retaliated. 'It was my idea to make her more comfortable, and she wasn't at all hysterical—'

'In which case,' Cam interrupted, 'you should have pointed her in the direction of the Raven Hall Hotel.'

'Perhaps, but I didn't!' There were times when Reg disliked his business partner intensely. 'I felt sorry for the woman, and what she said made sense to me. No way could she have spent the next few weeks sitting on thin, flimsy cushions in front of a one-bar electric fire.'

'My point precisely,' Cam reminded him acerbically. 'A woman like that would be far better off in a five star hotel with waiters dancing attendance on her!' He added gruffly, 'Sorry, Reg, I'm a bit jet-lagged at the moment. What I need is sleep. But this Mrs What's-her-name will have to stump up the money for the removal. I'm not prepared to pay for it!'

The trouble with Cam, Reg thought after he had gone, was that he'd allowed his judgement of women in general to become clouded by one woman in particular, his ex-wife Gloria. Not that Reg blamed him entirely for his bitterness towards Gloria. It must have come as one hell of a shock when she'd told Cam she was three months pregnant by another man.

In Reg's opinion, Cam's mistake had been marrying the lass in the first place, a girl fifteen years younger than himself, and his 'you should have known better' remark still rankled. A bit like the pot calling the kettle black. Cam should have known better than to marry an empty-headed girl with whom he had nothing in common—who had so obviously married him for his money.

If the old 'love is blind' adage was true, Cam must have turned up at the registrar's office five years ago, blinkered like a dray-horse. The poor devil, Reg thought, scratching his chin which was itching like crazy since he'd started re-growing his beard.

A sudden thought occurred. Reg wondered if Peter Augustine, who had a key to Cam's cottage and often spent his off-duty hours there, knew that Cam was back? Of course not, how could he? Cam had only just arrived. Picking up the phone, Reg rang the New Moon Hotel in Whitby to warn Peter to steer well clear of the cottage until Cam had slept off his jet lag.

'Thanks for the tip-off,' Peter said gratefully.

'You're welcome to pop round to my place,' Reg reminded him. 'Mother will be in this afternoon and she'll be pleased to see you.' Reg, who had never had much luck with the opposite sex, still lived with his mother.

'Yes, thanks again, Reg.' Hanging up the phone, Peter glanced at his watch. He would call on Mrs Rossiter first, he decided, then drive to Driftwood to find out how Caroline Fraser was faring, taking with him a fresh consignment of logs for her drawing room fire.

The thought of seeing her again filled him with a pleasurable feeling of anticipation, and though he scarcely knew her, Peter was suddenly determined to change that as soon as possible.

McCauley slept heavily for three hours, then got up, showered and shaved, and went down to the kitchen to make himself a pot of strong black coffee. Just as well that he preferred it black, he thought wryly. His refrigerator was empty of milk or anything else for that matter. But this was Friday, the supermarkets stayed open till all hours. He would shop later for milk, bread, eggs and so on.

Filled with a kind of restless energy—not unusual in his case—plus a strong feeling of resentment that Reg Rossiter had catered to the whim of some silly woman who obviously knew a fool when she saw one, and in exactly the right frame of mind to give her her marching orders to leave Driftwood first thing Monday morning, Cam pushed to the back of his mind the underlying reason for his dislike of women in general; engendered by the betrayal of one woman in particular.

Not that he was aware of pushing thoughts of his ex-wife to the back of his mind any more. The divorce had happened three years ago. So far as Cam was concerned, that shattering episode in his life was over.

He prided himself that he'd forgotten all about the woman who had caused him so much anguish, so much pain—which proved he had not forgotten at all.

59

Driving to Driftwood, Cam parked his car on the clifftop next to a red Mercedes and a white Volkswagen. Looking down at the beach he saw a man and a woman, deep in conversation, walking by the sea's edge.

What the hell was Peter Augustine doing here? Unaccountably angry, he strode down the cliff path, intending to find out.

'It's Cam,' Peter told Caroline, spotting the approaching figure. 'Reg said he was at the cottage sleeping off his jet lag.'

'Does he make a habit of calling on his tenants?' Caroline asked coolly. 'Perhaps he's come to check up on me. Does he usually look so aggressive?' He reminded her of a strutting rooster; a cocky, ugly little man, she decided, with his determined jaw and reddish brown hair turning grey at the temples.

'Oh, Cam's all right when you get to know him,' Peter assured her. 'He's not as grim as he pretends to be. Come on, let's go and meet him, shall we?'

'You mean we have an alternative?'

'Hi, Cam,' Peter called out to him. 'Did you have a good holiday? Reg told me you were back.' He paused awkwardly, puzzled by his benefactor's lack of response, then, 'I don't think you've met Mrs Fraser?'

Brushing aside the introduction, 'It's Mrs Fraser I came to see on a matter

60

of business,' Cam said coldly. 'I'll speak to you later, Peter, if you'll excuse us.'

'I was just about to leave in any case,' Peter said quietly, deeply hurt by McCauley's dismissive attitude.

'But you haven't had the cup of coffee I promised you,' Caroline reminded him. 'Perhaps Mr McCauley would care to join us?' her voice heavy with sarcasm.

'Some other time perhaps?' Peter suggested.

'Of course. But don't forget our appointment next Wednesday, will you? I'll meet you near the hotel at eleven-thirty as arranged, all right?' Holding out her hand to him, 'Goodbye, Peter, and thanks for coming.'

He smiled gratefully, 'I'll be there.'

When Peter had gone, 'You'd best come indoors, Mr McCauley,' Caroline said calmly, 'unless you prefer to discuss business matters in the open.'

Cam's expression registered his amazement that the woman confronting him was not, as he had imagined, some elderly biddy who had inveigled Reg Rossiter into an invidious situation with floods of tears, but a clear-sighted woman of roughly his own age, who obviously had a mind of her own.

Leading the way to the kitchen, she said, 'I take it you'd prefer cash? If you'll tell me how much I owe you? I shall, of course, require a receipt.'

'Just hold your horses, Mrs Fraser. I haven't told you why I'm here yet.'

'You don't have to, Mr McCauley. I know precisely why you're here. I take it you have brought an itemised account for the removal. I did ask Mr Cooper to send the account to me, by the way. It hasn't arrived yet, so I might just as well settle up with you.'

'I don't care for your attitude,' Cam said grimly.

'Really? I can't say I'm mad about yours either,' she countered coolly, suppressing her anger at the man's arrogance. 'Your treatment of Peter Augustine was nothing short of insulting in my opinion.'

'I was surprised to find him here, that's all. I had no idea that you and he were on such intimate terms with one another.'

'I shall treat that remark with the contempt it deserves,' she said, her anger rising. 'Now, if you don't mind handing me the account, I'll settle up with you before asking you to leave.'

'You seem to forget that this is *my* property, not yours,' Cam said grittily, fast losing patience. 'You had no right whatever to alter the existing character of Driftwood without my permission.'

Facing him squarely, 'The existing

character of Driftwood? That's rich, I must say, coming from someone so greedy, so insensitive as to have ruined an Edwardian cottage in the first place!'

Cam said heatedly, 'If you thought that, why do you imagine I had the furniture put into store?'

'Until you get around to opening that antiques shop Reg Rossiter mentioned, I imagine,' Caroline thrust back at him. 'Think what a killing you'll make then, Mr McCauley, selling the contents of the cottage at a handsome profit! But of course that has been uppermost in your mind all along, hasn't it? The longer it remains in store, the more it will be worth in the long run?'

'My God,' Cam observed, sizing up his opponent, 'you believe in speaking your mind, don't you?'

'If so, it's a lesson newly learned, believe me. Now, about the money—'

'Oh, to hell with the money!' Cam knew when he was beaten. 'You mentioned coffee, I believe?'

The heat had gone out of their quarrel, Caroline realised. She said quietly, 'You can stay for supper, if you like. There's plenty of food and I've taken to eating supper early since I came to Driftwood!'

Glancing about the room, Cam noticed the wealth of gleaming china gracing the

63

dresser, the polished silverware, and felt ashamed of his outburst to Reg earlier that day; the dark thoughts he'd harboured about giving Mrs Fraser her marching orders.

Was he really a greedy, insensitive man? He had never seen himself as such. An astute businessman certainly, with a knack of making money; an eye for a good investment. But money had never been his god. There were other far more important things in life—books, music, good food and wine, intelligent conversation. Love.

The trouble was, he'd never got around to savouring the good things in life. He'd been too busy making money. As for love—he'd fallen in love once. Never again.

Caroline had prepared her supper earlier that afternoon, before Peter Augustine arrived with a fresh consignment of logs.

Shopping in Whitby that morning, she'd treated herself to a whole salmon which she had gently poached with shallots and capers. Lettuce, tomatoes, spring onions, French bread, a block of farmhouse butter and a selection of cheeses from a tucked away delicatessen completed the feast, served with freshly ground coffee, and a bottle of Chardonnay.

Beginning to regret her rash invitation to Cameron McCauley, she wondered what the man was thinking, standing there, arms folded, watching her as she set the table. Putting the finishing touches to the salad and searching in a drawer of the dresser for the two silver napkin rings, she said, 'If you'd like to make yourself useful, Mr McCauley, this bottle of wine needs opening. No need to tell you the whereabouts of the corkscrew and glasses, I imagine, since this *is* your property, not mine.' She smiled briefly, taking the sting from her rebuke.

'Yes, of course,' he mumbled apologetically. 'Sorry, I was miles away! I'm still suffering the effects of jet lag, I imagine.'

Caroline knew the feeling. 'In which case you'd better not open the wine. The sooner you get back to bed, the better. How long since you've eaten, by the way?'

'Far too long,' he said wryly. 'Not since the early hours of this morning. Driving home from Teesside Airport, I stopped off at a transport café for a cup of coffee and a bacon butty.'

'Really?' Caroline regarded him thoughtfully across the supper table. Somehow she'd earmarked him as a three course luncheon at a posh hotel man, not a bacon butty at a transport café individual. Quite frankly, she couldn't make head or tail of him. Nor did she particularly wish to do so. She just wanted rid of him as quickly as possible.

'Sorry about the red and white checked tablecloth, by the way. Not entirely in keeping with the Edwardian character of Driftwood, I know, or His Majesty's napkin ring—but then neither is the fridge, the washing-machine or the microwave oven.'

Frowning, tucking into the salmon, salad and French bread, 'I'm not with you,' he said, swallowing a mouthful of food. 'What napkin ring?'

'The one by your side plate,' Caroline said amusedly, tongue-in-cheek, 'though they were, I imagine, manufactured in bulk around the time of Edward the Seventh's coronation, along with the china mugs and so on.'

'Not this one,' Cam uttered sharply, balancing the ring on the palm of his hand. 'Not *this* one, if any! My God, woman, where did this come from?'

'From Sam Cooper's repository, where else? You mean you didn't know? It was jumbled up with the rest of the silverware, along with the ring engraved with the initials S.S.J.—there, on the table in front of you.'

'S.S.J.,' McCauley mused excitedly, 'those initials ring a bell with me. If I could only remember more clearly!'

'Perhaps you will,' Caroline suggested quietly, 'after a good night's sleep. Shall we have coffee in the drawing room?' She just wanted to be alone again. She'd had more than enough of her frenetic landlord for the time being.

Mistake number two, she thought, as Cam, settling himself in the armchair, returned to the subject of the napkin rings. She should have served coffee in the kitchen then firmly ushered him through the front door. Now, comfortably ensconced, he might well stay put for the next hour or more.

He was saying enthusiastically that he would make it his business to delve into the history of Driftwood to discover the name of the original owner.

'Research is a particular hobby-horse of mine,' he said, holding out his cup for a refill. 'A necessary hobby when it comes to assessing the true value of antique furniture. There are so many fake items on the market nowadays and not just furniture—paintings, copies of Old Masters cleverly aged to resemble the originals. You wouldn't believe the jiggery-pokery prevalent in the art world in this day and age.'

'That's where you're wrong, Mr Mc-Cauley,' Caroline said coolly, 'this world is full of trickery and deceit, in my experience.' Rising to her feet, she added, 'Now, if you don't mind, I am rather tired and in need of an early night.'

'I see,' acerbically, 'so I've outstayed my welcome, is that it?'

'I think you mean my "hospitality," don't you?'

'Oh, I get the picture! No need of enlargement! You really are a superior kind of bitch, aren't you? No holds barred! You took pity on me, fed me. Now you can't wait to see the back of me, am I right?'

'Perfectly right, Mr McCauley,' Caroline smiled faintly, 'except that I didn't take pity on you, why should I? All I did was to invite you to supper. Now I'm inviting you to leave because I wish to be alone. Is that so difficult to understand?'

'Alone to do what?' he demanded roughly.

'To listen to music,' she said quietly, 'by firelight; read a little, perhaps, stand on the verandah for a little look at the stars; to savour the silence. Later to listen to the shipping forecast on Radio Four. I'm not a very sophisticated person, you see? Not at all a—"superior kind of bitch". But you are entitled to your opinion.'

Walking up the cliff path to his car, Cam felt that he had reached a watershed in his life. Why, he was not quite sure, but he had a feeling that damned cottage—and its occupant—had more than a little to do with it.

Entering his own cottage, Cam remembered that he had not been to the supermarket to do his shopping. So what? He had dined royally this evening. Moreover, he had been given food for thought; not that he'd relished that entirely.

Why had Mrs Fraser come to Driftwood? he wondered, and what was the nature of her friendship with Peter Augustine?

Inured to speaking his own mind, he'd been surprised by the woman's scarcely concealed hostility towards him; the way she'd thumped into him his own shortcomings, calling him greedy and insensitive.

The encounter still rankled, and yet there had been moments when he'd glimpsed a less aggressive person behind the cool belligerent facade: a woman who had taken the trouble to wash china and polish silverware; to cook and serve good food. A woman who enjoyed music, books. Silence ...

Deeply aware of the silence, as if the world had ceased suddenly to spin on its axis, troubled in mind and spirit, and having downed the better part of a bottle of duty-free Scotch, Cam McCauley went upstairs to bed.

Switching on his bedside radio, he heard the tune 'Sailing By', heralding the late night shipping forecast. The names 'Irish Sea', 'Dogger', 'Mallin Head', 'Faroes', 'Fair Isle', 'Trafalgar', conjured up vast stretches of gently rocking water beneath a star-washed sky, imparting a strange feeling of comfort, a sense of permanence in an uncertain world.

On the brink of sleep, he wondered if Mrs Fraser was also listening to the shipping forecast.

Switching off her radio, Caroline reflected thoughtfully on her encounter with Cameron McCauley. A difficult man to come to terms with, she surmised: arrogant, self-centred, greedy, insensitive; a touchiness in keeping with the colour of his hair.

And yet, despite her first impression of him, he was not an ugly man. Rugged would be a more fitting description. She wondered at his hostility towards her. Did he really mind so much about the removal of a few items of furniture from Sam Cooper's repository, or could there be a deeper, underlying reason for his harshness?

Certainly he had been displeased by Peter Augustine's presence that afternoon.

Perhaps he regarded the man as his bond-servant without a soul to call his own? If so, he'd better think again. Peter was a free spirit, a proud man, a sensitive soul who had taken badly McCauley's dismissive attitude towards him, which was why she had taken the trouble to remind him of their pre-arranged meeting within McCauley's hearing.

Quite simply, she had decided to drive the Mercedes to Pitman's Garage hopefully to get rid of the damned thing. She had asked Peter to go with her on his day off to help her discover the whereabouts of the second-hand car-dealer Zach Cooper had mentioned, a Mr Ron Collier, who just might have a half-way decent 'banger' for sale.

Drifting to sleep, she failed to hear the monotonous creak of the rocking-chair on the verandah beneath the balcony window.

Chapter Five

On an impulse, the Tuesday before her meeting with Peter Augustine, Caroline drove to the country town of Helmsley where she bought herself a blue cotton dress, high-heeled sandals and a wide-brimmed straw hat. Afterwards, she had lunch at the picturesque Black Swan Hotel overlooking the market square.

How ridiculous, she thought, delving into roast duck and orange sauce, a woman of her age wanting to dress up like a teenager on her first date. Perhaps this Indian summer weather had gone to her head? Possibly it would rain tomorrow? What price then her sandals and straw hat? But she knew somehow that it wouldn't rain.

Wednesday dawned fair and clear. Driving to Whitby in the red Mercedes—anxious to be rid of it—she felt curiously light-hearted and happy at the thought of seeing Peter Augustine again.

And there he was, standing beside his white Volkswagen, awaiting her arrival, wearing cream trousers and a coffee coloured silk shirt, smiling like a sunburst as she drew up at the kerb fronting the New Moon Hotel.

They had planned that Peter would guide her to Pitman's, on the outskirts of town, then drive her to the housing estate where the second-hand car dealer 'hung out'—in Zach Cooper's words. And so Caroline played follow-my-leader to the handsome garage-cum-showroom where, hopefully, she would see the last of the car she loathed, for the time being at any rate.

Reluctant to intrude in her private affairs, Peter elected to wait for her outside in the sunshine of that perfect September day.

There remained an element of mystery about Caroline, he thought. He still had no idea why she had been so upset at their first meeting, and he would never ask why. All he knew was that a deep bond had been forged between them that day. Sensing her loneliness, her vulnerability, he had offered her a shoulder to cry on. Holding her in his arms, he had experienced an unaccountable spark of physical attraction between them—or thought he had.

At least she seemed happy today, and he would do everything in his power to make this a day to remember.

The sun warm on his skin, he watched the traffic streaming downhill to the town centre, caught the glint of sunlight on the showroom windows, and noticed that the leaves of the trees spaced out along the thoroughfare were beginning to change colour from green to gold.

Hearing voices, he turned to see Caroline emerging from the showroom, smiling, shaking hands with a tall, businesslike man in a grey suit.

No need to ask if all had gone well. Obviously a satisfactory deal had been concluded between the pair of them. Moving forward to greet her, he thought how young and attractive she looked in her blue dress and straw hat; far different from the way she had looked that first day at the cottage, pale and strained, her eyes dark with worry—as if she were staring into a void.

She said brightly, 'Well, everything's taken care of. Mr Pitman is keeping the Merc, thank heaven.' Glancing at her watch, 'Now, how about lunch? I don't know about you, but I'm so hungry I could eat fish and chips from a newspaper.'

Peter laughed. 'I think I can do better than that. I know a restaurant overlooking the sea. The owners are friends of mine, and the food's terrific!'

They lunched at a table on a terrace overlooking the estuary of the River Esk, to which they had been conducted personally by Sally Griffiths, who managed the restaurant with her husband and business partner, Bill.

'It's great to see you again, Peter,' she said. 'Bill and I were talking about you the other day, wondering how you were getting along. He'll be sorry to have missed you. He's having a business lunch with our accountant! Accountants, yuck!' She pulled a face, then smiled at Caroline, drawing her into the conversation. 'Are you on holiday?' she asked.

'Yes. I've rented a cottage near Robin Hood's Bay for a month or so,' Caroline told her demurely, understanding the woman's curiosity about her relationship with Peter. Not that she had the least intention of satisfying that curiosity—even if she could. How to describe a relationship which she herself did not understand?

When the waitress came, they ordered sea bass cooked in wine, crusty garlic bread, endive and cucumber salad and sparkling Perrier served in tall glasses with ice and lemon.

Laughingly, Caroline refused dessert. 'Why spoil perfection?' she said lightly, allowing Peter to pay for the meal, not wanting to offend him in any way; glad of his company, his presence in her life—his friendship. Or was this feeling more than friendship?

No, of course not! How could it be? And yet there was this subtle body language between them, impossible to deny or disregard. Why else had she bothered to dress up for him? Why the quiet tide of sympathy and understanding running so strongly between them?

She was being ridiculous, she told herself sharply, on the verge of making a complete fool of herself if she didn't watch out. And yet she couldn't help remembering that day at Driftwood, when, in the circle of his arms she had known, however briefly, how it felt to be in love again.

After lunch, Peter drove her to the address Zach Cooper had given to call on the second-hand car dealer, whose premises comprised an open space, car-cluttered, adjoining a three up, three down pebbledashed council house with a gnome-infested front garden.

Preceding Peter down the path to the front door, steering well clear of the gnomes, Caroline rang the bell, and, 'Mr Collier?' she enquired charmingly on the appearance of an overweight male with shoulder length hair and a nose-ring, wearing jeans, a T-shirt and trainers, 'My name is Caroline Fraser. Zach Cooper gave me your address.'

'Oh yeah? What about it?' he asked

suspiciously. 'If you're one of them "do-gooders" from the Social Services about our Tommy, you're wasting your time! He went off to school as good as gold this morning!'

'Well no, Mr Collier,' Caroline explained, holding her laughter in check. 'Actually, I'd like to buy a second-hand car; if you have anything suitable, that is.'

'You would? Oh, right then! Good! Great! Oh, right then! Come this way, lady. You too, sir! If it's a good second-hand car you're wanting, you've come to the right place! I've some real little beauties here, going for a song. Take a look around. Tell me if there's owt you fancy an' I'll have it tidied up for you in no time at all! I can't say fairer than that, now can I?'

Standing aside, Peter watched as Caroline moved about the car lot, wondering what had possessed her to come to a dump like this in the first place. Then suddenly he knew why. It had to do with her sense of loyalty towards the Cooper family, and Zach in particular who, according to Reg Rossiter, had been especially kind to her on the day of the furniture removal from the repository to Driftwood.

Decent, well-meaning Zach, not quite as 'with it' as his elder brother Jake. He was the reason Caroline would rather waste her money on a clapped-out banger than offend someone who had been kind to her.

So now what was happening? Peter wondered. Caroline was signalling to him to join her; standing beside a little red Mini as if she had been given a gift worth more than gold.

She said huskily, 'Oh, Peter, it's just like my old one. The same year, the same colour. My last car, before the Merc, was a Mini. It nearly broke my heart when I had to part with it.'

'Then why did you? Part with it, I mean.'

'I couldn't very well look a gift horse in the mouth.' Caroline spoke lightly, but Peter sensed his remark had touched a raw nerve.

Ron was extolling the virtues of the Mini, saying it had passed its MOT test with flying colours after a few minor repairs. The documentation was in order, and if she'd allow him a couple of hours, he'd give the car a good spit and polish, check the oil and tyres and fill the petrol tank for her. All part of the service.

'Thank you, that'll be fine.' Unzipping her shoulder bag, she took out her cheque book and pen.

Peter wandered away to stare at the garden gnomes, faced with the realisation that there were secret compartments in Caroline's past which remained closed to him. Above all, he felt unreasonably jealous of a man, whether alive or dead, who had meant, or still meant more to Caroline than he ever could. Jealousy—an emotion he had never experienced before—at odds with his normally equable disposition.

Catching him unaware, tucking her hand into the crook of his elbow, 'Is anything the matter, Peter?' she asked.

Smiling down at her, 'No, of course not,' he said. 'So where shall we go from here?'

'I'd like to look round Whitby, if you don't mind,' she said eagerly. 'I haven't seen much of it so far apart from the main street shops and the supermarket. I'd love to poke around a little, make discoveries, and I could murder a cup of tea.'

'Sure. Why not?'

Later, on their way back to Ron Collier's to pick up her car, having poked about the tucked away streets of Whitby to her heart's content; buying this, that and the other as her mood dictated, including a small, framed watercolour of Whitby Abbey—a surprise gift for Peter she'd managed to smuggle into one of her carrier-bags without his knowledge—she said, 'I've been thinking, Peter. Why not come back to Driftwood with me? I'll cook paella. We'll have supper on the verandah, then dance barefoot on the beach! Would you like that? I would!'

'I'd like nothing better,' Peter admitted, 'except that I'm on duty this evening. The head waiter walked out this morning, and I have to stand in for him.'

'I see. Well, it can't be helped!'

She followed in the wake of the Volkswagen again to the New Moon where, opening the window of her newly acquired Mini, she said, 'Thank you, Peter, for a lovely day and for all your help. I couldn't have managed without you.'

He said desperately, 'We still have an hour or so left. Won't you come in for a cup of tea, coffee, a glass of wine?'

'No. I think not. I am rather tired. I'll just go home, take a shower, put my feet up and relax, if you don't mind. Goodbye, Peter, and thanks again for a lovely day.'

Driving home, she might have known, Caroline thought bitterly, that nothing worked out as one imagined or hoped for. Well, what had she expected? Romance at her age was utter nonsense. She should be grateful she'd been spared the humiliation of making a bloody fool of herself.

Dancing on the beach barefoot, indeed! She must have been out of her mind to suggest such a caper. This, she reminded herself, was precisely the kind of fantasy that lonely women of a certain age were prone to.

She parked the Mini on the clifftop, making sure it was securely locked. Walking down the path to Driftwood with her burden of carrier-bags, the thought occurred that Peter had, perhaps, dreamed up the 'duty' excuse to get rid of her. Possibly he viewed the evening she had planned as a trap to lure him into her bed? If so, and if he had wanted to take things further, how would she have handled the situation? Badly, she suspected, the way she had handled every situation in her life so far.

Thank God for the benison of hot water, an old towelling bathrobe to shrug into, a pair of comfy slippers to cosset her aching feet.

Standing on the balcony looking out to sea, calm and still, washed over with the fast fading colours of an autumn sunset, Caroline realised she was glad, not sorry, to have been spared handling any situation to do with matters of the heart. With love. Love? She scarcely knew the meaning of the word.

Closing the balcony window and drawing the curtains against the night, she went down to the kitchen to begin her evening meal, to stash away the various items of food she had bought in Whitby earlier that day—brown rice and mushrooms, chicken pieces, prawns, pimentos and garlic—for the paella of her imagination, destined never to be cooked now or eaten on the verandah in the company of Peter Augustine.

And what had been the point or purpose in treating herself to that emerald silk outfit, the clip-on earrings; the framed watercolour of Whitby Abbey she'd intended giving to Peter later this evening, as a reminder of their perfect day in the sun? Well, no fool like an old fool she thought, walking down the verandah steps to the beach, hearing the wash of the tide on the shore, aware of moonlight on the sea. The clustered lights of Robin Hood's Bay in the distance a comforting glow; bespeaking the presence of other people in the world.

Deep in thought, she scarcely noticed the moon-washed rockpool at her feet, in which shimmered the reflection of a Woman in White. Startled, heart pounding, Caroline realised that the Woman in White was nothing more than a reflection of herself in her white bathrobe.

Then, glancing upward, she saw that someone, carrying a torch, was hurrying down the cliff path towards her.

Peter! It must be Peter, Caroline thought joyously. Thank God. They would have their evening together after all. But she was wrong. Cameron McCauley, not Peter Augustine was the torch-bearer. The last person on earth she wished to see.

'What are you doing here at this time of night?' she asked abruptly, marching back to the house, feeling foolish in her robe and slippers, hoping he'd have the courtesy to apologise and leave her alone.

'This time of night? It's only eight-thirty for heaven's sake. Scarcely the witching hour,' he said, hurrying after her, following her up the steps of the cottage into the hall.

Really, the man was insufferable, she thought angrily. 'If you don't mind,' she said icily, 'I was planning an early night. As you can see, I'm not dressed for entertaining.'

'That's all right. I shan't keep you long. I don't mind waiting if you want to change into something less—compromising.'

'Very well then.' Short of telling him to get out, she had no alternative but to do as he suggested. She certainly had no intention of conversing with him in her bathrobe. 'You'd better go through to the drawing room. I'll be down in a minute.'

Upstairs in her room, she hastily exchanged her bathrobe for trousers and a lightweight sweater, her slippers for sandals, fuming inwardly at his intrusion, his high-handedness in telling her what to do. Something 'less compromising' indeed! And why had he come in the first place? Only one way to find out.

He was sitting in the armchair when she entered the room. 'I see you've made yourself comfortable,' she said pointedly. 'Please don't bother to get up!'

'Sorry,' half rising from the chair, 'I tend to forget the social niceties at times, so far as women are concernd.'

'So I've noticed.'

'I didn't come here for another slanging match,' he said sharply.

'Then why have you come?'

'If you'll stop hovering in the doorway like a thundercloud and sit down, I'll tell you why. It's about the initials S.S.J. on that napkin ring, remember? Well, I've found out who owned that ring. Her name was Sarah St Just—a wealthy recluse for whom Driftwood was built in the first place.' He paused. 'I say for whom it was *built*, advisedly. She certainly didn't fork out for it herself. The records show that the bills were paid by a firm of London solicitors acting on behalf of a Mr Henry Brown in the year 1870—at which time, I imagine, Sarah St Just was far from being either wealthy or reclusive. Exclusive, perhaps. There *is* a difference.'

'I see. So you're saying that Sarah St Just was a—kept woman?'

'It looks that way to me.'

'So? What exactly are you driving at, Mr McCauley?'

'Can't you guess? I have a gut feeling that the mysterious Mr Henry Brown was none other then Edward the Seventh!'

'You mean because of the other napkin ring engraved with the Prince of Wales's feathers? That's a pretty wild assumption, isn't it?'

'Not at all. Edward was a well-known philanderer with strong connections in this neck of the woods. Take the Londesborough family for instance. Edward was a frequent guest of theirs, in Scarborough. In fact, if my memory serves me correctly, it was during a weekend visit to the Londesboroughs that Bertie contracted typhoid fever, which damn near put paid to him.'

'Yes, I've read about that, but I don't quite see ...'

Leaning forward in his chair, fingers interlocked, tense with excitement, Cam said eagerly, 'There's more. Sarah St Just had a companion housekeeper called Margaret Roberts, to whom she bequeathed her entire estate, including Driftwood, her town house in Scarborough, her jewels and a considerable amount of money, along with strict instructions that after her death, all her private papers and diaries were to be destroyed, unread.

'Unfortunately, Margaret Roberts did not live long enough to enjoy her legacy. She died a few days later and was buried alongside her mistress in Scarborough's Dean Road Cemetery. A sad story, but they were both in their eighties. Possibly poor Margaret Roberts died of a broken heart.'

Caroline glanced at McCauley in some surprise at this evidence of finer feeling on his part. Even so, she could not quite understand what he was driving at. She said, 'Yes, it is a sad story.' Frowning slightly, 'If Margaret Roberts didn't live long enough to enjoy her legacy, presumably she didn't get around to destroying Sarah's diaries? So what do you suppose happened to them?'

Cam said quietly yet intently, 'I think they are here, in this house, right now!'

'But that's ridiculous! How could they be?'

'No, it isn't! Think about it! Think about that bedside chest in the turret room. The missing key! It makes sense, doesn't it? Sarah trusted Margaret Roberts to carry out her wishes, to destroy those diaries. How could she possibly have known that Margaret wouldn't live long enough to carry out that request?

'I think Margaret held the key to that chest, that it was among her possessions when she died, that no one realised its true significance. As Sarah's housekeeper, there would be many keys on her chatelaine! God dammit, woman, at least admit that I may be right about this, that those diaries may well be in that locked chest in your bedroom!'

Caroline rose swiftly to her feet, 'Very well then, supposing you *are* right. What do you intend doing about it?'

'Break the lock, of course. What else?'

Caroline said hoarsely, '*No*, you can't do that! I won't let you! Can't you see, it wouldn't be right? If those diaries do exist, they must be destroyed, unread, according to Sarah St Just's last will and testament. Anything else is unthinkable!'

Rounding on him fiercely, 'I realise, of course, that when I leave Driftwood at the end of October, you'll be free to do exactly as you wish; break open that chest, read the diaries, sell them to the highest bidder most likely. But *not now!* Have I made my feelings perfectly clear? If so, would you mind getting the hell out of here?'

'Gladly, Mrs Fraser,' Cam said, confronting her angrily. 'Just one thing sticks in my throat, that you believe me capable of selling those diaries to the highest bidder. What kind of man do you take me for?'

'A—businessman,' she said shortly, closing the front door behind him.

Going upstairs to her room, Caroline thought the day had ended badly despite its hopeful beginning.

How strange that, leaving London behind her, coming to Yorkshire, she'd envisaged finding only peace of mind, not the substitution of one set of problems by another.

Parting the curtains, Caroline stepped onto the balcony, gazing at the moon and stars riding high in the sky. Poor Sarah St Just, she thought, who must have also suffered the pain of rejection during her lifetime, especially here at Driftwood, in her declining years. In little more than a whisper, Caroline murmured, 'Goodnight, Sarah, God bless you, and please stay with me. I really do need your help.'

Nothing untoward happened; no sudden lightning flash, no billowing out of the curtains, no ghostly visitation. And yet something *had* happened—a subtle warmth, a feeling of peace, quietude of spirit, a renewed feeling of hope for the future, as if her worries had dissolved suddenly like spindrift on a wave.

Caroline slept profoundly, dreamlessly that night.

Chapter Six

Reg Rossiter looked up and smiled when Caroline entered his office early next morning, thinking how much better she looked. The sea air obviously agreed with her. He was not so sure of his own appearance. The growth of hair on his face had not yet flourished to its full potential as a beard and moustache. He simply felt scruffy.

'Nothing wrong, I trust?' he said warily, used to life's mishaps along the way; niggling complaints from one quarter or another, especially at the height of the summer season when the artist colony descended on Robin Hood's Bay.

'No, nothing's wrong,' Caroline assured him. 'I'd just like a word with Mr McCauley, if possible.'

'Cam? Sorry, he hasn't been in yet. Like as not he'll be at home, though he might have gone off to a house clearance sale or whatever. He's a hard man to keep track of at times.'

'Really? I hadn't noticed! Driftwood appears to attract him like a magnet!'

'You mean he's been pestering you?'

Knowing Cam, this was a distinct possibility, Reg thought, once he'd got a bee in his bonnet, about money in particular. 'If so, I'm the one to blame, and I told him so at the time. *I* authorised the removal from Sam Cooper's repository, and that you had asked Sam to send the bill to you!'

'No, Reg. Please stop worrying. This is a personal matter, nothing whatever to do with the removal.' Caroline felt sympathy for the poor man, a kindly, conscientious human being in partnership with a far stronger, less endearing personality. 'All I want is Mr McCauley's address. Or is it a deep, dark secret?'

'No, of course not. Cam lives at Gull Cottage, near the slipway. All you need to do is walk downhill until the road runs out.'

Robin Hood's Bay intrigued Caroline. The estate office, shops, some of the larger hotels, the main car park, school and newer houses, were situated on the clifftop. The older part of the village cascaded downhill to the sea via a series of steps and twisting alleyways negotiable only on foot, as if the village had somehow sprung, mushroom-like, from the earth and rocks beneath.

There, oddly shaped and strangely angled stone cottages clung to the hillside like limpets, interspersed with unexpected, small open spaces, flower-filled gardens, cafés, tea-rooms, antiques and curio shops, an art gallery and a few ancient pubs. It was as if everything had been built in miniature with regard to the irregular nature of the terrain; to accommodate communities of fisherfolk, long gone, whose lives had been centred on wresting a living from the sea on their doorsteps; including the occasional running of contraband too, by all accounts.

At the height of summertime, Caroline imagined, the steeply curving main thorough-fare would be alive with visitors armed with cine-cameras, crowding into the shops and cafés in search of gifts and refreshment. In which case she thanked her lucky stars that on this fresh, warm September morning, she had the place almost entirely to herself, with time enough to reflect on her reasons for wanting to visit Cameron McCauley; to say to him what needed to be said to ease her conscience regarding their last meeting.

She found Gull Cottage without diffi-culty, near the coble landing, a small, stone-built house with crooked steps to the front door. The door was nail-studded with an iron knocker in the shape of an anchor.

Caroline hesitated momentarily before wielding the anchor, uncertain of her welcome, not relishing the forthcoming exchange with her tetchy landlord.

'Oh, it's you,' he said ungraciously. 'I'm busy. What do you want?'

'Just a word or two—about last night.' Losing patience slightly, 'Well, can I come in—or would you prefer I sent you a message in a bottle?'

'Come in,' he said dourly, leading the way down a narrow passage to a cluttered kitchen overlooking a paved yard hemmed about with iron railings.

The sink was filled to overflowing with unwashed pots and pans. Surfaces were littered with polystyrene food cartons, empty milk bottles; the table with coffee-stained mugs, piles of paper, a full to overflowing ashtray crowded with cigarette stubs and spent matches, a recently opened pack of Benson and Hedges, a half empty whisky bottle and a cut glass tumbler.

'So now you know,' Cam said bitterly. 'The rest of the house is in a hell of a muddle too. Would you care for a conducted tour?'

'How you choose to live is your business, not mine,' Caroline said. 'I just came to apologise for my behaviour last night. My remark about selling Sarah's diaries to the highest bidder was uncalled for, and I'm sorry. I had no right to question your integrity or to lay claim to the chest the way I did. After all, Driftwood and its contents are your property, not mine.'

'So what are you saying?' Cam regarded her intently.

'That if you want to open the chest, that's up to you entirely. Just one thing, I'd rather not witness the breaking of the lock. If you intend to pry into the past against Sarah's wishes, I'd rather you did so elsewhere, not at the cottage.'

'Don't tell me you believe in ghosts?' Cam said mockingly.

'I never used to, but I do now,' Caroline said quietly. 'I've been aware of something—someone—a presence, call it what you will, ever since I came to Driftwood. Oh, nothing in the least frightening, quite the opposite—a gentle spirit, sad and lonely ...' She stopped abruptly, 'You think I'm mad, don't you? Imagining things?'

'No, I don't, as a matter of fact,' Cam confessed. 'Look, Mrs Fraser, why don't you sit down? I'll make some coffee.' He grinned ruefully, 'Sorry, I don't appear to have any clean mugs.'

'That's easily remedied.' She smiled, feeling more at ease with him. 'I'm a great washer-upper. Is there any hot water? And my name's Caroline, by the way.'

'Oh, I see.' Back on the defensive, 'So you intend "mucking me out", is that it?

If so, forget it! As you so rightly pointed out a moment ago, the way I choose to live is *my* business. I hate interfering women! Just what are you trying to prove, Mrs Fraser?'

'More to the point, what are *you* trying to prove, Mr McCauley? That you enjoy living in a pigsty? I'd have given you credit for more common sense! A successful, well-respected businessman like you! And just how long do you think that will last if you carry on like this?'

Her words had struck home. He said despairingly, 'You don't know what it's like, how could you, when someone you loved and trusted is no longer there; when everything shatters suddenly like broken glass and there's nothing left to fill the emptiness. It's been that way since my wife left me.'

'I *do* know,' she said quietly. 'Tell me, have you heard of the author Felix Felton?'

'You mean the crime writer? Of course, hasn't everyone? The papers have been full of him recently and his affair with some artist woman or other.' Cam frowned bemusedly, 'But why drag him into the conversation?'

'Because he happens to be my husband, and the—artist woman's name is Francesca Delgado! So now you know why I came to Driftwood; it's because I too have lost someone I loved and trusted. The difference between us, Mr McCauley, is that I am attempting to pick up the broken pieces of my life to form a new pattern. The only alternative left to me, wouldn't you say?'

'I'm so sorry, Caroline,' Cam said contritely. 'I had no idea.'

'I'd rather no one else did, either,' she said stiffly, picking up her shoulder bag and marching along the passage to the front door. 'I can't think why I told you. The last thing I want is publicity. I left London to get away from all that.'

'You have my word. I'm glad you told me.' He was standing close to her, his hand on her arm. 'Please stay.'

She knew he had drunk more than was good for him, and this was the result, the reason for his sudden change of mood. She had been through all this before, with Felix, whose mood swings had kept her on a knife-edge of uncertainty for days on end.

She said, 'Betrayal in any shape or form is a bitter pill to swallow, but drinking won't help in the long run. Neglecting yourself and your home won't help either.'

'You want me to sign the pledge, is that it?' The bantering tone was back.

'Oh, do people still do that? I hadn't

realised. I thought that went out of fashion with "The Primrose League".' She tugged open the door. 'Please let go of my arm,' she said lightly.

Walking back the way she came, no matter how hard she tried, Caroline thought, she always seemed to end up at loggerheads with Cam McCauley. But did that really matter? In no way was she committed to stay on at Driftwood. She could pack her belongings, leave the keys with Reg Rossiter and move on elsewhere—yet deep down she knew she was wrong.

Driftwood had become a haven, a sanctuary, and the people she had met —Reg, the Coopers and Peter Augustine, meant a great deal to her. Could she really bring herself to leave without a word of explanation?

That time would come soon enough when, her brief tenancy ended, she must perforce return to London to institute legal proceedings. Not that she had any intention of going back to her so-called marital home. She would rent a furnished apartment until the whole sorry mess of the divorce and the financial entanglements involved had been sorted out.

All she really wanted was what belonged to her by right; certain items of furniture bequeathed to her by her parents—her mother's wedding ring and other small items of jewellery, several watercolours painted by her father of the family home in Hampstead; a grandfather clock, and her Grandmother Heritage's rocking chair.

Financial entanglements? These, she suspected, would devolve upon Felix's greed for money, not hers. More than likely he would claim reimbursement for the Mercedes, the various items of jewellery he had given her as birthday or Christmas presents—none of which she had wanted or cared for, to his disgust! So be it.

Walking uphill to the car park, deep in thought, Caroline dreaded her return to London at the end of October, the inevitable finale to her stolen days of freedom at Driftwood. And then what? she wondered. What would she do when winter came?

Returning to the kitchen, Cam stared about him in distaste at the mess he'd created.

Picking up the whisky bottle, he poured himself a sizeable shot, raised the glass to his lips, shuddered, set it down untasted. Then, turning to the sink, bottle and glass in hand, he poured away the contents.

Caroline was right: drinking wouldn't help, and he knew the habit was gaining the upper hand—a habit begun three years ago to dull the pain of his wife's betrayal.

Looking at the chintz curtains above the sink, he remembered the day he came home to discover that Gloria had taken down the old curtains in favour of the new ones, bought from a market stall to 'pretty up the place', as she put it.

He had hated those curtains on sight. Not that he'd said so, making allowances for her youthful exuberance and lack of taste. Trying his best to feel pleased that she was showing an interest in their home; as if she were a little girl playing at doll's house.

'Mac,' she had called him, twisting his heartstrings round her little finger, playing games with his emotions, knowing he could deny her nothing within his power to give her. Above all, money.

He had known from the beginning that she disliked Gull Cottage; had her heart set on a bungalow in the new town area of The Bay—one of those brick 'boxes' with all mod cons.

His utter refusal to even contemplate moving away from his roots had triggered their first serious quarrel, when Gloria had come up against the harsher side of his nature. Then had come the tears and recriminations. 'You say you love me, that you'd do anything to please me.

Now, something I really want, and you won't even listen!'

'I *do* love you. But Gull Cottage has been in my family for generations. I was born here, I belong here. So no more talk of moving!'

'All right then, I'll find myself a job! You can't expect me to stay cooped up here all the time with nothing to do! It's all very well for you, Mac, you're set in your ways, but I'm not! I'm young, I need excitement. Friends of my own age to talk to!'

He'd said patiently, 'Things will be different when you start a—baby. You'll have plenty to do then.'

'Start a baby? In this poky hole? You've got to be joking! Where would I hang the washing? Where would I take it for walks?'

And that, Cam thought, conjuring up the past, had been the beginning of the end, because he had been too stubborn to move with the times. Inevitably, he and Gloria had drifted apart as a result of their misunderstanding. That first ever quarrel of theirs had brought sharply into focus Cam's realisation that he was too old for her, too set in his ways to cope with her 'little girl' outlook on life. That all she had ever really wanted from him was his money.

Now here he was, desecrating the place

he loved, his childhood home, allowing it to run to seed because of an ill-fated liaison with a girl he should never have married in the first place.

So now what? The last thing on earth he needed was some damned female preacher to point out his defects ... And yet, holding on to Caroline's arm, asking her to stay, he'd been aware of a strange compulsion to draw her into his arms, to bend his lips to hers, to kiss her ...

He was a healthy male, for God's sake, in desperate need of female companionship —sex, to put it bluntly. The kind of panacea to the pain of living that no amount of alcohol could begin to alleviate.

Walking slowly upstairs, like a man in a dream, he gathered together an armful of damp towels from the bathroom, shirts and underwear from the linen basket. Next he stripped the sheets and pillowcases from the divan bed he had once shared with Gloria, imbued with a drunken desire to restore Gull Cottage to some semblance of order once more—the way he remembered it from the days of his childhood.

Downstairs in the kitchen, he bundled the soiled linen and towels into the washing-machine, added what he deemed to be the appropriate amount of washing-powder, and punched the starter button.

Next, he swept the empty takeaway food

cartons littering the work surfaces into a bin-liner; turned on the hot water tap, and started washing-up the mountain of pots and pans in the sink, scraping away as best he could the burnt on remains of too many meals, the coffee-stained mugs and a pile of nicotine-stained ashtrays.

Damn Caroline Fraser to hell he thought, and yet there was something about her he respected and admired. Her plain-speaking for one thing, plus more besides. She really was a very attractive woman, disturbingly so, in fact. That was half the problem.

Returning to Driftwood, Caroline saw Peter's Volkswagen parked on the clifftop. And then she saw him walking on the beach, head bent deep in thought, as if he had the weight of the world on his shoulders.

Hurrying down the path, 'Peter,' she called out to him. 'I'm here. I'm coming!'

Hands outstretched, he came towards her smiling, but she knew instinctively something was wrong. She had never seen him like this before, drained of his usual *joie de vivre*. He said, 'I thought you might have gone away for the day. I didn't know what to do, where to find you.'

'I've been to Robin Hood's Bay to see Cam McCauley,' she said. 'A spur of the moment impulse, now regretted, so far as

I'm concerned. I wasn't given a very warm welcome.'

'I'll need to see him myself, pretty soon,' Peter said. 'We haven't been in touch ...' he added hesitantly, 'since Cam came back from Jamaica.'

'I remember,' Caroline remarked drily, recalling McCauley's rudeness on that occasion, 'But he said he'd contact you!'

'I know, but he hasn't.' Attempting a smile, 'I have the feeling he's angry with me, that I've done something to upset him.'

'That wouldn't take much doing, I imagine,' Caroline reminded him. 'The man's a walking disaster area. His own worst enemy, to put it mildly.'

Peter knew what she meant. All too often in the past, calling at Gull Cottage, he'd found Cam sprawled on the front room sofa, hoisted him to his feet and hauled him upstairs to sleep off his hangover.

Still clasping Caroline's hand, Peter said huskily, 'Something unexpected has happened. The reason why I came. I *had* to see you, to tell you ...'

'Tell me—what?' Caroline's heart skipped a beat. She was holding his hands just as tightly in hers. Their fingers interlinked, the strength of their feeling for one another evident in the warm pressure of palms and fingertips; a bridge of desire between them,

103

albeit a destructible one, Caroline realised, in their present circumstances.

She said softly, anticipating his reply. 'You're going away, aren't you? Back to Jamaica?' Blinking back tears, 'I knew you would sooner or later, of course,' she said bleakly, 'but I'll miss you so much! Just tell me when, and why.'

Stunned by her perception, he said quietly, 'The owner of the New Moon told me last night, that he's closing the hotel the first week in October, prior to his retirement. I can't blame him for that, staff problems being what they are, and at his age. So I guess I'll be going home the second week in October.'

'I see,' Caroline murmured, wondering where the days had fled to? They had passed by so quickly, like a dream. Now September was drawing to a close, and October was almost here.

Drawing her into his arms, Peter said hoarsely, 'I have no right to say this, I know, but I *must!* I couldn't go away without telling you how much I care about you; how much your friendship has meant to me! But there's more to it than just friendship, isn't there? You care for me too, that's true, isn't it? I know it's true! That's why I'm asking you to come back with me; to return with me to Jamaica as my wife!'

For one brief, blinding moment, Caroline visualised the utter joy of spending the rest of her days on an island in the sun with this wonderful man beside her; until she realised the impossibility of that dream.

He was so young, so naïve, so trusting, utterly oblivious to the many obstacles between them—her age for one thing. More importantly, the fact that she was already married. Possibly he believed her to be widowed? If so, the sooner she told him the truth about herself, the better. But not here on the beach, with the sea rolling in on the shore and the seagulls screaming overhead.

Gently, she led him by the hand towards the cottage and the quietude of the drawing room where, however painfully, she would recount the story of her life so far.

Chapter Seven

Cam McCauley, who had not set eyes on Peter since their brief encounter on the beach, suddenly wondered where he was.

The fellow should have been in touch by now, he thought irritably, forgetting that he had promised to contact his protégé first. Wasn't the man interested in his visit to Ocho Rios, news of his parents and family, the hotel venture? And why, in God's name had he been at Driftwood that day, deep in conversation with Caroline Fraser?

He had been more than kind to Augustine, Cam thought, in giving him the chance to better himself, offering him a career in hotel management, finding him a job at the New Moon, sponsoring his trip to England; going so far as to give him a key to Gull Cottage during his absence and inviting him to make use of the place. And this was his repayment—silence. Not a word of gratitude.

The more Cam thought about it, the more incensed he became until, ringing up the New Moon, he told Peter he wanted to see him that night, after work.

'Yes, of course, Cam,' Peter responded warily, sensing trouble.

He had liked McCauley enormously at their first meeting in Ocho Rios eighteen months ago, when Cam had outlined his plan to develop the old plantation house he'd bought into a first class hotel. The man's enthusiasm and energy had struck sparks initially. Now, having come up against the rougher side of McCauley's nature when he'd spoken so dismissively to him and so rudely to Caroline, Peter disliked the idea of a confrontation with the man he had previously regarded as a friend and benefactor.

Driving to Robin Hood's Bay late that evening, Peter thought about Gull Cottage, which Cam used as a kind of repository for all manner of objects and pieces of furniture that would one day form the nucleus of the antiques business he had in mind.

The trouble with Cam, he felt, was his energy spilled over in so many different directions he seemed never to be at peace with himself. Incapable of relaxation, of stopping to ask himself where he was going, what he really wanted from life—apart from money. A continual striving towards financial security to replace the real values which no amount of money could buy.

Parking his car on the clifftop, Peter walked down to the cottage, savouring the magic of the old streets and buildings washed with moonlight, the sound of the sea in the distance, thinking of Caroline; holding the thought of her to his heart like a talisman. Knowing that she loved him.

Not that he had been sure at first. He knew now. And where there was love, there was hope.

Cam answered the door. 'Come in,' he said shortly, leading the way to the cluttered sitting room with its preponderance of saleable *objets d'art*. A room familiar to Peter, who had spent many a night on the rug-draped settee near the fireplace before returning to the hotel early next morning.

He said, 'I'm sorry, Cam, I'd have come sooner except—that day at Driftwood—you said you'd be in touch with me, remember? You wanted a word in private with—Mrs Fraser.'

'Ah yes, Mrs Fraser,' Cam said coolly. 'Tell me, Peter, is she reponsible for your change of attitude towards me?'

'Change of attitude? I don't know what you mean!'

'Then I suggest you think about it. At the same time you might spare a thought for all I have done for you. In case you've

108

forgotten, it was *I* who sponsored your trip to England, who assumed certain responsibilities on your behalf. It never occurred to me at the time that you would make a damn fool of yourself with a woman twice your age!'

'I suggest you leave Caroline out of this!' Peter clenched his hands into fists.

'It's true then? I thought so,' Cam continued relentlessly. 'I sensed there was something between you that day on the beach! My God, man, are you out of your mind?'

'If it's any of your business,' Peter said tautly, 'I'm in love with her. I-I've asked her to marry me!'

'You've done *what?* You *are* out of your mind, then. You must be! A girl of your own age I could have understood. But *this!* The woman's using you!' Cam laughed bitterly, 'I can see why, of course! A middle-aged married woman wanting a bit of romance on the side. Or didn't she bother to tell you she was married? Well, who could blame her? But she told *me!* Oh yes, she told me all about her unfaithful husband and his artist girlfriend—'

'Stop it, Cam!' Peter uttered savagely. 'Of course she told me! It made no difference, why should it? We're in love! Nothing else matters!'

Changing tack, 'Look, Peter,' Cam said

less forcefully, 'the Ocho Rios project is well under way. The workmen have almost finished. With luck, the grand opening of the Full Moon Hotel—that's what I've decided to call it—will take place early next year.

'This has cost a great deal of money, believe me. But just think of the great future ahead of you when the hotel is up and running. So take my advice, forget about Mrs Fraser; concentrate on your career prospects. Think about your family—what it will mean to them to move up in the world.'

'I'm not sure what you mean by that,' Peter said, frowning. 'In what way would my family "move up in the world"?'

'Oh, didn't you know?' Cam said condescendingly, 'I've offered them both jobs at the Full Moon.'

'Doing what, exactly?' Peter wanted to know, his hands still firmly clenched.

'Nothing too strenuous, I assure you,' Cam said. 'Well within their capacity, if that's what's worrying you. I've offered your father the job of commissionaire, car park attendant and part-time gardener, and your mother, work as a cook-housekeeper with their own private accommodation, of course—a modern bungalow in the hotel grounds.'

'You call that "moving up in the world"?'

110

Peter said contemptuously. 'We Jamaicans are simple-hearted, not simple-minded! Hasn't it occurred to you that my parents might prefer to go on living in their own home? Oh, it may not seem much to you, but it does to them. And if they came to work for you and you decided to dispense with their services, what then?

'Oh, of course, I see it all quite clearly now. What you are really saying is that their future depends on my toeing the line? Well, I'm not into emotional blackmail. If you imagine for one moment that I'd give up the woman I love at your say so, then you can count me out as the manager of your blasted hotel.'

'As cut and dried as all that, is it?' Cam spat back at him. 'But what about the money you owe me? The money I squandered on your air fare to England, for one thing; not to mention the clothes I bought you, the food I put into your mouth, the fees I paid for your catering course, the books you needed. I even gave you access to my cottage; the use of my electricity and so on!'

'Not to worry on that score,' Peter said harshly, 'I'll pay back every cent I owe you sooner or later!'

Lowering his voice, 'You're not thinking straight, Peter,' Cam said urgently. 'Very well, then, if you are serious about Mrs

Fraser, presumably you'd want to offer her a decent standard of living? I hardly think that a woman of her age and financial standing would enjoy life as the wife of a "drop out", a beachcomber. Unless, of course, you wouldn't mind living on her money?'

'You really are an ace-in-the-hole bastard,' Peter said pityingly, unclenching his hands. 'All right, Cam, you win. Just one more thing, before I leave. I've been made redundant. The New Moon's closing down soon. Mr Sykes is retiring, putting the hotel on the market.'

Cam looked startled. Peter said grimly, 'Oh, no need to worry, I'll pay for my own fare home. No doubt you'll tell me what you want done when I get there, but I'm giving you fair warning, I'll do my damndest to talk my parents out of working for you.' Turning at the door, 'About Mrs Fraser. She isn't "using" me, as you put it, nor has she been dishonest! The trouble with you Cam, is you judge everyone else by your own yardstick. In any case, my private affairs are none of your damn business!'

Leaving Gull Cottage, striding up the moonlit streets of Robin Hood's Bay to the car park, unsettled by the angry exchanges between himself and McCauley, Peter wondered if Caroline would still be awake at this late hour—a quarter past midnight? Only one way to find out.

Walking down the cliff path towards Driftwood, he saw her bedroom light was on. Approaching the front door, he knocked gently, not wanting to frighten her. Moving away from the verandah, he stood in the moonlight, looking up expectantly.

In a little while, she came onto the balcony, saw him standing there on the moon-washed beach below, and hurried down to let him in.

'Come in,' she said quietly. 'Let's go through to the kitchen, shall we? I'll put the kettle on. I could do with a cup of coffee, how about you?'

'Yes, coffee will be fine.'

Something had happened to upset him, she realised. Experience had taught her to keep calm in an emergency—with one possible exception: the day she marched into Alec Porteous's office to give Felix's agent a piece of her mind.

But this was a different matter entirely. Peter Augustine was as far removed from a lecherous, money-grubbing agent and a constantly carping, in need of cosseting husband as the moon from the sun. This she understood, and valued immensely. So, busying herself about the kitchen, she waited patiently until Peter, gaining control of his emotions, felt able to explain the

113

reasons for this late night visit.

He said at last, hands clasped about the coffee mug she had offered him as if deriving warmth and comfort from its contents, 'I've been to see Cam. He sent for me. It wasn't a happy meeting, I'm afraid. We both said things far better left unsaid.'

She knew exactly what he meant. Cam had a way of putting people's backs up. Wisely, she remained silent.

Peter continued hoarsely, 'He's involved my parents in his hotel project, as— servants! I don't want that to happen! I can't bear the thought of my mother working in a hotel kitchen, my father in a commissionaire's uniform, in charge of the car park!' Close to tears, 'They haven't a clue what they're letting themselves in for, and all because of me!'

'Because of you? In what way?' Caroline asked gently. Then, not waiting for his reply, 'Oh, I see! Of course, a form of emotional blackmail! How despicable! But there's more to it than that, isn't there? Something to do with—us?'

'I—I told Cam I had asked you to marry me,' Peter said huskily.

Caroline smiled grimly, 'Let me guess his reaction. I imagine he told you, in his own inimitable way, that you must be out of your mind wanting to marry a woman nearly old enough to be your mother—a married woman into the bargain! I'm right, aren't I?'

'Something like that,' Peter confessed.

'Then, knowing McCauley, he'd throw money, career prospects, your parents' future into the melting pot for good measure. Did he go so far as to threaten your future as his hotel manager? I wouldn't put it past him.'

Peter smiled ruefully, 'I called him an ace-in-the-hole bastard!'

Caroline laughed, 'Good for you! About time someone told him a few home truths! Oh, I'm sorry, that wasn't very kind of me, knowing how upset you are. But managing Cam's hotel isn't the be-all and end-all. You're young, you've worked hard, carved out a career for yourself. There'll be other jobs, other opportunities ahead of you.'

'That's just it,' Peter said quietly, 'I didn't carve out a career for myself. Cam offered it to me on a plate. Oh sure, we quarrelled, I was angry, I threatened not to work for him when the time comes, but I couldn't leave him in the lurch after all he's done for me. It wouldn't be fair.'

Caroline had never loved Peter more than now, a proud man willing to stand up for his principles yet possessing the humility and grace to want to act fairly in the long run. She felt proud and deeply touched that a man of his calibre had asked her to share her life with him, despite the vast obstacles between them. Insurmountable obstacles, perhaps? Who could tell?

The only future she could see ahead of her right now had to do not with personal happiness or fulfilment, but the weary, distressing business of disentanglement from her abortive marriage to a man who possessed neither principles nor humility.

The late night shipping forecast had long since ended when Peter left Driftwood to return to the hotel.

Standing close together on the steps of the verandah, they saw with delight the shimmering path of moonlight on the sea, and felt the tide of love flowing strongly between them—a love they would both remember with joy for the rest of their lives, no matter what the outcome might be.

Drawing her into his arms, Peter murmured intently, 'We have so little time left together. Let's make the most of it, shall we?'

'Yes,' she replied quietly, leaning her head against his shoulder, 'let's make every moment count from now on!'

Cam had not enjoyed being referred to as

an ace-in-the-hole bastard.

His confrontation with Peter had left a nasty taste in his mouth. Amazed by his attitude, his outspoken anger, Cam could only suppose that Peter's liaison with Caroline Fraser was to blame. The woman must be out of her mind to have forged a passionate relationship with a man of his age.

Had the stupid female even considered the ramifications of marrying someone of a different race, a different colour? Peter's parents, devout Catholics, would scarcely take to a middle-aged divorcée as a daughter-in-law.

McCauley's frustration centred on the thought that he could do nothing to prevent Peter making a fool of himself. A man accustomed to having his own way, making his presence felt. There was one thing he *could* do, at any rate, he thought darkly.

Caroline was in the kitchen when Cam called on her the next evening.

The front door open, he entered un-invited, and called out to her from the hall. Obviously startled, she appeared in the doorway clutching a tea-towel. 'Oh, it's you,' she said defensively. 'I didn't hear you knock!' Was there no end to this man's incivility, she wondered, his constant, far from welcome appearances in her life? 'Well, what is it this time?'

'A word about that bedside chest,' he said coolly.

'What about it?'

'I've made arrangements with Sam Cooper to have it removed first thing in the morning.'

'Really? You might have consulted me first,' she said tautly, 'I may not be here first thing in the morning.'

'In which case I suggest you leave the key under the doormat. Better still, in that tripod on the verandah.'

She knew the object he meant—a metal artefact supporting a shallow bowl filled with trailing lobelia and geraniums which she had watered assiduously since her arrival.

'Very well, then, do as you wish.' Too tired to argue with the man; loathing his aggressiveness, his lack of sensitivity, she said dully, 'I came to Driftwood in search of peace, which you have so far denied me. Well, it won't be for much longer: three weeks at the most. When I'm gone, think of the pleasure you'll derive from re-boarding the drawing room fireplace, taking down the overmantle, re-hanging that print of the green-faced woman; returning Sarah St Just's furniture to Sam Cooper's repository! Oh, not to worry, I'll pay the bill! So take the bedside chest! Open it! Read the diaries! Do what the *hell* you like with them! Sell them to *Paris Match*, *The New York Times* or *The News of the World*, for all I care!'

Cam laughed briefly, 'The amazing thing about you, Mrs Fraser,' he said scathingly, 'is your self-righteousness, your "holier than thou" attitude towards others; myself in particular! Well, I suggest you take a long clear look at yourself and your own behaviour before passing judgement on me! I'm referring to your affair with Peter Augustine. It seems pretty sick to me, a woman of your age carrying on like a lovesick teenager.'

He continued relentlessly, 'Do you really imagine you stand a cat in hell's chance of happiness with a man scarcely old enough to know his own mind? You're a proud, independent woman, for God's sake, wanting everything on your own terms. We're a lot alike in that respect! Frankly, Caroline, you are heading for disaster if you believe for one moment that Peter's family would welcome you with open arms!'

Rounding on him fiercely, 'And you're telling me all this from the goodness of your heart, are you, *Mr* McCauley?' Caroline kept her anger in check as best she could. 'If so, you are wasting your time! Believe me, you couldn't say anything that I haven't said to myself time and time again regarding my so-called "affair" with Peter Augustine.

'What you fail to realise is that it is *his* future that concerns me, not mine! Why? Because, loving him so much, I would do nothing to hurt him! People of Peter Augustine's calibre are rare indeed in the present day rat-race we laughingly refer to as life. The reason *why* I love him so much is because he has restored my faith in human nature.

'Now, Mr McCauley, regarding the removal of the chest, I'll leave the key in the flower-bowl as you suggested. Just one thing more before you leave. From now on I shall keep the front door securely locked after dusk. Is that perfectly clear? And when I leave Driftwood at the end of October, God willing I'll never have the misfortune to set eyes on you ever again!'

Chapter Eight

Peter broke the news of his flight home to Caroline as gently as possible.

'But that's only a week from now,' she said bemusedly. 'Couldn't you have stayed for a while longer? Till the end of October perhaps?'

They were on the beach walking together near the sea's edge, stopping now and then to talk earnestly to one another: Peter explaining quietly that he'd had no say in the matter. Cam McCauley had made the travel arrangements on his behalf, sending him a brief message to that effect—a type-written letter enclosing a one-way ticket to Jamaica.

'Cam McCauley,' Caroline said bitterly, 'I might have known!' Had he done this deliberately to make herself and Peter suffer for the simple, unaccountable human act of falling in love?

Peter said levelly, with his inborn sense of justice and fair play, 'I gathered from his letter that Cam had been in touch with the owners of the New Moon beforehand, to make certain the hotel was closing its doors to visitors on the thirtieth of September. I guess he didn't want me hanging round there like a spare part for longer than necessary, helping out with the clearing up process: occupying my room in the staff quarters, when he had other, more important things in mind for me.'

'I see, then so be it,' Caroline said coldly. 'By all means, Peter, get your priorities right! At least accord me the dubious pleasure of driving you to Heathrow a week from now; of waving you goodbye from the departure lounge!'

Gathering her close in his arms, 'My God, Caroline,' Peter said intently, 'don't you know, don't you realise how much I want you to come with me to Jamaica? Please, Caroline, I'm begging you, please say you'll come with me!'

'I can't, Peter! I'm sorry! Please say you understand. I can't keep on running away from the past!' Close to tears, 'Let's not think about the future, just live for today!'

'I'll do whatever you want.' The thought of losing her, of not being there for her when she would most need his help and support, was unbearable. But the die was cast. His only hope was that one day, when her affairs had been settled, when she was free to decide where her future lay, she would come to him.

Deeply conscious of the coming separation, the bittersweet nature of the little time left to them, this was the way women must have felt during the war, Caroline thought, when their menfolk came home on leave; wanting to make every moment count, when every word, every smile, tear or the touching of hands would be tomorrow's memories.

When Peter had gone away from her, she would remember till the end of time the sweetness of the Indian summer days they had spent together. All the little things which meant so much, the creaming of the waves on the shore, the wild, freewheeling of the seabirds overhead; rock-pools glinting in the sunlight, the fires he had lit for her, the dawning awareness of love. In the words of an old song: *Love is lovelier the second time you fall; like a friendly home the second time you call ...*'

Peter said, attempting a lightheartedness he did not feel, 'We could drive over to Scarborough this afternoon, if you like. You could wear that dress you bought in Whitby, remember?'

'And those crazy gilt earrings?' she responded gratefully.

Peter laughed. 'Sure. Why not?'

Wanting to please him, she exchanged what she thought of as her beachcombing gear for the emerald silk outfit, clip-on earrings and high-heeled sandals she'd worn that day when she and Peter had lunched at the Griffiths' restaurant overlooking the Esk.

'You look lovely,' Peter said, when she came downstairs.

Pulling a face, 'Who are you kidding?' she laughed. 'More like mutton dressed as lamb!'

'That's the real hang-up, isn't it?' Peter said huskily. 'If only you could see yourself as I see you—a lovely, desirable woman on the threshold of life.'

'If only that were true.'

'It *is* true! Look at yourself in a mirror if you don't believe me. Look at your hair, your eyes, your skin; the bloom about you. Happiness becomes you, Caroline; days spent in the sun and fresh air.' Urgently, 'Given the chance, I'll do everything in my power to make sure you remain happy.'

He was speaking the truth, Caroline realised. The sun had brought colour to her skin and lightened her hair, which had grown slightly, making her feel more feminine—she preferred it that way. It was Felix who had insisted on her weekly visits to the hairdresser to keep it cut short. How odd, she thought, as though he were inflicting on her some kind of punishment for being a woman ... the wrong woman.

Walking up the cliff path towards Peter's Volkswagen, she wondered what Francesca

Delgado's reaction would be to the rape of her locks at her lover's request. More than likely, she thought with a degree of grim satisfaction, Felix playing Samson to Francesca's Delilah, would be the one to end up with a short back and sides! No way would Francesca ever part with that cloud of shoulder length hair so in keeping with her *femme fatale* persona.

By the same token, Caroline decided, never again would she submit to some scissor-happy cliptomaniac in a West End salon. From now on she would grow her hair and keep on growing it until it was long enough to swirl into a French plait, a chignon, or whatever, suitable for her newfound identity as a woman in her own right; a woman in love, despite the obvious barriers between herself and Peter Augustine.

Cam McCauley's harshly spoken words, 'Frankly, you are heading for disaster if you believe that Peter's family would welcome you with open arms' had found their target. Common sense warned her that this might well be true. The Catholic Church, she knew, and Peter's parents in particular, would have strong reservations about a young Catholic man marrying an older divorced woman unable, through no fault of her own, to give him children. One child perhaps, if she was lucky. Even so, there would be a risk factor involved at her age. Not that she would mind taking such a risk, for Peter's sake.

The question remained: would their love survive the many powerful obstacles raised against them if, against her better judgement, throwing caution to the wind, she promised to marry him in the fullness of time? What did that mean exactly? It might take months, even years, before her legal affairs were finally settled.

Knowing Felix as she did, he would more than likely demand a share of her inheritance, contest her father's will if necessary; do everything in his power to hurt and humiliate her for the simple reason that she had walked out of his life one September morning, six weeks ago, leaving behind her no word of regret, no forwarding address—how could she have done since she had had no notion where she was going that morning?

One thing was certain. Felix would make her pay dearly for her dereliction of duty when, returning home from America in need of her help and support in scotching rumours of his affair with Francesca, he would have found the house empty of all save the housekeeper, Mrs Gordon, stoutly reiterating that Madam had left the house in the early hours of the morning, and where she had gone to she had no idea.

Driving across the moors towards Scarborough, his hands on the steering wheel of the Volkswagen, 'You're very quiet, Caroline,' Peter remarked. 'Is anything the matter? If so, please tell me. Have I hurt or offended you in any way?'

'No of course not.' She smiled, 'I was just thinking ... what magnificent countryside!'

She meant what she said. Heather-clad hills rolled away to blue horizons as far as the eye could see, dotted here and there with flocks of grazing sheep. Bracken had changed imperceptibly from green to russet now that autumn was here, imparting a sombre quality to the landscape despite the watercolour blueness of the sky; a subtle reminder of November waiting in the wings to change the autumn scenery to winter in a few weeks' time.

The moors behind them, the road curved downhill through villages with pubs, churches and stone cottages whose flower filled gardens were ablaze with dahlias, chrysanthemums and Michaelmas daisies. A more familiar landscape, contrasing sharply with the vastness of the moorland scenery painted in shades of purple and brown.

Soon they were on a main approach road

to Scarborough, with more closely-packed houses, shops, garages, bus shelters, traffic-lights and signposts.

'Not to worry,' Peter said cheerfully, 'it's not all like this.'

'You've been here before, then?' Caroline asked.

'Yes, many a time. This really is a very special town. Just wait awhile and you'll see what I mean.'

Standing beside him on a vantage point overlooking the South Bay, Caroline knew exactly what he meant.

She saw with delight, the old town of Scarborough nestling in the lee of a majestic headland crowned with the towering, age defiant stones of a Norman Keep; ancient streets and alleyways leading down to the harbour; a scene of industry with trawlers, cobles and timber-boats hawsered alongside the quays.

There were wooded gardens sweeping down to the Spa, with its Victorian theatre and concert hall set like jewels against a backdrop of shining blue sea and sky, golden sand and moss-covered rocks.

The sun warm on her face, inhaling the subtly blended scents of sea air, seaweed, long grass and gently falling leaves, half closing her eyes, 'I wonder if Sarah St Just ever stood here,' she murmured, 'just as we are standing here now.'

'Sarah St Just?' Peter queried gently. 'A friend of yours?'

'Well, yes, in a manner of speaking ...' A brief pause, then, 'Tell me, Peter, do you believe in ghosts?'

'I'm not sure.' Tentatively, 'Why do you ask?'

'Driftwood was built for Sarah,' Caroline explained, 'and I have reason to believe she has never really left it. I've felt her presence so strongly there. It does happen, I imagine, that spirits cling to the places they loved best on earth. What do you think?'

'Yes, that's possible,' Peter said thoughtfully. 'I don't know much apart from what I've read, but there could be other reasons. Some—ghosts, spirits—remain earthbound seeking absolution from sin, perhaps? Some act; committed during their lifetime, that prevents their moving on to ... Well, you know what I mean?'

He wondered where all this was leading, this conversation about ghosts when the flesh and bood woman he loved was beside him, time running away from them as swiftly as the outgoing tide on the shore below.

Laying his hand on hers, needing to know, to understand what was going on in her mind, 'Tell me more about this ghost of yours. Who was she? Where did she come from?'

'I'm not sure, except that St Just is a Cornish name. All I know for certain is that Driftwood was a gift from a rich admirer of hers. She also had a town house here in Scarborough, and a loyal housekeeper-companion called Margaret Roberts. They died within days of one another apparently, and were buried here in the old cemetery.

'Oh, I'm sorry, Peter, forgive me! I didn't mean to be morbid. It's just that I ... ouch! these earrings are really hurting me! Clip-on things can be excruciatingly painful at times!' She laughed.

Leaning forward, gently Peter removed the earrings. 'Why suffer unnecessary pain?' he said quietly, pocketing the offending articles.

Scarborough had captured Caroline's imagination. And one day, she thought, when Peter had gone, she would come here again in search of Sarah's house and her grave in the old cemetery. She would need to do something positive to fill the lonely days without him.

In vain, Peter had tried to talk her out of driving him to Heathrow, fearing the journey would prove too stressful for her—particularly the homecoming. She would have to face the London rush hour traffic in a state of emotional upheaval which might affect her powers of concentration in a bewildering mass of road signs, junctions and traffic-lights.

Caroline said simply, 'No need to worry, I'll stay somewhere overnight and return to Yorkshire the next day. I just want to be with you for as long as possible.'

Planning ahead, knowing that Peter had sold his Volkswagen, Caroline continued, 'I'll drive over to Whitby the day beforehand, bring you back here to Driftwood, cook you a meal, and then ... We could set off for London early next morning.' She added brightly—a shade too brightly perhaps— 'We'll share the driving, shall we? Stop off for lunch along the way? Make the most of our last day together?'

'Yes, of course,' Peter said gently, 'if that's what you want,' wishing, at the same time, that this situation had never arisen. Dreading the forthcoming parting from Caroline as he had seldom dreaded anything in his life before; he knew that alone with her on the eve of his departure, he would want to spend the night making love to her.

On their last evening together, Peter stowed his luggage in the hall, then lit the drawing room fire whilst Caroline went through to the kitchen to cook their supper.

All day long, Peter had half expected a word or message, a note even, from Cam McCauley. No such message arrived.

In the kitchen Caroline prepared a simple meal of fresh plaice fillets, green salad and thickly sliced French bread. A celebratory dinner of rich food would have been totally inappropriate in the present situation.

She had never felt less like celebrating in her life. She was dreading what tomorrow would bring—the long drive to London, Heathrow Airport with its packed concourses and the relentless cacophony of crackling tannoys and shrill human voices; the impossibility of even a moment's respite from the hubbub to say all the important last minute things one needed to say when faced with a long and painful separation. All this before the plane finally took off from the runway, its navigation lights gradually fading from sight in the enfolding darkness of an October evening.

Tomorrow there would be no time. Tonight was all she had to prove her love for Peter; to sleep with his arms about her—if he wanted her. But how could she be sure? She had never slept with any man apart from her husband. Committing adultery herself would be tantamount to condoning Felix's affair with Francesca;

shattering her inborn belief in the sanctity of her marriage vows.

In this delicately balanced emotional situation, the last thing she wanted was to cheapen her relationship with the man she loved. And yet deep down she knew that if she let tonight slip through her fingers without offering herself to Peter body and soul, she might regret for the rest of her life not possessing enough courage to follow her heart.

After supper, they sat together in the drawing room, Peter in the blue velvet armchair, Caroline at his feet, her head resting against his knees, gazing into the fire. Peter stroked her hair, aware of the ticking of Sarah St Just's marble clock on the mantelpiece relentlessly eating away the time they had left together, minute by minute, hour by hour, until the first stroke of midnight when the fire had sunk to its last glowing embers.

Before the clock had finished striking, drawing Caroline into his arms, Peter said quietly, 'Let's go to bed together now, shall we?'

Looking up at him, 'If that's what you really want,' she murmured. 'But only if you are certain ...'

'I've never been more certain of anything in my life,' he whispered against her hair.

'I love you so much, my Caroline. More than you'll ever know—unless you let me prove it to you.'

They walked slowly upstairs to the turret room, his arm about her waist, her head against his shoulder.

Chapter Nine

Opening her eyes to the dawning of a new day, to sunlight filtering through the bedroom curtains, turning her head on the pillow, Caroline saw that Peter was still asleep, his warm-skinned body totally relaxed, and remembered with an overpowering feeling of joy, the passion, power and gentleness of his lovemaking throughout the long, slow, silent hours of darkness spent in each other's arms. And she had wanted the night, the all embracing darkness, to last forever, dreading what tomorrow would bring.

She gazed at him, committing to memory every detail of his face, as clear-cut as a cameo. His dark eyelashes sweeping his cheeks, generously curving lips slightly open in sleep. At least they would have that one night to remember, no matter what the future might bring.

Rousing slowly from sleep, Peter looked at her and smiled. Never had he felt more confident, more certain of a happy future for himself and Caroline, the woman he now regarded as his wife. He had realised all along that his parents might well express doubts about her suitability as a daughter-in-law. They would change their minds when they met her and came to understand how much she meant to him.

Getting up, Caroline drew back the curtains, opened the balcony window and stood for a moment breathing in the sea air. Then, opening the top drawer of the dressing table, she took out the picture she had bought for him that day in Whitby.

Standing by the bed, she handed him the package. 'Can you find room for this in your luggage?' she asked. 'It isn't very big.'

Sitting up, propping his back with pillows. 'What is it?' Eagerly, he untied the red ribbon bow and folded back the tissue-paper, reminding her of a little boy on his birthday.

Never would she forget his reaction to the gift, his expression of delight when he saw the painting. The way, gazing at it, his eyes filled suddenly with tears. The huskiness of his voice when he said, 'It's beautiful. I shall treasure it all the days of my life.'

It was time to leave. Caroline wearing her beachcombing gear, Peter in jeans, his holdall and anorak on the back seat of the Mini alongside Caroline's shoulder bag, anorak and overnight case, in accordance with her promise not to attempt her return journey to Yorkshire without a decent dinner, a good night's sleep, and a hearty breakfast to sustain her.

'Yes, yes, I promise to find myself a hotel room for the night,' she'd reiterated patiently as the Mini headed south towards London, 'and yes, I shall have dinner in the dining room, stagger to my room replete with Brown Windsor soup, steak Diane, braised liver and onions, or whatever! Oh, Peter darling, please stop worrying! I'll be fine, just fine!'

He was silent for a long while, turning over so many unanswered questions; so many what ifs, maybe and perhaps rang through his head. What about the future? *Our* future, he wanted to shout. Please don't forget me, Caroline, he prayed to himself.

'There's something bothering you,' she said astutely. 'Something you're keeping to yourself. I can tell. Whatever it is, I'd like to know. I *need* to know!'

'It's nothing really,' he said reluctantly, 'just that I had hoped for a word from Cam, a message of some kind to wish me luck. I hate the thought of being at loggerheads with anyone, especially Cam. I'm sorry, darling, but you did ask.'

'I know. I wish now that I hadn't.' Keeping her eyes on the road ahead.

'I understand why you dislike him so much, but he has his good points,' Peter said.

'Really? Well you know him better than I do, so I'll take your word for it, though you did recently refer to him as an ace-in-the-hole bastard—or had you forgotten?'

'No, and neither apparently, has he. But everyone says things they don't mean in the heat of the moment. It was late, I was tired, and he'd been drinking.'

The last thing Caroline had envisaged was dragging McCauley into the conversation on this of all days. Useless, and pointless to even try to explain her dislike of McCauley. The way he had walked into Driftwood uninvited one evening a week ago, the bitterness of that encounter when he had called into question her affair with Peter; telling her abruptly that he had arranged for the removal of Sarah St Just's chest from the turret room the next day and ordering her to leave the key to the front door in the flower pot on the verandah.

And when she'd returned to Driftwood later that day, the chest had been missing, replaced by a common-or-garden bedside cabinet; the key to the front door back in the metal container where she had left it early that morning.

Somehow she'd wanted to believe that

McCauley would not carry out his intention to remove Sarah's chest from the house which had once belonged to her. She might have known better.

And yet, despite his innate meanness and insensitivity, his egocentricity and ruthlessness, Peter continued to regard the man with an unwarranted degree of affection—as a kind of misguided knight in shining armour—worthy of respect and admiration.

She said at length, changing the subject, 'Would you mind driving for a while now, Peter? Let's find somewhere to have lunch, shall we?'

Glancing at her watch, she saw that the hands were nearing ten minutes to twelve. Peter's flight was scheduled at five o'clock, which meant they had exactly five hours and ten minutes left to them.

Strangely, Caroline dreaded a possible hiatus, some long delay spinning out the final leavetaking, stretching emotion to breaking point and beyond. Far better to say their goodbyes as quickly and as quietly as possible.

Her wish was granted. In the departure lounge, when Peter's flight was called at five-fifteen, they clung together tightly, smiling through their tears, saying over and over again, 'I love you!'

Then suddenly he was gone. A distant

figure hurrying away from her, turning back to wave, raising his hand in a final gesture of farewell, leaving Caroline to face the first, soul shattering moments of loneliness without him.

The last person she expected to see entering the departure lounge as she was leaving was Cam McCauley.

They looked at each other momentarily, without speaking. Then, 'I'm too late, I take it?' he said brusquely.

'So it would appear.' Conversing with McCauley was something Caroline could well do without, now or at any time in the future. 'Now, if you'll excuse me,' she said abruptly, brushing past him.

He called after her. 'Just a minute! Please don't go yet! We need to talk, but not here!' Clasping her arm, 'Let's have a drink, shall we? You look like you need one after your long journey. I'm not wrong in thinking, am I, that you drove that clapped-out Mini of yours all the way from Driftwood to Heathrow? The things one does for love!'

Rounding on him fiercely, angry beyond belief, 'That's enough!' she said grimly, 'Let go of my arm or I'll call security! I mean what I say! How *dare* you lay a hand on me? My God, McCauley, you really are a pathetic excuse for a human being, aren't you? Didn't you know, didn't you even *begin* to realise how desperately Peter needed some kind of message from you before his return to Jamaica? Just a note, a word, a phonecall?

'The things one does for love! Well, yes, you're right about that at any rate! The trip from Yorkshire to here in a "clapped-out Mini", was a small price to pay for the privilege of saying goodbye to the man I love. And I *do* love him, make no mistake about that, despite your ridicule! Or could it be that you are simply jealous of two people who have found happiness together, despite the age gap between them. You weren't so lucky. I wonder why not?'

'You don't understand,' Cam said harshly, 'I tried to contact Peter all day yesterday. I rang the New Moon, Sam Cooper's repository, Reg Rossiter's mother. No one knew where he was, or they weren't saying. I missed the obvious place, of course. I might have known he'd be with you at Driftwood—not on the phone unfortunately, otherwise I'd have told him I intended flying down to London from Teesside Airport to wish him *bon voyage*. So there you have it, the story in a nutshell. Now, why don't you stop behaving like a prima donna and sit down and talk to me?'

'About what? There's nothing more to

say.' Turning, she hurried out of the building.

Staring after her retreating figure. Cam deeply regretted the devil inside him which made him say the wrong thing at the wrong time. What she'd said about Peter had struck home. He should have tried to contact him long before yesterday. Stubborn pride had stood in the way. Peter had called him a bastard, had threatened to leave his employ; bitter pills for a man of his temperament to swallow. So he had played the martyr; his way of showing who was boss. Moreover he'd lied when he told Caroline that his decision to fly from Teesside had been reached the day before. It had been an early morning decision, arrived at too late to serve any useful purpose. He had missed Peter by minutes.

Now he had further antagonised Caroline Fraser. But why? For what possible reason? But beneath his bluster, he knew why. She was right. He *was* jealous of her relationship with Peter Augustine.

Caroline drove through the heavy traffic by instinct. Coolly and calmly, as she had done so many times before, keeping her emotions severely under control, heading north towards Biggleswade where she would branch off from the motorway and find herself somewhere to stay overnight. She didn't care where, a small hotel, even a pub would do, just as long as she could have a hot bath, a meal, however simple, and a comfortable bed to lie down on afterwards.

Luck was on her side. The Hotel Anatole, in a tree lined avenue on the outskirts of Biggleswade, proved to be a family run business of the olde worlde variety, with chintz covered armchairs, softly shaded lamps, a small bar and a well appointed dining room.

The atmosphere was restful. The single room she booked for the night had an adjoining bathroom, a TV set, tea and coffee making equipment, central heating, rose velvet curtains at the window, and a well-sprung bed with a rose pink duvet and matching pillows. There was also, thank God, a digital clock radio on the bedside cabinet.

The dining room was empty apart from herself and an elderly couple on the far side of the room, who smiled vaguely in her direction as she sat down and picked up the menu.

The woman who came to take her order was plumply attractive, in her mid-fifties, at a rough guess, Caroline decided, smiling up at her.

'I'm the proprietress Maisie Overton,'

the woman explained. 'My son Eric usually does the waiting, but this is his night off, so you'll have to make do with me, I'm afraid.' She laughed happily. 'My husband John does the cooking; our other son Stevie's in charge of the bar, which reminds me, would you like something to drink with your meal? I can recommend the sole *bonne femme*. Or perhaps you'd prefer the roast chicken?'

'The sole will be fine, thanks,' Caroline said, 'and a glass of Perrier with ice and lemon. Nothing more. I'm not very hungry.' She added apologetically, 'It's been a long, hard day, and I'm feeling a bit jaded.'

'Been seeing someone off?' the woman asked sympathetically.

'Well, yes, but how did you know? I mean, how could you tell?'

'Just a gut feeling.' Maisie sighed, then smiled. 'You're not the first, you won't be the last. What you need is a good night's sleep. I'll send up a cup of Horlicks and a few chocolate biscuits, if you like. And you needn't hurry down to breakfast tomorrow. We're not busy.'

A pretty young woman came up with the Horlicks and biscuits an hour later. Another member of the Overton family, presumably; confirmed when she said, 'Mum sent this, and she said to be sure to ring down if there's anything else you want.'

How kind they were, Caroline thought, getting ready for bed. Not that she expected to sleep immediately. Alone at last, her mind was filled with disconnected impressions of the day, coloured pieces of a kaleidoscope tumbling in confusion in her tired brain; the swift running away of the road beneath the car tyres, the flashing past of the scenery, her mounting feeling of dread nearing the journey's end.

Thank God there had been no protracted delay at Heathrow. She couldn't have borne that. Who had written the lines, *"Since there's no help, come, let us kiss and part"*? She couldn't remember. Whoever he was, the poet had put into words her own dread of spun out goodbyes; the meaningless platitudes uttered when there was nothing meaningful left to say.

She simply thanked God for that last night at Driftwood; the blissful silence of those long hours of darkness during which she and Peter had said all that needed to be said to one another, so that what they had said at their moment of parting, scarcely mattered—except, 'I love you'. But they had known that anyway, and no matter how many times the words were uttered, could neither add to nor detract from their full implication, once the ultimate proof of love had been given and received.

Now Caroline's thoughts were centred on a silver-winged plane crossing the Atlantic Ocean; a tiny speck in the vastness of a starry night—her lover aboard that plane.

Up early next morning, anxious to get back to Yorkshire as soon as possible, she showered, dressed and went down to breakfast.

Mrs Overton was in the dining room, placing the breakfast menus on the tables. 'Another lovely day,' she said cheerfully. 'My word, what a lovely summer we're having!' Her face fell, 'Not so wonderful for some though. A terrible thing about that air disaster, isn't it? Did you hear the six o'clock news? All lives lost, apparently. Not that the poor souls would stand an earthly chance of survival. Not over the Atlantic, I mean.'

The woman stopped speaking to stare at Caroline, then, 'What is it, Mrs Fraser?' she asked anxiously as, rising unsteadily to her feet, Caroline stumbled unseeingly from the room.

Chapter Ten

In vain, Maisie Overton begged Caroline not to travel that day. In her opinion Mrs Fraser was not fit to drive her car any distance if at all.

'You don't understand,' Caroline said dully, 'I *must* go home.'

'I blame myself,' Maisie said tearfully, 'for breaking the news to you the way I did. It just never occurred to me ... I'm so sorry.'

'It wasn't your fault. You couldn't possible have known.' Caroline smiled sadly, deeply touched by the landlady's concern for her welfare.

'But you've had a terrible shock! What you need is a doctor, a sedative, a day or two in bed!'

'No, what I need is to go home! Please don't worry, I'll be perfectly all right, I promise. You see, that's what Peter would want. I'll feel closer to him there.'

'Yes, well I can understand that,' Maisie admitted. 'I'd feel the same myself if I lost my husband. I'd just want to stay on here and get on with my life, for the sake of the children. I dare say you feel the same way?'

'Yes,' Caroline murmured. What more could she possibly have said? How to tell a comparative stranger that the man she had lost was not her husband but her lover, in whose arms she had discovered a new meaning of life?

Now, for Peter's sake, she must continue to live her life as he would have wished; rejoicing in the memory of their love and all it had meant to them during their brief time together. Anything less would seem a betrayal of their love; all the joy and happiness he had given her from the depths of his warm, generous nature; his bubbling sense of fun, his laughter. Above all, his tenderness, expressed in so many ways.

It had been a long, tiring journey. Perhaps Maisie Overton had been right in attempting to dissuade her from driving that distance in a state of shock, Caroline thought, but nothing short of physical disability could have prevented her return to Driftwood.

There and only there could she come to terms with her grief, in the room above the verandah with its poignant memories of Peter, and all that he had meant to her on that last night together.

Stumbling upstairs to the turret room, flinging herself on the bed, she gave way to uncontrollable tears, not for herself but Peter, whose young life had ended so tragically. But *why?*

The cause of the disaster remained a mystery. Steeling herself to listen to news flashes on the car radio, she had gleaned that a Mayday signal had been received from the pilot of the stricken aircraft shortly before eleven, after which no further signal had been sent or received. The plane, its crew and its passengers had simply disappeared without trace mid-Atlantic, with little hope of recovery of the wreckage, the victims' bodies or the aircraft's Black Box flight recorder.

So how exactly had Peter died? Struggling for survival in the deep, cold water of a hostile ocean? Oh dear Christ, if only she knew for certain that he had not suffered too long or too painfully before the end came. But she would never know, and this was the cross she would have to bear for the rest of her life—the uncertainty of not knowing ...

How long she had slept, she had no idea. Time had ceased to exist. All she knew was she had come home to Driftwood in daylight; now darkness had fallen. The sky beyond the turret room window was pitch black, or so it appeared until, getting up, her limbs stiff, her face still wet with tears, she stepped out on the balcony to find that the night sky was littered with stars.

'Oh, Peter,' she whispered, 'Peter, where are you?'

The tide was on the turn. She could hear the gentle refrain of the sea lapping the shore, and thought of the oceans of the world, of tides governed by the moon, the vastness of the universe governing the whole of human life, the unfathomable mysteries of life and death; of life after death, the survival of the human spirit. She wanted to believe in the continuance of life after death, never more so than now. But where was the proof? Had she merely conjured up Sarah St Just's presence at Driftwood at a time of personal distress? Had she imagined those voices she'd heard the first time she'd entered the house? Had that strange feeling of *déjà-vu* been nothing more than a mental aberration born of fatigue? It must have been. What other explanation was possible?

At that moment she saw on the beach below, near the water's edge, what appeared to be a glimmer of light shining through the darkness—as if the moon had glinted momentarily in a rock-pool. But there was no moon, only starlight.

Then the strange light began to move slowly across the beach towards the barrier of rocks on the far side of the cove, emitting a kind of radiance, with the outline of a human being—a woman.

Transfixed, Caroline followed the progress of shimmering light with her eyes until it disappeared from sight near the breakwater. Gripping the edge of the balcony, heart racing, she knew beyond a shadow of doubt that what she had seen was the ghost of the Woman in White: Sarah St Just.

The message was clear enough—'*You have seen me, as I intended you should. Now do you believe in the continuance of life after death?*'

Trembliing violently with emotion, clinging to the balcony, looking up at the stars, Caroline realised that she must reshape her future entirely; that she no longer cared about her husband's affair with another woman.

Somehow, she had stepped into a different dimension of understanding; a kind of spiritual release linked to a newborn sense of freedom. A blessed escape from a past no longer necessary or even important to her now, with a man who had never really loved her.

Where she would go from here, she had no idea. Certainly not to London to begin the dreary business of divorce proceedings. She would decide where to go, what to do with her life from now on, when the time came to leave Driftwood.

Blessedly, she was no longer afraid.

Fixing her eyes on the brightest star, 'Goodnight, Peter my darling,' she whispered, 'sleep well, my love. You too, Sarah, and thank you. Thank you for being with me tonight, when I needed you so much.'

Next day came a procession of visitors to pay their respects.

Reg Rossiter was the first to arrive. Handing her a bunch of red roses, 'I thought you'd like these,' he said stiffly, ill at ease under the circumstances.

'Oh, Reg, they're lovely! Please do come in. I'll make some coffee.'

'Well, no, I'd rather not, if you don't mind. I've left the office unattended; hung a sign on the door. "Back in half an hour". I just wanted you to know how sorry I am about—Peter. My mother too. We thought the world of him, and, well, we knew how he felt about you.'

'Thanks, Reg. And please thank your mother.'

'I will, and if you'll forgive my saying so, you and Peter were two of a kind, the salt of the earth!' His voice roughened suddenly, his eyes filled with tears, 'Well, I'd best be off now, but Ma told me to tell you you'll be welcome any time to have tea with her, if you feel in need of company.'

'Nothing would please me more.' Caroline smiled at him. 'By the way, your beard's coming along quite nicely now, and it suits you. Keep up the good work.'

He seemed pleased. 'Do you really think so?'

'Yes, I do. Have you a girlfriend, by the way?'

He blushed, 'Well, not so you'd notice. She's more into the macho type of bloke, if you know what I mean.'

'I know exactly what you mean,' Caroline assured him, 'so take my advice, find yourself a girlfriend who will be more than happy to love you just as you are—one of the kindest human beings I've ever known.'

Later, Sam Cooper arrived on her doorstep. 'Please forgive my intrusion, my lady,' he said, handing her a bunch of white chrysanthemumus, 'but I reckoned you might feel in need of a comforting word or two right now. What I mean is, Peter made no secret of the way he felt about you, with good reason, I'd say. You are a lady, he was a natural-born gentleman. The world will be a poorer place without him.'

'Thanks, Sam. I'm glad you came, I'd like to talk to you, to put forward a proposition I have in mind.'

'Oh? What proposition might that be?'

He doffed his cap, crossing the threshold, and followed her through to the kitchen, looking puzzled, somewhat alarmed.

Caroline smiled mysteriously, 'Sit down, and I'll tell you,' she said, filling the kettle for a cup of coffee. 'Remember the day of the removal, when you warned me about the danger of leaving the Mercedes in the car park?'

'Well, yeah, of course I remember. Why do you ask?'

'Because your son Zach just happened to mention, when you weren't listening, that to own a Mercedes had been a lifelong dream of yours, never realised. Am I right?'

'I dunno for sure. I might hev said summat to that effect,' Sam floundered, acutely embarrassed, 'but I still don't see what you're driving at, my lady. The little toe-rag knew fine well it was nobbut a pipe-dream—a bit like Whitby Football Club winning the Cup Final! Chance'd be a fine thing!'

Caroline laughed. Handing Sam a mug of coffee, she said, sitting opposite him at the kitchen table, 'Even pipe-dreams come true now and then. I can't guarantee, of course, that Whitby Football Club will ever play at Wembley, but the Mercedes is yours. And if you don't believe me, here are the keys.'

'But I don't understand!' Sam stared at the keys open-mouthed, lost for words.

'Then I'd better explain,' Caroline said gently, 'I asked Mr Pitman to store the car for me, pro tem, until I'd decided what to do about it. Well, now I *have* decided. You see, Sam, I simply had to find a way to repay you for all your kindness to me.' She added mistily, 'No one had ever called me "my lady" before.'

'But that car's worth thousands. You can't just—give it away!'

'Kindness is beyond price, Sam, and there's no law that says I can't give away my own property if I want to.'

'Eh, I don't know what to say.'

'You could pick up the car tomorrow,' Caroline suggested, 'if you're not busy. I'll go with you to Whitby, if you like, to see Mr Pitman and make the handover official. How does that strike you?'

'Truth to tell, my lady, I'm struck all of a heap as it is,' Sam admitted bemusedly. 'All I did was shift a bit of furniture for you.'

'You did much more than that, Sam. More than you'll ever know. Remember the few extra bits and pieces you brought with you on the day of the removal? The sofa, so I could lie down near the fire? Let's just say that I'd forgotten what kindness meant when I came here to

Driftwood. Until I met you and your sons, Reg Rossiter and—Peter.'

Standing up, she added, not wanting to embarrass the man with sentimentality, 'So shall we say ten o'clock in the morning?'

Sam smiled, 'I guess so, if you're really sure that's what you want. But it'll tek a bit of getting used to. Me owning a Mercedes, I mean!'

He walked up the cliff path like a man in a dream. As if he'd won a prize in the National Lottery, without so much as a ticket.

Darkness was falling when Caroline's final caller of the day arrived on the doorstep. It was Cameron McCauley, the last person she wished to see. Even so, courtesy demanded inviting him in. He had, after all, taken the trouble to knock this time.

'Why have you come? What is it you want?' she asked.

'Just to talk to you about Peter,' he said wearily. 'Do you mind if I sit down? It's been a long, hard day.'

'You'd better come through to the kitchen,' she said, leading the way. She hadn't had the heart to light the drawing room fire. In any case, she wanted an early night.

Sitting down, he said, 'I really cared about Peter, you know. I knew from the moment we met that he was a very special person, and that was the reason why I pinned so much faith in his future.'

'Really?' she flung at him, 'Well, all I can say is if you cared about Peter, you had a strange way of showing it! Frankly, Mr McCauley, in my view all you have ever cared about is money! You didn't give a damn for Peter as a very special person, merely as a good investment as the future manager of your blasted hotel!'

Cam said unexpectedly, 'Would it surprise you to know that I have decided not to go ahead with that particular project? The fact is, I've spent the whole of today negotiating the sale of the property with a Kingston-based firm of estate agents.'

'For a handsome profit, I dare say,' Caroline said scornfully. 'Now, would you mind leaving? Why you came in the first place, I can't begin to imagine, unless—oh, I see—an assuagement of your guilt complex concerning Peter's death! That's why you came to see me, isn't it? Well, if you came here seeking absolution for your own sins of omission, you came to the wrong place, I'm afraid.

'Just one more thing, before you leave, Peter thought the world of you—God alone knows why! But that's the kind of person he was, thinking the best of everyone. The last thing he would have wanted was to burden you with guilt. So don't spoil all that, otherwise what would his time on earth be worth? Less than nothing, had he thought for one moment that you, a man he looked up to and admired, saw him, not as a human being, but a damned good investment.'

She added succinctly, opening the front door to speed McCauley's departure, 'By the way, I shall be leaving Driftwood the day after tomorrow. I shall hand in the keys to Reg Rossiter on the day of my departure, pay any monies due to you for electricity or whatever ... the re-removal of Sarah St Just's furniture to Sam Cooper's repository, for instance. I couldn't bear the thought of your being out of pocket on my account! Now, goodnight and goodbye, Mr McCauley. Hopefully, our paths will never cross again!'

Stepping on to the verandah, spreading out his hands, Cam said simply, 'It's raining! Oh, thanks be to God, it's raining! At long last, it's raining!'

It was then, stepping down from the verandah to feel the raindrops splashing on to her upturned face, like tears, Caroline realised that this brief Indian summer was over forever, apart from its everlasting memories of happiness which would remain with her till the end of time.

Cam said hoarsely, 'Well, goodbye, Mrs

Fraser, I'm sorry it had to end this way.'

Standing on the beach, seeing the wavering beam of the torch he was carrying moving erratically away from her up the path to the car park, Caroline wondered what Cam meant. But then, she supposed, returning indoors, locking the front door behind her, there would always be people stupid enough not to know when to come in from the rain. Herself included, perhaps?

Next day, she called for Sam at the repository. They drove to Whitby in her car. He would drive back in the Mercedes. When she remarked how smart he looked, he laughed and said he couldn't very well drive a posh car in his working clothes.

'The lads are that chuffed,' he said, 'they've bought a bottle of champagne to celebrate, when we get back. You will join us, won't you, my lady? An' there'll be a bite to eat, an' all. My missus was in the kitchen when I left home, making a few sausage rolls an' suchlike for the boys to take to the office.'

'Yes, thanks, Sam. Of course I'll join you, and I'll look forward to meeting your wife.'

'Not much chance of that,' Sam chuckled. 'She's a bit on the shy side is Maudie. Never mind, I've promised her a run in the Merc later on. A pity the weather's spoilt itself, but this rain will do good, that's for sure, what with the rivers an' reservoirs being so low.'

When Caroline told him she'd be leaving Driftwood the next day, Sam looked stricken, 'I'm sorry to hear that,' he said concernedly. 'Funny, really, I was hoping you'd stay on there. You seem to belong to that house somehow, as if it was a part of you.'

'It *is*, Sam,' Caroline said quietly. 'It always will be. But it's time I was moving on. My time at Driftwood is ended. It has served its purpose, if that makes sense?'

'So you'll be going back to London, I suppose?' Sam asked wistfully. 'Back to where you belong? I've never been one to pry into other folk's affairs. Reg just happened to mention that's where your home is.'

'It was, once upon a time.' Caroline smiled sadly, 'No longer, I'm afraid. The truth is, I no longer have a home as such, which is why I have to move on, to discover where I really belong; to create a new home for myself, God willing.'

'Have you any idea where, my lady?' Sam asked gently.

'Oh, yes,' Caroline said calmly, remembering that night on the balcony beneath the stars when, imbued with renewed hope and courage, a blessed sense of freedom so long denied her, 'I shall go to Scarborough. I think I'll find what I'm looking for there—whatever that may be. Not happiness exactly, but peace of mind.' She smiled through her tears, 'So wish me luck, Sam, and say an occasional prayer for me—okay?'

Sam said fervently, 'I will that, my lady. And if ever you need help of any kind, all you have to do is ask!'

Locking the front door of Driftwood behind her for the last time was the hardest thing Caroline had ever done in her life. Walking slowly up the cliff path, turning to look back at the cottage, the beach below, she remembered all that it had meant to her during the Indian summer days of her tenancy. As if she had lived, for a little while, the full drama of life against a backdrop of the flow and ebb of tides on the shore, the crying of the seabirds overhead, moon and starlit nights. All over and done with now the time had come to move on—except in memory. And memories of this place, Caroline knew, would remain with her for the rest of her life.

Part Two

Chapter Eleven

From the windows of her room in Scarborough's prestigious Crown Hotel overlooking the South Bay, watching storm-tossed breakers rolling in on the shore, Caroline longed intensely to find a place she could call home, to which end she had haunted the local estate agents' offices. But nothing she had viewed so far had come up to expectation despite the glowing reports handed out to her, one of which had captured her imagination until ...

The blurb had read: 'This newly converted top floor flat in the Old Town area of Scarborough comprises a fully modernised kitchen and bathroom, private parking space and panoramic views of the South Bay from the lounge windows.'

Viewing the property, Caroline had discovered that the 'lounge windows' were two attic dormers set so high up that one would need the aid of a step-ladder to see out of them at all, the so called lounge would scarcely permit the use of a fully extended deckchair and the single, dark bedroom resembled a cell. 'What you need here, as tenants,' she told the estate agent succinctly, 'is a Jesuit priest and a giraffe-necked woman!'

Other agents had introduced her to a series of detached bungalows with oil fired central heating, stone built fireplaces, picture windows overlooking gardens with fish ponds and larch fencing, on the outskirts of town. All well and good in their way, but not Driftwood.

The winding road across the moors had seemed to Caroline, during her first sad and lonely days in unfamiliar surroundings, like an umbilical cord linking her to Driftwood, imbuing her with the comforting feeling that, retracing that road, hurrying down the cliff path to the cottage, she would find the drawing room fire still lit for her, lights shining through the darkness, the rocking-chair on the verandah, awaiting her return.

Sadly, she realised that there could be no return to Driftwood except in memory. The cottage would be cold and dank now that November was here; the sea thundering in on the beach, wild and angry, with storm-ruffled breakers.

Moreover, Cameron McCaulley would have lost no time in returning Sarah St Just's furniture to Sam Cooper's repository, boarding up the drawing room fireplace,

166

removing the overmantle in favour of the print of the green-faced woman in readiness for the next influx of summer visitors. Expunging all evidence of her own brief tenancy as if she had never existed.

Even so, common sense told her that she must find somewhere of her own to live sooner or later. A house, for preference, not a flat. An old house, perhaps in need of modernisation, with a view of the sea from its upper windows?

Meanwhile, she must write to her solicitor and long time friend, Basil Pryde, and her financial adviser, Jon Carradine, for help and advice in her present circumstances.

Peter's death had brought with it the realisation that she no longer cared about her past life with Felix or the London house with its big empty rooms—empty in the sense that, bereft of love and laughter, they had resembled the film sets of old black and white movies: sumptuously furnished, but without substance. She had no wish to complicate her life with litigation, but Basil Pryde must be kept informed of her present whereabouts now that she had decided to settle in Yorkshire, and she needed Jon Carradine's confirmation that her financial affairs were in order.

Money, so far, had been the least of

her problems, but there was no guarantee of financial security, in which case she would have to cut her coat according to the cloth. Thankfully, her father had suggested postgraduate courses in business management in the event of needing to earn her own living at some stage in the future.

At home with her parents prior to her marriage, Caroline had happily made full use of her domestic skills, planning menus, shopping and doing the weekend cooking to give the elderly cook time off.

Too late now to regret that she had left the family home in Hampstead to marry a man her parents had disliked and distrusted. Not that they had put obstacles in her path. Her father had merely pointed out that she knew next to nothing about Felix, and suggested waiting a while before taking such an important step in her life.

He must have realised from the beginning that Felix was a fortune-hunter, and he had taken good care to ensure that his son-in-law would never be able to lay a finger on his own capital and investments after his death. Unfortunately, he'd held no power of attorney over Caroline's inheritance from her grandmother Heritage, which had dwindled alarmingly after the wedding.

The old adage, *'A fool and his money*

are soon parted', had quickly dawned on Caroline during the early days of her marriage. Perhaps she had been a fool in allowing Felix unlimited access to her money by way of a joint bank account, but surely any wife deeply in love with her husband would have done the same?

Her spirits at a low ebb in this sad, dark November, ill at ease in her opulent yet curiously negative and empty hotel environment; still grieving for Peter, missing his warm vital presence in her life, she longed for something positive to do to ease the dull weight of the future confronting her.

One rainy day, standing on the exact spot where she had stood with Peter what seemed like a lifetime ago when they had revelled in the warmth of a perfect October afternoon, Caroline remembered Sarah St Just's links with Scarborough, and her intention to find out more about her when Peter had gone away ...

She had not known then, how could she, that he would go away from her never to return? Now it seemed to her that she was not alone in the rain after all, that a warm presence had invaded the coldness of her heart, a gentle spirit breathing words of comfort and hope, telling her not to despair. The words, *'Seek, and ye shall find'* hung in the air about her. *'Seek, and ye shall find!'*

Yes, of course!

Her face uplifted to the rain, Caroline retraced her steps to the Crown Hotel. Entering the foyer, walking up to the reception desk smiling, Caroline said to the busy, efficient young woman in charge of the various telephones and computers, 'I'll be leaving here first thing tomorrow morning. I'll pay my bill this evening after dinner, if that's all right.'

'Certainly, Mrs Fraser,' the girl replied warmly. From past experiences with the rough diamonds of the hotel trade—money to burn, creating mayhem in the dining room as often as not—Mrs Fraser compared very favouably: a quiet lady who ate sparingly, and always left the dining room with a word of thanks to the chef. 'By the way,' she added, turning to the pigeon holes behind the desk, 'these letters arrived for you after you'd gone out.'

'Thank you.' Holding the letters in her hand, Caroline rang for the lift and went upstairs to her room to read them.

Jon Carradine's letter cheered her enormously. She could see him quite clearly in her mind's eye; tall, stoop-shouldered because of his height, grey haired and bespectacled, his eyes, behind the glasses, a vivid shade of blue.

'*My dear Caroline,*' he had written, '*Thank God for your letter! I thought, for one awful moment you'd discovered the world was flat after all, and dropped off it accordingly ...*' The letter went on to assure her that her investments were doing well. A full statement of her quarterly returns was presently being prepared, meanwhile he was sending her a printout to set her mind at rest.

On a personal note, he was sorry to have heard she had felt it expedient to leave London last September, but felt this had been a wise decision on her part in view of the distressing circumstances, and to avoid the media attention she had dreaded.

Most importantly, she need have no fear of her husband's gaining control over her finances unless she allowed him access to the capital sum of her inheritance and investments.

He concluded, '*A strong word of advice. Beware of trickery and deceit. Sign nothing without my knowledge and consent. Remember that you are your father's daughter, that his last will and testament was carefully devised to ensure your future financial independence. Yours and yours alone. Need I say more?*'

Her solicitor's letter, couched in more formal terms yet sympathetic towards herself and her matrimonial problems, nevertheless queried Caroline's reluctance to institute divorce proceedings against her husband in view of his liaison with Signora Francesca Delgado, admittedly his mistress, with whom he was now living openly in the house in Eaton Square—a deplorable situation in his opinion.

'As a long standing friend of your late father in particular, I have to say, without prejudice, that his deep regard for his daughter's future welfare and happiness would have centred upon a speedy end to an untenable situation, within the letter of the Law.

Therefore, my dear Caroline, having sought my advice, at the same time having indicated your unwillingness to enter into litigation for the time being, for personal reasons, I scarcely know how to proceed, apart from advising you most earnestly to reconsider your present viewpoint from all angles before reaching an ultimate decision.'

Sinking into a chair, staring into the past, shocked beyond belief by the news that Felix and Francesca were now living together, Caroline's imagination ran riot.

How could Felix have heaped upon her this final humiliation? True, she had never regarded the house in Eaton Square as a home, but to have allowed his mistress access to it beggared belief! Her blood ran cold thinking of Francesca clearing shelves, drawers and cupboards of a rejected wife's belongings to make room for her own; issuing orders to the servants, making her presence felt, sweeping aside convention with a wave of the hand. Flourishing by reason of her fame, beauty and something far more disturbing—the ruthless arrogance and evil Caroline had glimpsed in that self-portrait in the Purcell Galleries last spring.

Given a much smaller house with comfortably furnished rooms, in Bayswater perhaps, and if Felix had wanted children, their marriage might have stood a chance of survial, Caroline thought wearily. She, at least, would have found a reason for living in the creation of a home in the true meaning of the word. But Felix had wanted a palace not a home, to reflect his success as a bestselling author.

Fatherhood, he'd said carelessly, would tarnish his 'James Bond' image, besides which children were a damned nuisance; excess baggage he could well do without. But what if he wanted a child, children, by Francesca Delgado? What then? Or possibly his mistress was already pregnant by him?

Caroline rose unsteadily to her feet to

begin packing her belongings in readiness for her departure from the Crown Hotel early the next morning, wondering what on earth had possessed her to even think of leaving to find herself temporary accommodation in a furnished flat where she could cook and shop for herself once more.

Suddenly she knew: what she sought was independence; what she hoped to find was a fresh reason for living.

When she had finished her packing, apart from her night things and her radio, and before going downstairs to dinner, she wrote a letter to her solicitor asking him to go ahead with the divorce as quickly as possible. Stepping out into the wind and rain, she posted it before returning to the hotel dining room to sit at her usual table, wondering, as she did so where she'd be and what she'd be eating at this time tomorrow evening.

Curiously, she was no longer sad, or afraid of the future. She felt suddenly alive once more, strangely happy and contented having reached this watershed in her life. As if she had reached a crossroads with a signpost pointing in different directions, so that it was entirely up to her which path to follow. Pray God she had chosen the right one.

Only time would tell.

Finishing her meal, she passed a word or two of appreciation to the chef via her favourite waiter, went through to reception to settle her bill, then walked slowly upstairs to her room to sit by the window overlooking the rain-washed promenade, remembering all the moments of her life which had led to this one in particular. All the hurt and disappointment she had suffered along the way, mitigated by the happiness of loving, and being loved in return, she saw as a balancing of the scales in her favour.

Now she had her sights set on tomorrow. A new day. A new beginning, God willing. *'Seek, and ye shall find.'*

Later, lying in bed, listening to the shipping forecast, she thought briefly of Cam McCauley, of Driftwood, of starlight on the sea. Inevitably of Peter Augustine, of summertime; of tides washing in on the shores of so many faraway places —Hebrides, Stornaway, Mull of Kintyre, Wight, Dogger, Finisterre ...

Sleet, chivvied by a strong sea wind, scurried the promenade next morning when a porter carried Caroline's luggage to her car and stowed it in the boot.

'I hope you'll have a pleasant journey, madam,' the man said respectfully touching his cap, when she was settled in the driving seat. 'Going far?'

'No, not very,' Caroline smiled, handing him a tip, wondering what his reaction would be if she told him she was heading for an accommodation agency in the town centre, in the hope of finding a furnished flat to rent for the time being.

Her luck was in. The receptionist seated behind a wide desk in an overheated office, the walls of which were plastered with details of accommodation currently on offer, recorded Caroline's name and address plus requirements on a form bearing the logo, 'We Aim to Please'. Her remark, 'You've come at the right time,' revived memories of Reg Rossiter, whose beard should have reached fruition by now, Caroline thought wistfully.

'So what you want is a self-contained, fully furnished flat, one bedroom, bathroom, kitchen, lounge and parking space,' the girl reiterated. 'Any particular location?'

'As close to the town centre as possible,' Caroline said, 'near the shops and the library, for preference.'

'Hmm.' The girl, neatly dressed, obviously efficient, gave the matter some thought then, 'I may just have the very place for you. The flat I have in mind came in quite recently. Yesterday, as a matter of fact. The owners are going abroad for three months—Australia, to stay with their daughter who's having a baby. But,' she added, 'there are certain drawbacks ...'

'Such as?' Caroline enquired mildly.

'Well, it's quite expensive, and high up in the world. Also, a bond and references are required. It is a rather superior flat, you see, in The Crescent ...'

'In other words, a desirable residence in a posh part of town?' Caroline suggested, tongue-in-cheek. 'How high up in the world, by the way?'

'The fourth floor, and there's no lift, I'm afraid.'

'Tell me, is it anywhere near Londesborough Lodge?' Caroline asked the question diffidently to conceal her excitement, the sudden swift beating of her heart.

'Yes, just across the road, and the library and shops are round the corner. In fact it's a lovely position, bang in the middle of town, but secluded, with a central garden. Would you like to take a look at the flat? I could let you have the keys.'

'That would be lovely.'

'Right. And if you like it, we could take it from there.'

The owners of the flat were obviously people of taste and discernment, Caroline realised the moment she crossed the threshold. The spacious rooms were exquisitely furnished. There were deep pile carpets in the lounge, lined velvet curtains, inlaid side tables with shaded reading lamps, comfortable armchairs and a sofa upholstered in a restful shade of moss green draylon, bookshelves flanking the fireplace, gilt-framed oil paintings on the walls. Best of all, a view of the sea from the windows.

The master bedroom contained a king size bed, built-in cupboards, a floral skirted dressing table with a triple mirror, walnut chests of drawers and bedside tables. The adjacent bathroom contained a shower unit, bidet, bath and hand basins with gold plated taps; the kitchen, pine floor to ceiling units, a split-level cooker, a Bendix washing-machine, a microwave oven, and a dining area comprising a pinewood table and chairs.

Little wonder that the owners required references and bond from a potential tenant of their property Caroline thought, standing at the drawing room windows looking out to sea. They'd be crazy to let it to just anyone. This after all, was *their* home, no one else's—and whilst she would be happy to stay here for a little while, she would never truly belong here, as they did. Nor would she wish to do so.

Returning to the agency, she handed

back the keys to the receptionist.

'Well, what did you make of it?' the girl enquired brightly.

Caroline smiled faintly, 'I feel inclined to take it,' she said thoughtfully, remembering Driftwood, 'though I might feel somewhat inhibited there in the role of custodian of other people's property. That's what it amounts to doesn't it, in the long run?'

'You mean because of the bond and the references?' the girl asked anxiously, eager to do business at this slack time of year.

'No, not really,' Caroline said, 'there's more to it than that. What I'm really looking for is a small flat where I'd feel more at home. Somewhere not quite so—daunting.'

The receptionist sighed deeply, 'Then you'd best take a look at the basement flat at the same address,' she said, 'not that it's much cop compared with the one on the top floor. But you can't blame me for trying, can you?'

Handing over the keys, 'This one's been to let for a couple of months now,' she admitted, 'for obvious reasons, as you'll see for yourself. The furniture's functional, to put it mildly. It belonged to an old lady who died recently in hospital due to a stroke, whose relatives decided to let the flat furnished, until they find a buyer for it. No luck so far, I'm afraid. But at least

179

they're not asking for a bond and taking up references!'

The basement steps led down to a glass panelled door opening onto a narrow passageway. The sitting room to the right of the passage was comfortably if not spectacularly furnished. There was a three piece suite near the fireplace, a standard lamp, an oak sideboard, a marble clock on the mantelpiece, plus various brass ornaments. The carpet, a colourfully patterned Axminster, though well worn, was by no means shabby or threadbare. There were pictures, not oil paintings on the walls, one of which, a reproduction of Millais' *Bubbles,* recalled memories of Caroline's childhood nursery of long ago; imparting a sense of familiarity and homecoming.

The lady who had lived here she decided, had been of the old school, as proud of her possessions as the couple in the top flat were of theirs, though obviously less well off.

Wandering from room to room, gaining an overall impression of cleanliness and simple, ordinary comfort, Caroline knew she would be far happier here than in the overwhelmingly smart apartment on the fourth floor.

She liked the kitchen in particular, with

its common or garden electric cooker, functional work surfaces; the homely touches here and there—a small kitchen dresser with shelves of household china, an old fashioned egg-timer, a japanned tea caddy, a metal teapot plus handknitted cosy; a wall clock, and a row of busy-lizzies and geranium plants on the windowsill above the sink.

Instinctively, Caroline knew that she could be happy here in these unpretentious surroundings, shopping and cooking for herself: jaunting to the shops and the library whenever she felt like it. Maintaining her privacy while at the same time making discoveries about the town she had elected as her future home, reading up on its history; finding out more about Sarah St Just and her faithful companion Margaret Roberts—where they had lived, and where they were buried.

Returning for a second time to the agency, 'Well, what comes next?' Caroline asked the receptionist. 'Signing on the dotted line, perhaps?'

'You mean you—*liked* the flat?' The girl stared up at her in surprise.

'Yes. Quite a lot, as a matter of fact. So, how soon can I move in?'

'Right away, if you want. But I'd better check with the owners first, if that's okay with you.' She added bemusedly, 'Hang on just a sec, you haven't asked about the rent yet! I'm sorry, Mrs Fraser, but the owners are bound to ask about your credentials. All I have here is your name and your London address. I'll need more to go on than that!'

'Yes, of course,' Caroline agreed, 'so how much is the rent per week?'

'Sixty quid. I mean—pounds!'

'That seems reasonable. Any hidden extras?'

'Well, there'll be a proportion of council tax and water rates. Apart from that, I can't think of anything except gas and electricity, but those items have nothing to do with the landlords. They'll want you to sign a tenancy agreement of course, and an inventory.'

'Yes, of course,'

'Any idea how long you'll be staying there?'

'Difficult to say. Two months, perhaps three, or until I come across somewhere more permanent. A home of my own, preferably a house. I haven't found anything I feel inclined to purchase so far,' Caroline said.

The girl, whose name was Lara West-wood, glanced up at her with renewed interest. 'So you're thinking of settling here in Scarborough?' she asked. 'Funny,

I'd got it into my head you were on holiday, because of your London address, I suppose.'

'I shall not be going back there,' Caroline said quietly. 'I just need somewhere to stay for the time being. Frankly, I'm tired of hotel life. I've been staying at the Crown these past few weeks ...'

'The Crown?' Lara looked suitably impressed. 'That must have cost you an arm and a leg!'

Caroline smiled ruefully, 'Money is the least of my problems, I assure you. Indeed, it might be helpful if I paid, say three months rent in advance. That would set your clients' mind at rest. Would a cheque be in order? Or would they prefer cash? A silly question, really. Anyone in their right senses would prefer cash! I'm not sure if I have that much on me, at the moment. Let me see!'

Opening her shoulder bag, unearthing her wallet, 'No, I'm sorry, all I have with me right now is three hundred or so, and I shall need a little cash in hand to purchase food and so on.'

Lara said shamefacedly, 'I'm sorry, Mrs Fraser. I'll ring the landlords, tell them the flat's let for an indefinite period and that you're willing to pay a month's rent in advance, by cheque. They have my personal guarantee that this is a bona fide transaction. Okay?'

Deeply touched by the girl's trust in her, 'That's fine by me,' Caroline said gratefully. 'So I'd best start moving in, hadn't I, and stocking the larder? Strange, really. Last night, at the hotel, I wondered where I'd be and what I'd be having for dinner tonight. Now I know! I'll be in a basement flat in The Crescent, eating—well, who knows? Baked beans on toast, I imagine!'

Chapter Twelve

She had settled well in her new surroundings, which she thought of as a 'bolt hole'; somewhere she felt safe and anonymous, able to choose where she went and what she did with her time.

The Crescent, with its tall, gracious buildings and central garden pleased Caroline enormously. Apart from Londesborough Lodge where Edward VII had once stayed with Lord and Lady Londesborough, to her delight she had discovered the building next to it was an art gallery, and the house adjacent to that, Wood End now a museum, had once been the home of the illustrious Sitwell family, the renowned writers Osbert and Sacheverell and their eccentric poetess sister, Edith.

It seemed to Caroline that she had chanced upon a treasure trove of historical significance on her doorstep. Even though Londesborough Lodge, the art gallery and Wood End were now owned by the local borough council, it was still possible for members of the public to walk, via a veritable maze of paths and gardens, to St Nicholas Cliff with its magnificent

Victorian edifice, the Grand Hotel, or to the Valley Road leading to the seashore.

Warmly clad against the raking December winds blowing in from the sea, Caroline had taken to exploring this fascinating area of the town she had begun to think of as home. This would have been impossible had she remained at the Crown, where she had felt trapped by the overheated rooms and being waited on hand and foot; the necessity of appearing suitably dressed at breakfast, lunch and dinner.

Now she could please herself how she dressed, mainly in jeans, thick-knit sweaters and an anorak. No one knew her or cared a damn how she looked. Paraphrasing the poem, *'I care for nobody, no, not I, and nobody cares for she'*.

But was this strictly true? She cared for a great many people: Jon Carradine, her financial adviser for instance; her solicitor, Basil Pryde—both of whom she had written to recently advising them of her change of address. She also cared deeply for Sam Cooper and his sons, and Reg Rossiter, none of whom she had been in touch with since leaving Driftwood.

What must they think of her? She hadn't meant to close the door on them. She had simply been too sunk in her misery over the death of Peter Augustine to care about anyone except herself. Nor had she bothered to write to Peter's parents to offer her condolences on the death of their beloved son. But surely, they of all people should have been made aware of the tender, loving relationship which had sprung up between herself and Peter prior to his death?

Call it cowardice on her part that, leaving Driftwood, she had felt unable to communicate with anyone—not even herself. In retrospect, she had stumbled through her days at the Crown like a zombie scarcely knowing how to live from one minute to the next, weeping alone in her room unable to sleep properly. Wishing to God that she had been aboard that flight to Jamaica with Peter Augustine; that she had died with him in the deep, cold waters of the Atlantic Ocean.

But fate had decreed otherwise. Now, here she was, still alive and kicking, attempting to create a new life for herself from the ruins of the old. With Christmas looming on the horizon, the wheels of her divorce petition against Felix set in motion, and with so many threads of her Driftwood days to pick up again, she scarcely knew where to begin.

Buying Christmas cards in town in the second week in December, it struck Caroline forcibly how few she needed. Half a dozen would suffice. One for Jon

Carradine, another for Basil Pryde; the rest for Sam Cooper and family, Reg Rossiter and his mother, Lara Westwood at the agency, and the remaining one for Mrs Gordon, her trusty housekeeper, addressed to their former home in Eaton Square.

How strange, she thought, that she had reached maturity with so few friends or relations to call her own. With neither uncles nor aunts to turn to at this, the most emotive time of year, when families drew closer together to celebrate Christmas.

She had never felt so lonely, so alone in the world as she did then, choosing six Christmas cards to send to people whose lives she had scarcely touched at all, apart from Jon Carradine, Basil Pryde, and Mrs Gordon—who may well have left Eaton Square now, for all she knew, since Francesca Delagado had become the new mistress of the house.

Somehow, Caroline could not envisage the down to earth Ginny Gordon knuckling down to a new regime. The elderly Scotswoman had made abundantly clear her dislike of the master of the house from time to time, especially when Felix had switched menus at the last minute.

'I'm sorry, Mrs Fraser,' she'd complained bitterly, times without number, 'but I'm a housekeeper, not a clairvoyant! How you put up with his shennanigans, I really don't know!'

'Because I have to, Mrs Gordon,' Caroline had reminded her, 'otherwise my life wouldn't be worth living!'

'Then all I can possibly say, madam, is there must be a much better way of living,' had come Mrs Gordon's quick-as-a-flash reply, 'being what you are, a lovely lady in the prime of life! If I were you, I'd be over the hills and far away in two shakes of a lamb's tail. So now you know!'

Her Christmas cards posted, Caroline derived pleasure from decorating the flat in a way she felt the former occupant would have approved of, with flowing plants, holly and candles for the brass holders on the mantelpiece.

Some mail had arrived for Mrs Gladys Farmer from people who had not heard of her death, which Caroline took round to the agency for Lara's attention.

'Oh, thanks. I'll readdress them to her family right away,' she promised. 'How are you getting on at the flat, by the way? Doing anything special for Christmas?'

'I haven't decided yet.' Lara was of the age where the thought of spending Christmas alone would be incomprehensible, a cause for concern, Caroline realised. In any case, she didn't think it necessary to explain that she wouldn't mind being alone, cooking for herself, reading, walking along the seashore.

She had written to Peter's parents, explaining that he had been a dear friend of hers whom she had driven to Heathrow on the day of his departure; had gone on to say how much he'd been looking forward to his return to Jamaica.

It had been a difficult letter to write. In the event, she had decided not to dwell on the closeness of their relationship. What would be the point? Putting herself in his mother's place, or trying to, a grieving woman would only want to know details of her son's last days on earth, and so Caroline told her about Driftwood, how Peter had come to the cottage to deliver wood for her fire; of their trip to Whitby to buy a second-hand car, and lunching together at a restaurant overlooking the estuary. Remarking on how well and happy he had been; making no mention of Cam McCauley, simply recounting the pleasure they had derived from a visit to Scarborough, where she was now living.

Reading between the lines, possibly a mother would realise and understand that their relationship had been more than a casual friendship. It had been impossible to even write about Peter without betraying the warmth of her feelings towards him.

She had ended the letter: '*Your son was*

a fine human being whose kindness and friendship enriched my own time on earth, just as his love for his family enriched his. So vivid were his descriptions of Ocho Rios, and yourselves, that I feel I know all of you quite well. Above all, I think that Peter would wish to be remembered with smiles, not tears, as a continuing source of happiness in all our lives.'

Had she gone over the top? Caroline wondered, posting the letter enclosed in a suitably worded card of sympathy. How could she possibly know? She had simply expressed what was in her heart: people like Peter Augustine did not quit the world to be mourned over and forgotten, the vital flame of them somehow lived on.

In the days preceding Christmas, she bought and posted gifts for Sam Cooper, his wife, his sons Jake and Zach, also Reg Rossiter and his mother. A road map of the British Isles for Sam, a flagon of 4711 perfume for Maudie, Havana cigars for Jake and Zach, a silk scarf for Mrs Rossiter, a 'Noel Coward' cravat for her son plus various boxes of chocolates, colourful Christmas crackers and hampers containing Drambuie-enriched Christmas puddings, duck pâte, caviare, smoked salmon and champagne: the contents of each hamper chosen with care from a delicatessen in the town centre. Caroline had also ordered for herself, for Christmas Eve, a hamper containing Parma ham, a selection of cheeses including her favourite Tome de Savoie; a jar of pickled gherkins, a tin of anchovies, a bottle of seafood dressing; smoked mackerel, and crystalised fruits.

For Christmas Day itself, she'd decided she'd treat herself to a plump little capon which she would stuff with homemade sage and onion stuffing, accompanied with vegetables, which she could then eat cold the next day and the day after.

What would Felix and Francesca be having for Christmas lunch? she wondered. Champagne and canapés, most probably. And a real 'blow out'. Caroline thanked God that this Christmas, despite her solitude, she would be spared the horror of watching her husband making a fool of himself during dinner. Stuffing himself to excess ending up so drunk that the servants would be obliged to see him upstairs to his room afterwards, to sleep off his champagne induced hangover. There were worse things than loneliness to endure, Caroline realised. She would far rather have baked beans on toast for her Christmas dinner than ever return to her former way of life.

Thinking in terms of battening down

the hatches over the Christmas period, Caroline remembered the day she came to Driftwood, desperate for solitude. Now that longing had been fulfilled, her desire granted. She wondered if Cam McCauley would spend Christmas alone at Gull Cottage, a case of Scotch for company?

In the sitting room later that morning, arranging the fresh flowers she had bought for Gladys Farmer's sideboard, glancing out of the window, Caroline noticed a red Mercedes drawn up at the kerb. Almost immediately her doorbell rang. Her heart leapt. Hurrying to answer, opening the door, 'Sam!' she said breathlessly, 'Sam Cooper, of all people! What on earth are you doing here? Well, don't just stand there! Come in! Come in!'

'You're pleased to see me then, my lady?' he murmured shyly.

'Pleased? I'm delighted! Sit down! Let me make you some coffee!'

'Nay, I'm not stopping. I just came to give you this.' He handed her an envelope.

'What is it?'

'Open it and you'll see. My missus wrote it special like, just for you. An' it were her idea, though we all agreed it would be the nicest Christmas present of all.'

Opening the letter, Caroline read:

193

'Dear Mrs Fraser,
Thinking you'll be alone at Christmas,
and maybe feeling a bit lonely, Sam and
me and the boys hope you'll see your way
clear to spending it with us. We're not posh
folk, as you know, but you'll be given a
warm welcome.
Yours sincerely,
Maude Cooper.'

And this from a woman she had never even met!

'Well, what do you think?' Sam asked eagerly. 'Course, if you've made other arrangements, Maudie said not to worry, she'll quite understand.'

'No, Sam, I haven't.' Caroline's eyes filled with tears. 'I'd love to spend Christmas with you. In fact I can think of nothing I'd like better!'

She spent the next three quarters of an hour packing a small suitcase, clearing the refrigerator and making sure the electric appliances were switched off, having decided to take the capon and the hamper with her to Whitby as additional extras to supplement the Coopers' larder.

'Eh, there's no need, my lady,' Sam said. 'You've done us proud already. Happen you'll be glad of that there bird after the holidays.'

'No offence, Sam,' Caroline explained,

194

'it's just that I'd rather everything was switched off before leaving the flat, in case of accidents happening to someone else's property. This is a rented flat, you see.' She added, surveying the fridge, 'I defrosted it a couple of days ago, so it shouldn't drip too much. Even so, I'll leave the door open and pop a couple of towels on the floor, just in case.'

'A rented flat, you say?' Sam gazed about him, taking in the fresh flowers on the sideboard, the azalea plant on the table in front of the window, the burnished brass candlesticks on the mantelpiece, the tapering red candles and the holly adorning the mirror and picture-frames, 'Well, I never! But then, some people have it, others haven't!'

'Sorry, I'm not with you. Have what?'

Sam smiled. 'The knack of homemaking. Remember Driftwood, my lady? The evening you came to the repository to choose the bits and pieces you wanted to make it into a home? It's the same here, I can tell. I caught the whiff of furniture polish the minute I crossed the threshold. I really thought you'd put down roots at last.'

'Not yet, I'm afraid,' Caroline said wistfully. 'Some day soon, perhaps. Who knows?' Then, smiling brightly, 'Well, I'm ready if you are. Everything present and correct! Just let me make sure the door's securely locked!'

She had not thought to travel the road across the moors so soon, perhaps never again, and certainly not in the Mercedes with its unpleasant memories of the day Felix had handed her the keys as a *fait accompli*, having got rid of her red Mini without so much as a by-your-leave, so strong had been his determination that she should drive a car appropriate to the wife of a bestselling author.

"For Christ's sake take control of the damned thing, woman," he'd shouted at her the first time she'd taken the wheel in heavy traffic, unnerved by the length of the bonnet, the high windscreen, and the fact that her lack of height precluded her reaching the pedals without straining forward in the driving seat at an impossible angle.

It had started to rain heavily at the time, and she hadn't known the position of the windscreen wipers, so that the entire incident had assumed nightmare proportions, with traffic bearing down on her, stop signals and roundabouts looming ahead, and her husband's voice in her ear calling her a bloody incompetent fool, a nonentity, an idiot lacking the brains of a louse.

Little wonder she had wanted to get rid of the car, Caroline thought as the miles sped beneath its tyres on this grey December afternoon, wondering if she had done the right thing, after all, in agreeing to spend Christmas in Whitby; in crossing this moorland road with its memories of the man she loved.

Breaking into her reverie, 'You're upset and unhappy, aren't you, my lady?' Sam said concernedly, 'and I can see why. You're still thinking of Driftwood, aren't you? Longing to go back there, wishing nothing had changed? But life goes on, that's the way of the world. Even so, my lady, if you'd rather turn back, I'll take you home again right now. Just say the word. I'll tell Maudie you had made other arrangements. I can't say fairer than that, now can I?'

Smiling through her tears, warmed and comforted by Sam Cooper's common sense approach to life, thinking that here was a man who closely resembled her father in his way of thinking, his concern for her welfare, Caroline said quietly, 'You're right, Sam, life goes on, and I meant what I said. I can think of nothing I'd like better than spending Christmas with you and Maudie.'

'I'm glad of that, and you won't be pestered to do anything you'd rather not.

Maudie knows you're a quiet lady—what's known as a private person nowadays—so she's given you a nice quiet room on the top floor, with a bathroom next to it, just in case things get too boisterous downstairs.'

He said gently, 'The lads usually invite a few of their pals round on Boxing Day for a bit of a party. Maudie provides a buffet for them in the front room, then we leave them to it. What I'm trying to say is, don't feel obliged to sit with us if you don't feel like it. You see, we understand that Christmas is not always an easy time to live through, especially when you've just lost someone—someone you loved.'

'Bless you, Sam,' was all Caroline could manage. 'Bless you, and thank you.'

Maudie was on the doorstep awaiting their arrival when the Mercedes swung in to the driveway. A small, plump lady with greying fair hair drawn back in a bun, wearing an anorak and fur-lined boots against the cold, pink cheeked and motherly.

Hurrying forward, hands extended, 'Eh, I'm so glad you decided to come,' she said breathlessly. 'Come inside, my dear, and get warm. Sam will see to your luggage. I expect you could do with a nice hot cup of tea? Here, let me take your coat, and come through to the fire.'

Caroline hadn't been certain what to expect, a semi-detached modern house, with a neat front garden, in a cul-de-sac most probably. But this house bore little or no resemblance to what she had imagined.

Detached, set in a quarter acre or so of scythed grass, with gnarled apple trees dotted here and there, the house, a handsome building, bay windowed, with tall chimneys, must be at least a hundred years old, she realised with a sweet feeling of relief as, crossing the threshold, she found herself in a wide hall with a broad staircase rising to the upper landings.

'Oh, what a lovely house,' Caroline said appreciatively, following her hostess into a cosy parlour with a coal fire in the grate, feeling instantly at home.

'I'm glad you like it,' Maudie chuckled. 'Mind you, the first time I saw it, just after Sam an' me were married, I very nearly ran away, the state it was in! Gave him a proper telling off, I did? "If you think I'm moving into this hovel," I said, "you've got another think coming, Sam Cooper, so there!"

'"But Maudie, love," he said in that soppy way of his, "it's going for a song, an' we'll need plenty of space when the kid start arriving."'

'"So what are you expecting? A football

team?" I asked him.' Maudie smiled reflectively, 'But I'm glad now that I saw sense. It's a grand house, though it's taken all of twenty odd years to get it as we want it, or very nearly so. Now, about the cup of tea I promised you. You just sit there and get warm, Mrs Fraser, whilst I put the kettle on.'

'Thank you, Mrs Cooper.'

'My name's Maudie!'

'Mine's Caroline!'

They exchanged glances and laughed, setting the seal on their friendship.

'By the way, I'd like to thank you for all the lovely presents you sent us,' Maudie said shyly.

'And I'd like to thank you for inviting me to spend Christmas with you,' Caroline replied warmly.

'Ah well, I just didn't want you to be alone, that's all, not after all you've been through. We thought the world of Peter Augustine. We all did, including Reg Rossiter and his ma.' Maudie added hesitantly, 'By the way, we've invited them for dinner tomorrow. I hope you don't mind.'

'Mind? Of course not! I'll be delighted. How's Reg's beard doing, incidentally?'

'Hmmm. I think sparse is the word, but don't tell him I said so.' So saying, Maudie flitted down the passage to the kitchen to make the tea.

Sam came into the room seconds later, with Caroline's luggage.

Advancing to the fire to warm his hands, 'It's main parky outdoors,' he said. 'Beginning to snow. Looks like we're in for a white Christmas. Where's Maudie?' He sounded nervous.

'In the kitchen, making tea,' Caroline told him. Then, 'Is anything the matter?' she asked. 'You seem a bit on edge all of a sudden. Sam, we're friends, aren't we? You can tell me! What's wrong?'

Sam said heavily, 'I was putting the car away when I received a call on my mobile. It was Jake, ringing to say that Cam McCauley's been admitted to hospital—a suspected overdose of painkillers washed down with whisky!'

'Oh my God,' Caroline said bleakly, 'but *why?*'

Formulating the question, she knew the answer. Deep in her heart, she knew the answer. Because of loneliness and despair, the feeling that nobody really cared what happened to him any more. Because he had reached the end of a long road without a signpost in view to point the way ahead.

Sam said wearily, 'I'd better tell Maudie. I've arranged to meet the boys at the hospital. The least we can do. I'm so sorry, my lady, leaving you both on your own like this, you and Maudie. I'll just carry your case upstairs first ...'

'You'll do nothing of the kind! I'm perfectly capable of carrying it myself. You just go and tell Maudie what's happened, then do what you have to do. Believe me, Sam, I'm the least of your worries right now!' Caroline assured him. She added numbly, 'I hope and pray that—Cam—will be all right, that he'll recover.' She meant what she said. True, she and Cameron McCauley had not always seen eye to eye, but he, too, had, however unwillingly become an integral part of her life during her days at Driftwood, and the world would seem a much poorer place without him.

'Well, if this doesn't beat all,' Maudie said, when Sam had departed, and she and Caroline were drinking their tea in front of the fire. 'What a thing to have happened, on Christmas Eve of all times. Puts a damper on things, don't it? Not that I'm at all surprised Cam did what—what he's supposed to have done. I'm just hoping it's a mistake of some kind; an accident ...' Pausing, shaking her head, she continued, 'Oh, what's the use of kidding myself. I've seen it coming! He's been acting that strange lately, not wanting to see anyone. 'The fact is, he's never been the same since his wife left him, and I think he hasn't got over ... Oh, I'm sorry, Mrs Fraser, Caroline, I didn't mean to mention ...'

'Peter Augustine, you mean?' Caroline smiled sadly, 'Not to worry, Maudie, it pleases me to talk about Peter. There's been no one, you see, I could talk to once I'd left Driftwood. That made losing him harder to bear, somehow.'

'I know, dear. It's best not to keep grief bottled up. Perhaps that's where Cam went wrong, pretending not to care about his wife going off the way she did. As for Peter ... I have the feeling that something went wrong between them, and Cam's regretted it ever since.'

Later, Caroline went through to the kitchen with Maudie to help with supper, which they'd eat in the dining room when the men came home.

A housekeeper to her fingertips, Maudie had already cooked a York ham, peeled and salted the potatoes and prepared the rest of the vegetables, made a winter salad, and baked fruit pies, scones and sausage rolls.

'I like to give Sam and the boys plenty to go at,' Maudie explained, removing trays of mince pies from the Aga. 'I made the Christmas cake and puddings last month, and I've already stuffed the turkey ready for tomorrow.' She smiled happily, 'It's the way I was brought up, to keep one jump ahead where food's concerned. Take this here ham, for example, they can have it hot or cold, when they come in, as the fancy takes them, with taters and veg, salad an' pickles, or cut thick an' grilled with fried eggs an' chips; this being Christmas Eve, anything goes.

'Happen the boys will want to go down to the pub afterwards, to wet their whistles! Tomorrow they'll have what they're given, turkey, all the trimmings, and Christmas pudd'n! What's more, they'll wear collars and ties, and no messing!'

Setting the dining room table at her hostess's request, placing the knives, forks and spoons on a pristine white cloth, making herself useful, although Maudie could probably have done the job herself in half the time, Caroline kept on glancing at her watch, her thoughts centred on the hospital and, of all people, Cameron McCauley.

Half an hour later, the front door opened and closed, and the boys and their father entered the house, bringing in with them a gust of cold air and a flurry of snowflakes.

Immediately, Maudie bustled through

from the kitchen to greet them, a worried frown creasing her forehead, Caroline noticed, keeping well back, not wanting to make her presence felt in this moment of crisis, as Maudie asked the burning question: 'Well, what news? How is he?'

Sam said quietly, placing a comforting hand on his wife's shoulder, 'It's all right, love, Cam's out of danger now. He'll be fine in a day or two, the doctor said. They found him just in time.'

'*They* found him just in time. Who are *they?*' Maudie insisted, determined to get to the truth of the matter.

Jake, the gentle giant, stepped forward, stamping the snow from his trainers, 'What Pa really means is that *she* found him just in time. I dare say the kid hadn't a clue what was happening. Well, he wouldn't have, would he, not at his age, the poor little soul!'

Zach said patiently, 'What Jake's trying to say is, when we got to the hospital, Gloria and her kid were there before us. Apparently they'd turned up on Cam's doorstep out of the blue, seeking shelter. She'd let herself in with her latchkey and found him on the floor. Thank God she had the common sense to phone for an ambulance—otherwise who knows what might have happened?'

'You mean to tell me that Cam's ex-wife

has come back to him?' Maudie asked disbelievingly.

'It rather looks that way, Ma,' Jake said matter of factly, hanging his jacket on the hallstand. 'By the way, what's for supper? I'm so hungry I could eat a horse!'

Any minute now, Caroline realised, she would be given bearhugs by the Cooper brothers when they discovered her standing alone in the dining room, then it would be too late, overwhelmed by the warmth of their greeting, to decide whether she was pleased or sorry that Cam's ex-wife had come back to him.

But why should she care one way or the other?

Strangely enough, she *did* care. Cam, like herself, had been through a rough time. He deserved a second chance of happiness with the woman he loved. Everyone deserved a second chance of happiness ...

But happiness was not easy to hold on to as she knew only too well.

Chapter Thirteen

A hiatus occurred on Christmas morning when Reg Rossiter rang up to say that he and his mother wouldn't be able to come for lunch after all.

Caroline and Maudie were in the kitchen when the call came, Caroline washing up the breakfast pots, Maudie basting the turkey, Jake and Zach upstairs in their rooms, Sam in the hall, answering the phone, saying; 'Well, that does seem a pity, Reg ... Yes, I see your problem ... Maudie will be ever so disappointed, but you must do as you think best ...'

Returning the bird to the oven, Maudie marched through to the hall to demand what was happening, having caught half of the conversation. 'What do you mean, Maudie will be ever so disappointed?' she asked Sam forcefully, 'Disappointed about *what*, I should like to know?'

There followed a murmured conversation between husband and wife which Caroline, drying the dishes, could not make head or tail of, not that she was really listening, at least she was trying not to, until Maudie burst forth, 'Oh, tell him not to worry. The more the merrier. There's enough food to feed an army! Just remember to bring some toys for the little 'un!'

Seconds later, Maudie appeared in the kitchen. 'Well, what else was I supposed to do?' she asked Caroline, apropos of the mysterious phonecall. 'After all, this *is* Christmas, the season of goodwill!'

'I'm sorry, I'm not with you,' Caroline confessed, at a loss to know what was going on, yet realising that something had happened to upset Maudie.

'I suppose I should have let well enough alone,' Maudie said irritably, slamming a pan of potatoes onto the Aga to parboil. 'Me and my big mouth! But when Reg said that he and his ma couldn't see their way clear to coming for lunch because Cam's ex-wife and her child are staying with them until Cam comes out of hospital, I had to invite them as well.

'Oh, what a mess! Talk about fools rush in where angels fear to tread! And all because I hadn't the sense to button my lip! So bang goes our nice peaceful Christmas dinner. I mean, what price the conversation with Cam still in hospital, that daft young wife of his, and her child by another man at the same table?' Maudie's face puckered, 'I should have *thought* before I spoke, really I should!'

'On the other hand, Maudie,' Caroline

reminded her gently, 'how could you possibly have turned them away? Not just Cam's wife and child, but the Rossiters?'

'I know,' Maudie said, 'but that lass —that Gloria—put Cam through hell when she left him.'

'Try not to think of that,' Caroline murmured consolingly, 'imagine what might have happened to Cam if she hadn't turned up when she did. She must have had good and sufficient reasons for returning to Gull Cottage so close to Christmas. Shouldn't we give her the benefit of the doubt? As you so rightly said, this *is* the season of goodwill!'

'Then you really don't mind?' Maudie asked hesitantly.

'Mind about what?'

'Well, you know, having your Christmas Day ruined this way?'

'Look, Maudie,' Caroline said gently, 'if it hadn't been for you and Sam, I'd have been sitting alone in a rented flat, right now, feeling sorry for myself. So why don't I start setting the table? And why don't you see to those potatoes before they turn mushy?'

In an hour or so, Caroline thought, setting two extra places, she was about to come face to face with Cam's ex-wife Gloria, the woman he held responsible for ruining his life.

Reg had a rakish air about him when he appeared on the doorstep duly bearded and moustached—looking rather like Franz Hals's *Laughing Cavalier,* only darker, shepherding his mother, whom Caroline had not met before, a thin, dark-haired woman with sharp eyes, and the waif-like, flaxen-haired Gloria, and her child, a sturdy boy, clinging to his mother's skirt for comfort.

'Oh, do let go of me, Toby,' Gloria said irritably. 'Stop being such a pest!'

At that moment, in a split second, Caroline reached her verdict on Cam's ex-wife.

The usual flurry of greetings ensued, kisses and handshakes, remarks about the weather, introductions where necessary, the taking off of coats and boots in the hall, Sam and the boys standing back a little with Caroline; Maudie well to the fore, exhorting everyone to come into the back parlour and get warm. Trying in vain to cajole Toby into a less suspicious frame of mind with a stuffed toy she had dredged up from somewhere, whereupon he clung even more tightly to Gloria's miniskirt.

Reg's delight at seeing Caroline again had been obvious. The beard had enhanced his appearance and imparted an air of self confidence, she thought, a kind of rakishness in keeping with his neatly trimmed facial adornment. Introducing her to his mother, 'This is Mrs Fraser,' he said proudly.

'Please call me Caroline,' she responded warmly, taking Mrs Rossiter's hand, 'I'm so pleased to meet you, at last.' She paused uncertainly, daunted by the woman's lack of enthusiasm. Aware of those sharp, searching eyes of hers gazing at her intently. Caroline wondered if Mrs Rossiter had resented the kiss Reg had bestowed on her under the swag of mistletoe suspended from the hall lampshade?

'Humph,' Mrs Rossiter said eventually, 'I can see now why Reg has been singing your praises these past months; why Peter took to you the way he did. You're a bonny woman an' no mistake!' She sighed deeply, 'A pity about poor Peter. We thought the world of him, didn't we Reg?'

'I thought the world of him, too,' Caroline said quietly, 'and thank you, Mrs Rossiter, for your kindness towards him. He spoke of you often with great affection, and already I feel we are old friends.'

Mrs Rossiter actually smiled, albeit grimly. It was not in her nature, Caroline realised, to be overly effusive or easily swayed. She reminded Caroline of her former housekeeper, Ginny Gordon, inured to speaking her mind when necessary, and letting the chips from her sharp-edged tongue fall where they may.

Gloria, who seemed totally disinterested in the proceedings, conveyed the impression of acute boredom tinged with animosity. A pity about her lack of vivacity, Caroline thought, and her disdainful expression, because she was a very pretty young woman; tall and willowy, with waist length blonde hair, a peaches and cream complexion, and luminous blue eyes fringed with dark lashes.

Attempting to break the ice, and since no one had thought to introduce them, she said, 'I'm Caroline Fraser. What a lovely little boy you have. You must feel proud of him,' thinking that any mother would warm to praise of her offspring. Not in this case apparently.

'The trouble with him is he takes after his father,' Gloria said sullenly.

Reg started, 'Oh, I'm sorry, I should have introduced you.' All of a fluster, 'Caroline, this is Mrs Dennis—Gloria.'

'Take no notice of me, as usual,' Gloria said rudely, 'I'm just part of the furniture! Well, go on, take a good look at me, why don't you? I know what you're all thinking, but it's none of your damned business. Just think what would've happened if I hadn't turned up when I did!'

'No need to go into all that, lass,' Sam said levelly. 'You're here because you were invited to spend Christmas Day among friends.'

'Oh yeah?' Gloria said bitterly, 'Well you can tell that to the marines! I know when I'm not wanted! I wasn't born yesterday!'

'The sooner you get that idea out of your head, the better,' Sam said equably. 'I'm sure we're all grateful that you did turn up in time to save Cam's life. As you rightly said, why you turned up is none of our business, so come through to the fire, get warm, and have a glass of sherry.' He added, 'Let's remember what Christmas is all about, shall we?' Holding out his hand to the child, 'Come on, son,' he said gently, 'let's see if there's any lemonade in the kitchen.'

Not an auspicious beginning to a time of peace and goodwill Caroline thought uneasily, praying to heaven there'd be no more verbal fireworks ...

Jake had been up to the attic to fetch a high chair for Toby to sit in during lunch. Sam carved the turkey, and plates had been handed round along with the tureens of vegetables. Sitting next to the boy, Jake had cut up his meat for him and applied a liberal helping of gravy. Suddenly, the child banged his spoon experimentally into his food, splattering the tablecloth and the front of Mrs Rossiter's jumper.

'There,' she said crossly, glaring at Gloria across the table, 'look at the mess he's made. If you'd been seeing to him instead of staring into space, this wouldn't have happened. I suppose it's the modern way of doing things, walking out on your husband and expecting other people to take care of you. Well, things weren't like that in *my* day! Folk made vows and stuck to them, for better or worse!

'First you walked out on Cam Mc-Cauley. Next thing, you came running back to him when it suited you, expecting him to pick up the pieces, no doubt, to lumber him with another man's child! A disgrace, I call it! You should think shame on yourself, young woman, playing games with other folks' lives! Above all, the life of that child of yours. You had no right to drag him away from home the way you did, especially at Christmas! You should've stayed where you belonged, in your own home with your new husband, not come chasing after the old one!'

'Ma, *please*,' Reg said desperately, 'that's enough!' But the damage had been done.

Rising unsteadily to her feet, Gloria said hoarsely, close to tears, 'What's so bloody special about Christmas, I should like to know? The season of peace and goodwill?

Well, try telling that to Mrs Rossiter, the sanctimonious old hypocrite! And all because she got a gravy stain on her nice clean jumper! Well, I'm sick and tired of the bloody lot of you, if you really want to know! So far as I'm concerned, I'd rather spend the rest of Christmas in a—in a barn—than stay here with my so-called friends!'

'Oh dear,' Maudie murmured tearfully, surveying the wreckage of the Christmas lunch she'd worked so hard to provide.

Assessing the situation, extending a hand to Gloria, 'You and Toby had best come upstairs with me,' Caroline said calmly. 'With your permission, Maudie?'

'Yes, of course. Whatever you think best,' Maudie conceded, as picking up her child from his high chair, Gloria followed Caroline from the scene of combat and upstairs to her room on the top floor, albeit unwillingly, mouthing her contempt on the way.

'So just who the hell do you think you are? Joan of Arc? Or just another bloody do-gooder?' Gloria demanded hostilely. 'Whichever, you're wasting your time on the likes of me! You heard what that woman said about me didn't you? That Mrs Rossiter? No doubt you agreed with her, so where the hell do you fit into the picture?'

'I don't. I'm a stranger here myself,' Caroline said mildly. 'It simply occurred to me that discretion is the better part of valour. What you and your little boy need right now is a good rest. You must be tired out with all the toing and froing you've done recently. So please, just try to relax for a while. Sleep if at all possible.

'Just remember, it's up to you to decide where to go from here; where your future lies—with Cam or your present husband, bearing in mind your son's welfare.'

'How the hell am I supposed to know what's best for me and Toby, right now?' Gloria snapped back at her. 'I was hoping Cam would welcome me with open arms. He really loves me, you know? The last thing I expected was to find him unconscious, not knowing me from Adam!'

'But thanks to you, he's on the road to recovery now,' Caroline reminded her, 'and I'm certain that Sam or Reg Rossiter would be more than pleased, later on, to drive you to the hospital to visit Cam.'

'No way,' Gloria retorted quickly, 'I *hate* hospitals! All that pussyfooting about in those long corridors, and not knowing what to say to someone lying in bed with tubes and suchlike attached to his nose. I can't face that again, I can't, and I *won't!* You go to the hospital to see him, if you

216

want to. I suppose you know Cam? Most everyone does, though not everyone likes him. He can be hard and cruel when he feels like it, and I should know.

'The truth is, he drove me away, all because he wouldn't move away from Gull Cottage. I begged him to buy us a nice modern house on the estate, but would he listen? Would he hell as like! He wanted things his own way. That's when I met Chris Dennis. I'd found myself a job in a dress shop in Whitby, at the time, when Chris caught my eye. Leastways, I'd caught *his* eye, and yes, well, I suppose I was flattered when he started asking me out for a drink once in a while.

'He was so different from Cam, more my own age, and just as well off. He owns a fishing fleet, you see, and a fish cannery, and he's tons better looking than Cam. Well, to cut a long story short, we started an—affair. Then, when he'd got me pregnant and begged me to marry him, I asked Cam to divorce me, and he did—as if he was glad to get shot of me—though I still cared about him quite a lot, the silly old fool.'

'I see,' Caroline said quietly, 'so what happened to bring you back to Gull Cottage?'

'What do you suppose?' Gloria responded sharply. 'Chris and I had a blazing row about money, besides which he'd always been jealous of Cam, taunting me about him, wanting to know if Toby was really his kid, not Cam's. I couldn't stick it any longer so I cleared out.'

'Cam didn't know you were coming?'

'No. I thought I'd surprise him. I thought he'd be pleased to see me. If he'd known I was coming back to him, he wouldn't have done what he did.'

'Then you really intend staying with him when he comes out of hospital?'

Gloria coloured up, 'I suppose I'll have to,' she said defiantly, 'I haven't much choice now, have I?'

'That's not for me to say.' Caroline turned away, sensing more grief to come Cam's way if Gloria was using him as a stop-gap, a means of support until she decided about the future.

Realistically, it seemed unlikely that her fall out with her husband was more than a temporary hiccup in their marriage. Returning to Gull Cottage, the old dissentions between herself and Cam were bound to arise once more. Gloria, she suspected, cared for no one deeply, apart from herself, not even her child.

She said, 'Try to get some rest now, Gloria. I'll come up later to see if there's anything you want. Toby's half asleep already. I should pop him under the duvet, if I were you.'

Closing the door behind her, Caroline went downstairs to rejoin the party, who had repaired to the parlour to watch the Queen's broadcast on television; all except Maudie who, meeting her at the foot of the stairs, said resignedly, 'It's no use, Caroline, I just can't face the Queen right now. I'm going to clear the dining room table and make a start on the washing up.'

'Not on your own, you're not,' Caroline assured her. 'I'll clear the table and lend you a hand in the kitchen.' She smiled, 'I couldn't face the Queen either. So let's get started, shall we?'

'But you're the guest of honour ...'

'Then let's say the guest of honour will feel honoured to help with the washing up!' Caroline sighed deeply. 'Look, Maudie, I really need a job to do, to make myself useful; to feel—needed once more, the way I used to when my parents were alive.'

Maudie nodded understandingly, 'All right then. But what about her upstairs and that poor little lad of hers?'

'They'll both be fast asleep by now, I shouldn't wonder. I promised Gloria I'd look in on them later.'

In the kitchen, Maudie said, 'Sam, the boys and Reg are going to the hospital to see Cam after tea. Do you suppose Gloria will go with them?'

'No, but I'd like to, if that's okay. Cam and I haven't always seen eye to eye over lots of things. All the more reason to offer the flag of truce, wouldn't you say?'

Hands deep in washing-up water, Caroline doing the drying, Maudie said worriedly, 'Frankly, I can't see Gloria staying on with the Rossiters after what's happened and, to be honest, I don't fancy her stopping here with us. So what's to be done about her?'

Caroline said thoughtfully, 'What's wrong with Gull Cottage? She has her own latchkey. We have food enough to spare, and that's where she was heading anyway. That capon and the hamper I brought with me might come in useful after all. She'll need fresh milk for the child, of course, to see her through Boxing Day. At least, at Gull Cottage, she wouldn't be at loggerheads with Mrs Rossiter. *A consummation devoutly to be wished,* for both their sakes, if that makes sense?'

'Yes, of course,' Maudie admitted. 'Now why didn't *I* think of that?'

On her way to the hospital later that afternoon, having peeped in on Gloria and Toby beforehand to discover them both fast asleep beneath her duvet, sitting upright on the back seat of the Mercedes between the Cooper brothers and clasping the box of crystallised fruits gleaned from her Christmas hamper as a gift for Cam, Caroline wondered if she should have come. She simply felt that he needed all the goodwill possible after what he'd been through.

No longer in need of intensive care, he'd been removed to a side ward. The nurse in charge said he'd be kept under observation till after the Christmas period for assessment and primary counselling. In other words, his consultant would want to establish his present circumstances, attitude and state of mind before deciding the right course of action to take in his patient's best interests. 'Subject to Mr McCauley's cooperation, of course,' the nurse added wryly, 'and he's not being entirely cooperative at the moment, I assure you.

'A word of advice: don't go in all at once, and don't stay too long.' Turning to Sam as the senior member of the contingent, 'I suggest that you and the lady go in first, and remember what I said, don't stay too long.'

Preceding Sam into the room, Caroline saw a man she scarcely recognised as Cam McCauley, the adversary of her Driftwood days. Propped up with pillows, hands clenched on the coverlet she read in every line of his raddled face, brightly staring eyes and attenuated body beneath the hospital gown he wore, the intensity of the suffering he had endured since their last meeting.

'Hello, Cam,' she said quietly, approaching the bed, Sam following closely in her wake. Not bothering to ask how he was feeling, knowing exactly how he was feeling—weary, dejected, sick at heart, a shadow of his former self—'I imagine I'm the last person you expected to see, possibly the last person you wish to see.'

Cam said unexpectedly, 'Still listening to the late night shipping forecasts on Radio Four, are you, Mrs Fraser? Tyne, Dogger, German Bight, Irish Sea, Mull of Kintyre? Rain, showers, sleet and all that jazz?'

'Yes, as a matter of fact,' Caroline replied softly. 'A feeling of permanence in an uncertain world, wouldn't you say? Since Peter's death I've found myself clinging to those shipping forecasts as to a lifeline.'

'That figures, but there aren't any real lifelines to cling to when the going gets really rough, are there?'

'Well no, I suppose not, in your present frame of mind,' Caroline said levelly, grasping the nettle. 'Frankly, Mr McCauley, I saw you as a fighter, never as a quitter! I suppose, in attempting to end your own life, you never even stopped to think of the devastating effect it would have on other people? Just how selfish and self-deluding can one person become? What bothers me most, Cam, is how you could even contemplate throwing away the most precious gift of all—life itself!

'Peter Augustine died through no fault of his own—a young man who loved life and lived it to the full as long as it lasted, whilst you of all people simply chose to throw it away as if it didn't matter a damn. But life *does* matter. Think about it, Cam! It's all we have in this uncertain world. Something to be cherished and fought for, not thrown away, discarded like rubbish! Now, if you'll excuse me ...'

Quitting the room, Caroline marched past Reg and the Cooper boys without a word, along the corridor and into the fresh air outside. What on earth had possessed her to say what she did to a man recovering from a suicide attempt? How could she have done such a thing?

Sam came out to her eventually, when the other three had gone in to see Cam. 'I've always admired your honesty,' he consoled her, opening the car door for her.

'I doubt if Cam does.'

'Aye well, Cam's not afraid of speaking his own mind, at times, as you've probably noticed. You certainly gave him food for thought.' Sam chuckled deeply. 'Now about the other little matter. I broke it to him gently that Gloria's back.'

'How did he take it?'

'Difficult to tell with Cam. By the way, I'm taking her to Gull Cottage, as you suggested. Maudie's going to pack some groceries for her to see her through till the shops reopen. No way could she go back to the Rossiters after what's been said.' Sam sighed, 'I'm sorry, my lady, I'm afeared this Christmas hasn't come up to expectations so far.'

'Never mind, there's always tomorrow. Hopefully there'll be no alarms and excursions on Boxing Day. It's Maudie I feel sorry for, after all her hard work, having her dinner ruined the way it was.'

'Happen she'll be having a heart to heart with Freda Rossiter right now,' Sam said sagely, 'reading her the riot act, I shouldn't wonder.' He grinned broadly, 'My Maudie's soft-hearted, not soft in the head. Still, Freda's not a bad old stick at rock bottom, just a bit of a gaffer, that's all. Maudie'll soon set her straight, don't worry.'

It had all been a bit cloak and dagger, Caroline thought afterwards. Returning to the house, she had gone straight upstairs to discover Gloria up and complaining bitterly that she wasn't about to stay under this roof a moment longer, if she could help it.

'Your luck's in then,' Caroline said pleasantly, 'Sam's taking you to Gull Cottage right away. Mrs Cooper's packed some food to take with you. It's all been arranged for your benefit. All you have to do is walk out the front door, and you'll be on your way.'

'Oh, so it's all been arranged, has it?' Gloria said disagreeably. 'I'm to go to Gull Cottage whether I want to or not?'

Caroline said patiently, 'But that's the whole point, isn't it? Taking you to where you wanted to be in the first place? What's wrong with that?' She paused, 'Of course if you'd rather go back to the Rossiters, I dare say that could be arranged just as easily.'

Five minutes later, Gloria and the boy were in the hall putting on their outdoor things, helped by Caroline. Sam had carried out the box of groceries to the car, and the party, so far as Gloria was concerned, was over.

Sam would see her safely into Gull Cottage, break the news of the hospital visit earlier that afternoon, and probably give her a pep talk into the bargain. Knowing Gloria, she'd more than likely tell

225

him to mind his own damned business.

Watching the rear lights of the Merc disappearing through the garden gates, what happened between Cam and Gloria from now on was very much their own business, Caroline realised, closing the front door against the bitter wind blowing in from the sea.

Going through to the warm, cosy parlour she found to her infinite relief that the party was also over so far as Freda Rossiter was concerned, despite Maudie's half-hearted attempts to persuade her to stay for supper.

'No thank you, Maude,' she said with a martyred air, 'What I need is an early night. This hasn't been easy for me, you know, having that wretched girl and her child to contend with. I'm fair worn out with all the trouble she's caused me one way and another. Well, don't just stand there like a spare part, Reg! Fetch me my hat and coat and then we'll be off!'

'Yes, Ma,' Reg murmured resignedly, doing as he was bidden, overruled by his mother as ever. Turning at the door, he added, 'Thanks very much for a lovely dinner, Mrs Cooper. Well, so long everyone. Goodnight, Caroline.'

'Goodnight, Reg, and,' she slipped in, *sotto voce*, his mother out of earshot, 'I really do like your beard.'

'You do?' He nearly glowed in the dark.

Standing on the doorstep near Caroline, Jake called after him, 'See you in the pub, Reg, tomorrow around seven, before the party begins.'

'Party? What party?'

'Why here, of course, as usual!'

'Oh yes. I'll do my best, but it all depends ...'

Caroline helped Maudie with the supper, consisting of cold ham and turkey sandwiches, warmed through mincepies and Christmas cake which they would eat round the fire.

'If anyone wants owt else,' she said wearily, 'they can go through to the kitchen and help themselves.'

'You look as if you could do with an early night yourself,' Caroline remarked sympathetically. 'So could I, come to think of it. This has been a difficult day one way and another, hasn't it? Especially for you.'

'Eh, it's not myself I'm bothered about,' Maudie said weepily, 'it's you. What must you be thinking of us, I wonder? Inviting you here for a nice quiet Christmas and with everything going wrong the way it has!' Wiping her eyes on a piece of kitchen roll, 'I could have strangled Freda Rossiter

227

with my bare hands, carrying on the way she did at the dinner table. As for that Gloria! Whatever Cam McCauley saw in that little madam, I'll never know! But mark my words, he'll take her back as sure as night follows day! All I can say is, God help him if he does!'

After supper, alone in her room looking up at the night sky brilliant with stars, Caroline longed for the peace and privacy of her basement flat, her own environment, however makeshift. The day after tomorrow, please God, she'd be back where she belonged again—master of her own fate.

Coming here to spend Christmas with the Coopers, she had scarcely envisaged the dramatic events that had taken place in so delightful a setting. Not that the Coopers were in any way to blame for Cam's near fatal attempt at self destruction; his ex-wife's reappearance on the scene, or the almighty row between Mrs Rossiter and Gloria.

Possibly Christmas had been to blame, a time of heightened emotions and hard work, lacking the ordinariness of everyday life—rather like an idealistic picture of togetherness framed in coloured lights, tinsel and holly.

And yet, above and beyond the spurious glamour of Christmas, touched in this case with near tragedy, Caroline rejoiced in her newfound friendship with the Cooper family. Strengthened by their kindness towards her, their caring concern for her welfare; knowing that their friendship would endure—as if she had miraculously been given the priceless gift of a new family to fill the empty spaces of her heart.

Chapter Fourteen

A wild February wind rattled the branches of the trees in the old Dean Road Cemetery the day Caroline went in search of the graves of Sarah St Just and her faithful companion, Margaret Roberts.

Since her return to Scarborough in December, she had spent fruitful hours in the library and archives of the local newspaper, researching the history of the town and reading all the books she could lay her hands on pertaining to the Sitwells, the Londesboroughs, and 'the Royal Roué', Edward VII, a personal friend of theirs.

Present day royal indiscretions paled to insignificance compared with the sexual exploits of that particular monarch. How his lovely, Danish born wife Alexandra had borne so stoically his manifold extramarital flings, was incredible. The man had been sexually insatiable with a string of mistresses a mile long, including a Liverpool sea captain's daughter, a handsome dark haired Frenchwoman, La Barucci; La Goulue—'Queen of the Can-Can'; Bertie's 'Darling Daisy', Countess of Warwick; the actress Sarah Bernhardt and

Lily Langtry. Last but not least of the line, the Honourable Mrs Keppel.

So where had Sarah St Just fitted into the love life of a monarch of the realm? How long had their affair lasted? When had it ended? Where had Sarah sprung from? What had been her background? She must have been very beautiful to have caught the eye of a king.

At least Caroline now knew where she had lived, how she had died, and where she was buried. Not that she had discovered the whereabouts of Sarah's town house so far, nor the exact location of her grave in the sprawling Victorian cemetery close to the centre of Scarborough. The gatekeeper would have the necessary records.

The cemetery, with its winding paths, toward Victorian headstones, marble monoliths, skeletal trees and mounds of decaying leaves seemed in no way daunting or macabre to Caroline as, holding the bunches of chrysanthemums she had brought with her, she came at last to two headstones placed close together. One was inscribed with the words: *'Sacred to the Memory of Sarah St Just. I Believe, therefore I Live'*; the other, *'In Memory of Margaret Roberts, a Dear Friend and Companion. In Death they were not Divided'*.

There were rusted cylindrical vases on

the graves, empty of flowers, yet filled to the brim with rainwater. How long, Caroline wondered, since anyone had visited those graves to pay homage to two long dead and forgotten women of a bygone age, of little or no importance in the unheeding world of today? Few, if any. And yet their story, if told, might well create a morbid public interest in the resting places of a former mistress of a king of England and her humble companion whose dying wish, within days of her beloved mistress, had been to be buried as close to her as possible.

Now they lay side by side, and Caroline divided the flowers she had brought with her equally between them, as a mark of respect for their earthly remains but in no way relevant to their spiritual survival. Those voices she had heard from the kitchen, last September, on her first visit to Driftwood; that sudden feeling of *déja vu,* the creak of a non-existent rocking-chair on the verandah; that dancing will-o-the-wisp light she had seen on the beach following the tragic death of Peter Augustine. Somehow they had meant her to find them, she realised, to finally discover the truth.

Leaving the cemetery, she walked quickly towards the town centre in search of coffee and a sandwich, after which she would go to the library to discover the exact whereabouts of Sarah St Just's town house.

The first thing Caroline noticed about Sarah St Just's residence, was the 'For Sale' sign posted in the almost non-existent garden—a small area of soil planted with laurel bushes crowding the path to the entrance.

It was a strange looking house, turreted, uncompromisingly ugly at first glance, in a cul-de-sac near a built up area of the town. Unaccountably disappointed, she opened the iron gate and followed the overgrown path round an angle of the building.

Seek and ye shall find ... What she found, to her amazement, was that what she had imagined to be the main entrance was nothing of the kind, merely the side entrance, leading most probably to the kitchens and servants' quarters.

Rounding the corner, drawing in a deep breath of surprise and pleasure, she beheld sweeping lawns overlooked by vast Victorian bay windows flanking an imposing door beneath an ivy-covered grey stone arch.

Standing back to gaze up at the exterior of the house, Caroline saw that the downstairs bay windows were matched by those of the first floor rooms and realised that the house had been designed to ensure the privacy of its occupants, on land overlooking the Valley Gardens below.

What a magnificent house this must have been in its heyday, she thought, before the passage of time and years of neglect had taken their toll on its grandeur. Other people must have lived here, of course, since the death of its original owner; wealthy people who, for whatever reasons had drifted away, allowing the fabric of the building to fall into a state of disrepair, the lawns to become overgrown with weeds. The present state of the rooms she could only imagine. One thing was for sure, she wanted desperately to see those rooms for herself.

Retracing her steps, making a note of the estate agents' name and filled with a mounting sense of excitement, she walked quickly into town, not caring about the stinging hailstones slapping her cheeks; harbouring the strangest feeling that she was at last about to come home.

She had been right in thinking that the side door would lead to the kitchen and servants' quarters, Caroline thought, wishing the estate agent would go away and leave her alone to make her own discoveriess. She scarcely needed his presence to guide her through the cobwebby passages leading to the main part of the house; the half panelled hall with its imposing mahogany staircase and stained glass windows; the spacious bay windowed reception rooms with their fine marble fireplaces, peeling paintwork and torn wallpaper.

Poor house, she thought, so sadly in need of someone to love and take care of it.

'As you can see for yourself, a lot needs doing to it to make it habitable,' the estate agent said, stating the obvious.

Caroline guessed what he was thinking: why waste time on a woman wearing jeans, an anorak, boots, and with a woolly cap on her head, who looked as if she hadn't two ha'pennies to rub together.

'Yes,' Caroline said thoughtfully, 'I shall of course want detailed estimates of the cost involved, before making an offer.'

'An—offer?' The agent looked at her disbelievingly, wondering if this was a send-up. Some women filled in time wasting that of estate agents. 'Then you *are* interested in the property?'

'How long has it been empty?'

'Let me see. Five years or so.'

'Who does it belong to?'

'The legatees of an old gentleman who passed away some time ago, who are now living in America. Sadly, they had no interest in the place and returned to the States after the old gentleman's death and the sale of the contents,' The agent, Harold Smythe, close to fifty and well-upholstered, continued cannily, 'Naturally, a property of this size and importance has attracted a great deal of interest, a number of enquiries regarding its potential as a first class hotel.' Clearing his throat slightly, 'Er, may I ask what you intend doing with it, if, as you say, you intend making an offer?'

Caroline smiled, 'I intend living in it, Mr Smythe, along with the ghost. I mean, it *is* haunted, isn't it?'

The agent's mouth sagged open. 'Whatever gave you that idea?' he managed eventually, keeping a stiff upper lip. 'There have been rumours, of course, which I utterly refute! I am not attempting to sell you a—pig-in-a-poke—Mrs Fraser, I assure you!'

Caroline said kindly, 'But you are not attempting to sell me anything at all now. So far as I'm concerned you might as well take down that 'For Sale' notice in the garden.' She laughed delightedly, 'Oh, I dare say my financial adviser will throw a fit when he knows I've decided to pay the asking price after all. But why prevaricate? It isn't every day that one—comes home.'

She had tried hard to be sensible, but the house was going for a song, compared with London property, and she wanted it so much that she dared not risk losing it. But it would be some time yet before it was fit to move into. Meanwhile, whilst the builders were busy re-pointing the brickwork, mending the roof and knocking down interior walls to create the modern kitchen she envisaged, she'd have a ball choosing paint and wallpaper, carpets and curtains and items of antique furniture for her future home.

Then, in the spring, she would employ a team of gardeners to turf the lawns, plant rhododendrons, azaleas, lilacs and laburnum; to create herbaceous borders filled with delphiniums, larkspur, peonies and lupins.

And when all this had been achieved, when the house was ready to move into, she would invite the Coopers for a long weekend, possibly even the Rossiters and Lara Westwood, of the 'We Aim to Please' agency.

Pie in the sky? Perhaps. Caroline had lived long enough to realise that nothing ever ran all that smoothly.

Basil Pryde had written to inform her that Felix intended to contest the divorce on the grounds of her desertion and adultery. Sick at heart, she realised that

Felix had known her whereabouts all along, had had her followed and checked up on. Received detailed reports from some private investigator, spying on her, making inquiries about herself and Peter Augustine; providing ammunition for Felix to use against her in court.

Of course Felix would use every means at his disposal to gain access to her inheritance, including emotional blackmail, thinking that she would accede to his demands rather than have her affair with Peter dragged into the limelight. How well he knew her. How right he had been in calling her brainless, stupid, a nonentity. She must be all those things to have imagined for one moment that her ruthless husband would not have hired undercover agents to bring her to heel.

He must be laughing up his sleeve now, knowing he had her exactly where he wanted her, that she would do anything to protect her relationship with Peter. Worst of all was the realisation that they had been spied upon all along. Walking on the beach at Driftwood with Peter, had there been some apparently innocent bird-watcher on the cliff top viewing them through binoculars?

That day on the terrace overlooking the estuary of the Esk River, had there been someone at another table taking snapshots?

238

Basil Pryde wrote that he had not been entirely surprised by Felix's tactics, which he described as devious. He had, however, been deeply disturbed by the findings of his investigations into her own private life, which placed in jeopardy the foregone conclusion Basil had anticipated when the divorce hearing took place.

The letter went on to say that he had been in consultation with her husband's solicitor with regard to his client's counter claim of desertion and adultery, backed by strong evidence in support of the claim.

In short, Felix would put forward the argument that she, Caroline, had quit the marital home to pursue a long standing adulterous relationship with Peter Augustine. Asking the court's discretion with regard to his admitted adultery with Francesca Delgado, an indiscretion exacerbated by his wife's desertion.

Finally the core of the letter was revealed. Felix's solicitor had stated his client's willingness to destroy all documentary evidence pertaining to his wife's adultery on certain conditions: (a) That she withdrew her divorce petition against him forthwith, in favour of a similar petition brought by himself against her, citing desertion on her part, thus reversing their roles as claimant and defendant. (b) That she surrendered unconditionally all rights to the marital home, the fabric and the contents thereof, and signed a legal document to that effect. (c) That she would agree to pay him the lump sum of £250,000 in consideration of the distress her actions had caused him.

Basil Pryde had concluded: *'Only you can decide how you wish to proceed in these unfortunate circumstances. I shall, of course, act in accordance with your instructions. You will, no doubt, advise me of your decision in due course, when you have had time to reflect upon your husband's demands.'*

Caroline signed her immediate reply to Basil Pryde's letter with a flourish.

Her father's daughter to the marrow, no way was she prepared to submit to blackmail. Nor, when the chips were down, was she prepared to deny her love affair with Peter Augustine. To do so would be a betrayal of all that he had meant to her, and she to him.

'Tell my husband's solicitor,' she had written, *'that I very much doubt the legality of suppressing documentary evidence in any case, especially as an incentive to blackmail. You may also advise my husband that (a) I shall proceed with my divorce petition against him on the grounds of his adultery with Francesca Delgado, with constructive desertion and mental cruelty thrown in, if he so wishes; (b) I have no intention whatsoever of waiving*

240

my rights to the matrimonial home, fabric and contents, considering the fact that the deeds were drawn up jointly to reflect my financial input at the time, relating to the purchase of the property and its contents; (c) I do not intend to part with so much as £250, let alone £250,000 to satisfy my husband's insatiable greed for money; (d) Tell him to gird up his loins for battle, because he's in for one hell of a fight!'

Posting the letter, Caroline experienced an uplifting of the spirit, heart and mind, as if the old, nervous shadow of the woman she used to be in her pre-Driftwood days no longer existed. Albeit unwillingly at first, she had learned to stand on her own two feet; had discovered the true meaning of love: that love casts out fear; even the fear of being left alone in the world; with the ongoing battle for survival against all the odds. But survive she must, for Peter's sake, who would have expected nothing less of her than the courage to have written and posted that letter, whatever the outcome may be.

Three days later, she received a letter from Jon Carradine, saying he'd be coming to Scarborough at the weekend to see her, and inviting her to dine with him at the Crown on Saturday evening.

Ringing him immediately, 'Oh please,

not a hotel,' she'd beseeched him, 'come to me for dinner. I'll cook you braised steak with mashed potatoes and dumplings!'

'Well yes,' he demurred, tongue-in-cheek, 'I was rather afraid that you might, which is why I suggested the Crown. Oh, very well, then, you win. It might be interesting to discover how the other half lives!'

He arrived bringing flowers, chocolates and champagne. 'Well, let me look at you,' he said, holding her at arm's length. 'Hmm, better than I'd imagined you'd look after all you've been through. Blooming as a matter of fact! Must be all the sea air.'

Caroline laughed, delighted to see him, loving his wry, quirky sense of humour. 'Come in and sit down,' she said. 'Oh, daffodils, how lovely! Coffee creams *and* champagne! Just as well I decided against dumplings at the last minute, knowing your preference for *haute cuisine!*'

'So what are we having instead? Bangers and chips?'

'How did you guess?'

'So this is your bolt hole is it?' Gazing about him, 'Neat but not gaudy, as the devil said when he painted his tail pea green. And how's "Tara" coming along? Or haven't you decided on a name for your new abode yet?'

'No, not yet.' Knowing this was no

chance visit to Scarborough, she said more seriously, 'I take it you've been in touch with Basil Pryde?'

'Yes, my dear, and we both applaud your stand in the wretched matter of the divorce. Food for thought for Felix, I imagine, and serve him damn well right, the unprincipled swine! Sorry, but I never liked the man, as you well know, and with good reason. The thing is—the reason why I came really—is we must tighten up any and every possible loophole, financially speaking. Have you thought, for instance, what would happen if you met with a fatal accident tomorrow or the next day?'

Caroline knew what he was driving at. 'Because I haven't made a will, you mean?'

'Exactly so,' Jon nodded. 'A sobering thought. If you suddenly popped your clogs, so to speak, Felix would scoop the pool, the whole bang-shoot, as your next of kin. Frankly, my love, it doesn't bear thinking about.'

'Yes, I can see that,' Caroline frowned, 'but as you know, Jon, I have no close family connections, or none that I know of. I only wish that I had, however remote—a second cousin in Australia, perhaps—but Felix was all I had by way of next of kin, and I would have given him everything I had if only ... I'm sorry! Look, let's eat

243

now, shall we? You must be starving!'

'Well, this *is* nice,' Jon said appreciatively, uncorking and pouring the champagne. 'Duck à l'orange, asparagus and duchesse potatoes, no less. A feast fit for a king!'

'I've always loved cooking.' She smiled, 'My father wanted me to learn something useful in case I ever needed to earn a living. I've given some thought to investing in a small business—a café or a restaurant—to give myself a purpose in life when all the unpleasantness is over. What do you think?'

'That's a great idea! I'm all for it!' Jon realised how empty Caroline's life must seem now, robbed of that impossibly demanding husband of hers and whose prior existence revolved around entertaining his wide circle of hangers on. Luncheons, dinner and drinks parties, interspersed with lengthy holidays abroad, leaving the packing and the detailed travel arrangements to his wife to attend to—and God help her if so much as a minor last minute hitch occurred.

Little wonder the poor girl's nervous system had been brought to such a low ebb. But the mills of God ground exceedingly small at times, he reflected quietly. And with a certain sardonic relish, recalled that Felix's latest book had received a panning from the critics which had effectively removed his name from the bestseller list. The wicked did not always flourish ...

Later, in front of the sitting room fire drinking coffee Jon said, 'About the will. My suggestion is this: for the time being, leave your money, property and so forth to the RSPCA, Battersea Dogs' Home, your friendly neighbourhood butcher! Anyone at all until you've had time to ponder the matter more fully, bearing in mind that you'll be at liberty, whenever, to change your will.'

He smiled encouragingly, 'Under normal circumstances, of course, the matter of making a will would come under Basil's jurisdiction. In this case, I offered to act as his envoy, for obvious reasons—speed being of the essence in closing the legal loopholes as quickly as possible prior to the divorce hearing.'

'Yes, of course. So, the Battersea Dogs' Home it is!' Caroline said wryly. 'Now, where's the dotted line for me to sign on?'

Next morning, she and Jon visited her future home.

'Ye gods,' he said, 'what a magnificent house! But, forgive my asking, do you really need so much space? So many rooms? Won't you feel a tad lonely living here all on your own?'

'No, I don't think so, you see I've learned to value my own space, to embrace loneliness. There are far worse things in life than loneliness, you know. I'd rather live the rest of my life in seclusion than ever go back to the past with Felix!'

'God willing, you'll never have to, Caroline, my dear,' Jon told her reassuringly. 'The past is the past, or it soon will be, and the way you intend to face the future is entirely up to you. Nobody else's business but your own. Just as long as you remember that you are still a very attractive woman, in the prime of life, with a whole new future ahead of you!'

Wandering from room to room, keenly interested, 'There's something about this place I can't quite put my finger on,' Jon said, rubbing his chin reflectively, 'something vaguely mysterious. Those stained glass windows in the hall, for instance, the Prince of Wales feathers and the motto "Ich Dien." Could this have been one of Edward the Seventh's lovenests, I wonder? He had quite a few in this area, I imagine.'

'I hadn't realised you were an historian,' Caroline remarked.

Jon laughed, 'I'm not really, just a royalist at heart, a sucker for romance.

Take Edward the Eighth and Mrs Simpson, for instance: one of the world's great love affairs. I can't help wondering if his grandfather would have thrown his cap over the proverbial windmill, renounced his throne for any one of his mistresses. I doubt it. What a right royal rumpus that would have caused! Must have been pretty rough on the women in his life, though, especially if any of them had had the misfortune to fall in love with him. Rejection must have been a bitter pill to swallow.'

'Falling in love with a king would pre-empt that outcome, don't you think?' Caroline said softly. 'They would have known from the start that rejection was on the cards, and there was nothing they could do about it ...'

'Apart from accepting payment in kind for services rendered, you mean?' Jon interrupted astutely. 'A house like this one, for example? A carriage and horses, jewellery, a royal annuity to keep the wolf from the door?'

'Something like that.' Caroline smiled wistfully.

'So which of Edward's mistresses merited this particular grace and favour residence?' Jon asked.

'Her name was Sarah St Just.'

'How fascinating. Tell me the whole story.'

'I can't, I don't know the whole story yet. Just snippets gleaned from here and there, a bit like a jigsaw puzzle with the essential pieces missing.' Caroline shivered slightly. 'One thing I'm sure of, Sarah St Just lived here to a great age, and died of a heart attack in this room we're in now. Her body was discovered over there, near the window—an event described graphically in a local newspaper of that era, captioned *"Death of a Recluse".*'

'Heavens,' Jon murmured, staring first at the window, then at Caroline. 'I'm sorry, I'm out of my depth. It's a fantastic house, but are you quite certain you'll be safe here? Has it struck you that the place may be haunted?'

'Oh yes. I'd be surprised if it wasn't,' Caroline said, with a mysterious little smile. 'Let's go back to the flat now, shall we? I'll make some coffee and tell you all about Driftwood and the Woman in White.'

Chapter Fifteen

Jon left the flat around three o'clock that afternoon to pick up his luggage from the Crown Hotel and catch the four o'clock train to London, feeling rather like a male counterpart of Alice in Wonderland.

What an amazing weekend it had been, to be sure, complete with ghost stories to dwell on during the return journey to King's Cross, Caroline's will in his briefcase, duly signed, and witnessed by a young couple in the first floor flat. Called upon to ensure the legality of the document, they had been treated to a glass of champagne afterwards as a small compensation for their trouble.

'No trouble at all,' they'd said cheerily, returning to their Saturday evening's televiewing. 'Any time. Any time at all!'

Having changed platforms at York Station, entered a First Class compartment on the mainline York to London express and ordered coffee and brandy from the dining-car attendant, Jon sat back to reflect on his weekend in Wonderland.

Acquainted with Caroline Fraser for many years now, and her father before her, he had never really come close to her before as a friend, a warm, somewhat offbeat human being, rather than as a client. Possibly because, he reasoned with himself, hitherto he had regarded her in the light of the down-trodden wife of a husband who had her jumping through hoops at his command.

This weekend, he had gained an entirely new perspective on the woman he had once seen as a cipher, a limpet, desperately in need of friendship, help and advice. A woman who had startled him with revelations about her love affair with Peter Augustine, speaking proudly, tenderly of his simplicity of spirit, his innate honesty and charm.

He had listened enthralled to her graphic description of her Driftwood days and the people she had met there, the Cooper brothers and their father Sam; Reg Rossiter; her bullying landlord, Cameron McCauley and, whether or not he believed it, the Woman in White.

But whether or not he was prepared to accept the notion of life after death, he had to admit that he had been aware of an unseen presence that morning, in the house he thought of as 'Tara', and he felt more than a little disturbed that Caroline, devastated by the tragic death of Peter Augustine, and facing what promised to be an extremely acrimonious divorce, might turn to the occult as a means of solace.

True, she had spoken of investing in a small business, a café or a restaurant, to provide a new interest in life when the divorce trauma was over, but what about the long hours she would spend alone at night in the rambling, ghost-ridden mansion she was now lumbered with? Would she, in the fullness of time, become as sad, lonely and reclusive as its original owner?

He would write to Caroline first thing tomorrow morning to thank her for her hospitality, the splendid dinner and lunch she had given him, and suggesting she should give some thought to engaging the services of a married couple to occupy the servants' quarters as a cook-housekeeper and gardener-cum-handyman.

Pulling no punches, he would point out to her the necessity of having a man about the place to mow the grass, bring in the fuel for the open fires she had planned, to patrol the premises at nightfall as a security measure; a woman at hand to organise the dusting and polishing of the rooms with the aid of a part-time 'daily', most likely, who would also help with the washing and ironing.

He couldn't envisage Caroline humping

her own fuel indoors, lighting fires, clearing grates, washing and ironing, swilling the front steps, cleaning windows, doing all the shopping and cooking and the washing-up afterwards. The woman needed staff in a house of that size, and it was up to him to make her see sense.

Above all, she needed protection from the world outside. He shuddered to think of what might happen if a gang of burglars broke into the house at the dead of night, her defencelessness in the event of attack, a lone woman in a house overlooking a valley.

Jon realised, exiting the train at King's Cross, that Caroline's welfare had suddenly become of paramount importance to him during the past few hours he had spent alone with her—almost as if he was falling in love with the woman. A ridiculous notion, of course. He was nearly sixty, for God's sake, reputedly a confirmed bachelor, which meant, inevitably, that he was generally regarded as a non-practising homosexual by the much younger, more macho colleagues he occasionally rubbed shoulders with on the stairs, or in the lift to his office on the fourth floor of a tower block overlooking the Thames.

If they only knew! He'd been married once, long ago, to a beautiful young woman who had died giving birth to a stillborn child, their son, Roland. At least that was the name they had chosen for him in the early days of his wife Ramona's pregnancy.

Ramona, dark haired, brown-skinned, with Cherokee blood in her veins, had never doubted for one moment that their child would be a boy, or that this child would be the first of many—'a whole tribe of them,' she had teased him, referring tongue-in-cheek to her Indian ancestry.

They had met in Mexico City, Ramona's birthplace, Jon recalled, waiting in line for a taxi. Her mother was Mexican, she'd explained over dinner on their first date, describing herself as a bit of a hybrid. If so, she was the most beautiful 'hybrid' he'd ever seen, as slender as a wand, a rope of blue-black hair worn over one shoulder, eyes as lustrous as diamonds set in the honey-skinned oval of her face.

He had fallen deeply in love with her that night, she with him, across a candlelit table overlooking the twinkling lights of Mexico City, against a backdrop of brilliant stars in a black velvet sky. Jon remembered that he had requested the band-leader to play 'Ramona'—a romantic melody of the 1930s—to which they had danced closely together, looking into each other's eyes, as though asking and answering unspoken questions of one another.

'Ramona, I hear the mission bells above, Ramona, they're ringing out a song of love ...'

They had been married a month later, then, his working vacation over, he had brought his bride back to England with him to face his parents' strongly voiced disapproval of his choice of a wife: beautiful and charming admittedly, but even so, a misfit, an embarrassment in their view.

Thankfully, Jon thought, paying the taxi-driver his fare and walking slowly up the front steps of the apartment block in which he lived, few people raised so much as an eyebrow in the case of mixed marriages nowadays. He therefore totally understood and accepted Caroline's liaison with Peter Augustine. The pity of it was that the man had died so young and so tragically at a time of trauma and uncertainty in Caroline's life. What the hell did age, or anything else matter when two people were in love?

Entering his flat overlooking St James' Gardens, suddenly feeling his age, Car-radine glanced about him with distaste at the space he inhabited; the pin neatness of his spacious drawing room, devoid of a woman's touch: no flowers or magazines, no family photographs on the sidetables flanking the fireplace; no trace of perfume in the air, or warm smell of cooking from the kitchen.

Making ready for bed, showering first in the clinically neat bathroom, he remembered Caroline's bolt-hole, the tantalising smell of roast duck from the cluttered kitchen, the pleasure he had derived from her company, even, he thought wryly, when the conversation had centred on her love affair with Peter Augustine.

Caroline's thoughts turned frequently to her in-depth conversation with Jon in the days following his visit to Scarborough. She had always liked him enormously and regarded him in the light of the brother she'd longed for and never had, someone she trusted implicitly to handle her financial affairs. Even so, she had never felt as close to him as she had done this past weekend when, warmed by his understanding approach to her personal problems, she had recounted intimate details of her love affair with Peter, expressing clearly and simply how the affair had begun and how it had ended. And he had listened silently, attentively, to her revelations, as a priest in a confessional might have done. The room had been in darkness apart from the flickering simulated flames of the electric fire in the hearth, otherwise, Caroline realised, she might have lacked the courage to bear her soul so completely.

On their return from 'Tara', she had cooked a simple lunch of fresh plaice fillets broccoli florets, and warm, crusty garlic bread, followed by wafer thin crepes with lemon juice and caster sugar, after which they had returned to the sitting room to talk. It was then Caroline had told Jon about Driftwood and the Woman in White, Margaret Roberts, Sarah's diaries, Cam McCauley, the Coopers and Reg Rossiter, one topic leading to another until, finally, she had found the courage to tell Jon Carradine about her love affair with Peter. She'd been filled with a blessed feeling of release at the unstoppering of so much pent-up emotion, an overwhelming sense of relief that she had, at last, discovered a confidant capable of understanding the emotional hell she had lived through since that day, last September, when she had known for certain that Felix and Francesca were lovers.

Jon had been so utterly kind and sensitive towards her that she had felt reluctant to say goodbye to him. Now, on Tuesday morning, opening and reading the letter he had sent her thanking her for her hospitality, going on to say that he strongly advised her not to live alone at 'Tara', she knew that he was right in suggesting the instalment of a married couple to ensure her safety and peace of mind.

She had thought along the same lines herself. The only drawback was where to discover the ideal couple? From an employment agency or a newspaper advert? Possibly she'd find the answer when the house was ready to move into? She'd have to wait and see for the time being. Meanwhile, her days would be filled to overflowing with the restoration of 'Tara'; daily visits to ensure that the plumbers were forging ahead with the modernisation of the kitchen area, the decorators busily engaged in stripping, painting and re-papering.

She had kept in touch with the Coopers since the Christmas vacation. It was good to chat to Maudie on the phone, to hear the latest news.

Cam and Gloria were living together at Gull Cottage, Maudie told her, but the child had been taken away by his father to stay with his grandparents, or so she had heard through the local grapevine, meaning Mrs Rossiter, who had gleaned the information from Reg and cronies of hers resident in Robin Hood's Bay.

There had been a terrible scene, apparently, the day Gloria's husband arrived at the cottage to collect his son, Maudie said avidly, with Gloria shouting on the doorstep, yelling that she would have the law on him for kidnap, he had no right to take her kid away without a court order, interspersed with floods of tears.

Where had Cam been when all this was going on? Caroline wondered. Not the happiest of scenarios for a man recovering from a suicide attempt. Maudie said he was more taciturn than ever these days, unwilling to discuss his ex-wife's return, although he had started taking her about more, on his various business trips for instance, and they had been seen together more than once in the dining room of the Victoria Hotel on the cliff-top, not to mention various pubs in The Bay, as the lower half of the village was referred to by its inhabitants.

But despite her initial outburst at the removal of Toby from Gull Cottage, Gloria now appeared to be her old self once more, dressed to the nines, enjoying the turning of heads whenever she entered a bar with Cam in tow, obviously loving the 'buzz' her return home had caused, savouring her notoriety.

In Maudie's opinion, poor little Toby would be much better off with his father and grandparents, and Caroline had to agree with her, though whether Cam would be better off with Gloria was far less certain. Caroline could not help thinking that Gloria might act as an irritant in the shell of a touchy individual like Cam McCauley. But who was she to judge? And why should she, in any case? How McCauley chose to live his life from now on was none of her business. She had never liked the man anyway, so why should his past or his future matter a damn to her one way or another?

And yet, in retrospect, she had relished, to some extent, their verbal fencing matches, their sharpening of claws on one another, the realisation that beneath Cam's seemingly rough and uncompromising exterior, there lurked a hint of decency.

Memory recalled the night he had come to Driftwood after Peter's death, to tell her that he had decided not to go ahead with his hotel project in Ocho Rios, his wearily uttered words: 'I really cared about Peter, you know; I pinned so much faith in his future.'

In no mood to listen, she had shown him the door. If only, at that moment in time, she had been prepared to forgive and forget Cam's past sins, he might never have ended up in the intensive care unit of the local hospital, a potential suicide victim, Caroline realised, wishing she had been less unbending, more forgiving, when forgiveness really mattered to a man in need not of condemnation but understanding.

One morning, arriving early at 'Tara' to see how the workmen were getting on, the foreman in charge requested a word in her ear.

'Yes, what is it? What's wrong?' Caroline asked him more sharply than she'd intended, having become inured to delays along the way for whatever reasons—mainly due to missing consignments of slates, kitchen units, the correct shades of paint, wallpaper and so on.

'Well, nowt's *wrong,* exactly,' the foreman explained. 'It's just that the roof repairers have come across a cupboard in one of the attic rooms, stuffed full with trunks of clothes, books, ornaments, pictures and so on, and we just wondered what to do with them, that's all!' He added warily, 'Well, you'd best come upstairs an' take a look at them yourself.'

This was unbelievable. There was nothing to indicate the presence of the cupboard by way of a knob or a handle, and it had remained undiscovered for so many years. One of the workmen had noticed a discrepancy in the woodwork, a missing length of skirting-board. On investigation, he had found a gap between floor level and the cupboard door, allowing him to force the door open.

The man and his workmates had dragged the contents of the cupboard into the middle of the attic. There were four trunks in all, draped with cobwebs, the lids of which stood open to reveal dresses, hats, furs, shoes, bedding, paintings, photographs in tarnished silver frames, books spotted with mildew, a treasure trove from a bygone age.

'Do you want 'em left here or tekken downstairs?' the foreman asked patiently, thinking if he had his way he'd burn the lot at the end of the garden, apart from the silver photo-frames which might be worth a bob or two.

'Downstairs, please,' Caroline said, 'if you wouldn't mind. Put them in the hall for the time being, I'll sort through them later.'

'Well, you heard what the lady said.'

'We're slaters, not removal men,' one of the workmen grumbled.

'Would this help?' Caroline asked.

Pocketing the generous tip she handed him, 'Ta very much, Miss,' the foreman said. 'Okay, lads?'

'Yeah, fine! Let's get on with it, shall us?' The grumbler, she noticed, was first in line to rally to the call of a twenty pound note, the prospect of a free drink or two later in the pub round the corner. Whoever said, 'money talks', had hit the nail squarely on the head, Caroline thought wryly. Money, something she'd never been short of, was a mixed blessing at times. Would she have been happier without it, as the wife of a poor man?

She waited until all the workmen had gone home for the day to begin sorting through the chests, holding at bay her inner excitement at what she might find there, wanting to be alone and uninterrupted on her voyage of discovery into the past, realising as she did that the contents could be relevant to one person only, Sarah St Just—the Woman in White.

It was a strangely haunting experience, alone in a mansion at dusk, unpacking the belongings of a woman long dead, who had once known this house as intimately as her own reflection in a mirror, whose footsteps had crossed this hall times without number, whose hand had rested on the banister rail of the staircase leading to the upper landings, who must once have given instructions for the removal of unwanted items to be packed and stored away in that cupboard in the front attic, for what reasons Caroline could merely surmise; because she had grown tired of them, perhaps, or could no longer bear to look at them and the memories of happier times they invoked?

Essentially, Caroline thought, the wealth of folded garments stowed away in the first chest, once stunning green and crimson velvet evening gowns, day dresses, broad-brimmed flower and feather-trimmed hats, kid gloves, fans and elegantly-fashioned high-heeled shoes, belonged to the era of soirées when a slender young woman, a close friend of His Majesty, had been invited to attend dinner parties, balls or race-meetings by royal request.

Certainly the Londesboroughs, inured to Edward's philanderings, would have included, in their guest list the name of his current lady-friend, at his behest. Furthermore, the King would have made certain that his latest conquest would emerge impeccably well-dressed on each and every occasion on which they appeared together however fleeting their relationship might be.

The dresses spoke poignantly to Caroline of the swift ending of a love affair, when Sarah had known beyond a shadow of doubt that the affair was over and done with forever, so that she could no longer bear to look at the clothes he had given her, mute reminders of her days in the sun, and nights of passion in her lover's arms.

The second chest, containing diaphanous

nightgowns, embroidered silk shawls, lace peignoirs, satin dressing gowns, peach, turquoise and white lace-embellished lingerie: ankle-length petticoats, bloomers and wasp-waist corselettes, pure silk stockings, forget-me-not trimmed garters and narrow, satin slippers, touched Caroline deeply. They had been carefully laid away in layers of tissue paper interspersed with muslin bags of lavender and rose petals which still retained something of their former fragrance. The fragrance of a long dead love affair.

Unbelievably tired, Caroline decided to leave the other two trunks until next day to unpack. She had reached a saturation point of emotional excitement for the time being, but first she must repack the gowns and lingerie. She did not want the workmen, when they arrived in the morning, to touch the garments or make jocular, possibly crude remarks about the underwear in particular, knowing that Sarah would hate above all things a public display of her private possessions.

'It's all right, Sarah,' she murmured to the unseen watcher on the staircase, 'I'll take good care of your belongings.'

Chapter Sixteen

Every moment of the next day, Caroline lived in a state of febrile excitement, awaiting the coming of darknesss, the departure of the workmen, the opening of the remaining two chests, wondering what their contents would reveal.

Realising that she must do something positive to while away time, she drove to a country house sale she'd seen advertised in the local paper, hoping to find some suitable items of furniture for her future home. Not necessarily antiques, but comfortable sofas and armchairs, brass bedsteads, rugs, ornaments and pictures, bearing in mind the amount of space that needed filling.

Parking her Mini on the pebbled forecourt of the country house, Caroline thought how sad it was that the owners were obliged to part with their home and its contents. Making discreet enquiries beforehand, she had discovered that the former occupants of the Grange, an elderly couple in failing health, had recently moved into sheltered accommodation in Whitby.

They were certainly people of discrimination and good taste, she thought, viewing the household effects on display: china cabinets, sideboards, cretonne covered sofas and chairs, oil-paintings, occasional tables, lamps, mirrors and overmantles, china and silverware.

Referring to her catalogue, she marked several items she would bid for later when the sale got under way: an immaculate Chinese Rose dinner service, two fine oil-paintings of Whitby Harbour, a Sunderland lustre jug, a walnut bedroom suite, an Indian carpet and a circular rosewood library table.

Looking up from the catalogue at that moment she saw Cam McCauley and Gloria standing close together on the other side of the room. With luck, she'd escape unnoticed. The last thing Caroline wanted or needed right now was a face-to-face confrontation with her ex-landlord and his ex-wife.

Slipping quietly from the room, she found the auctioneer's assistant, who agreed to bid for the items she had selected on her behalf and took her name, address and phone number. Fortunately, she and the man had met before at various other sales in the area.

'Leave everything to me, Mrs Fraser,' he said cheerfully, 'I'll see to it you'll get what you want.'

'Thank you. Now, if you'll excuse me
...'

Getting into her car, Caroline drove quickly to the Mallyan Spout Hotel in the village where, seated alone in the bar, she ordered sandwiches and a glass of wine. This was a pleasant hotel facing the village green, and soon other cars began to arrive, the bar filling up with people seeking refreshment, women wearing tweeds, men in anoraks and quilted body-warmers, county folk on the whole, Caroline thought, who would probably head towards the Grange after lunch.

Suddenly the door opened and in walked Gloria Dennis, wearing a black mini-skirt, scarlet boots, a matching loose-knit sweater, black poncho, and with her long blonde hair swept back from her heavily made-up face to reveal gold earrings the size of curtain rings.

Caroline couldn't help wondering if Cam felt as uncomfortable as he looked as eyes turned to appraise the overdressed young woman framed by the doorway, posing as a fashion model or a film-star might pose for the paparazzi, before sweeping to the bar to demand a large gin and tonic with plenty of ice and lemon.

Leaving the remainder of her sandwiches and her scarcely tasted glass of wine on the table, Caroline threaded her way towards the exit in the hope of escaping unnoticed once more, this time to no avail. To her intense embarrassment, catching sight of her, 'Well, blow me down if it isn't Caroline what's her name,' Gloria burst forth with a merry peal of laughter. 'Well, aren't you going to say hello to the lady, Mac darling? No? Fancy, and there was I thinking the two of you were old pals from way back. Whatever gave me that idea, I wonder?'

'That's enough, Gloria,' Cam muttered savagely, turning his back on Caroline who, ignoring his ex-wife's tirade, quit the bar with as much dignity as she could muster, yet deeply conscious of the curious glances upon her as she walked stiffly from the room.

She was at the bolt-hole later that day when the auctioneer's assistant rang up to impart the glad tidings that he had bidden successfully on her behalf for the items she had marked in the catalogue, wanting to know where and when she wanted the items delivered, and would cash on delivery be acceptable as opposed to cash in advance?

'I'd rather cash in advance, if you don't mind,' Caroline said wearily, strangely disturbed by the events of the day.

She added, with an attempt at cheerfulness, 'I'll come to the saleroom some time tomorrow to settle up with you and make further arrangements. Meanwhile, thank you so much for all your help. I am most grateful, I assure you, Mr ... I'm sorry, I don't know your name.'

'Oh, just call me Peter, everyone else does,' the auctioneer's assistant said blithely.

Replacing the receiver, Caroline's eyes filled with tears. This time, making no attempt at bravery, she allowed them to run down her face, unchecked; tears long overdue for the sheer weight and sadness of life which seemed, at times, a burden too heavy to bear for one woman, alone in the world, trying her best to create a new life, a new future for herself without the one thing she needed and craved for beyond all else. Love. But her lover was dead, and the world was a much sadder, lonelier place without him.

And so she wept for Peter Augustine until there were no more tears left to shed. Then, rising to her feet, putting on her outdoor things, she drove slowly towards 'Tara' to discover the contents of the two chests she had been too tired to examine the night before.

The photographs were a revelation. Now

Caroline knew why a king had been attracted to a proverbial 'beggarmaid'. Sarah St Just's face, a flawless oval, was lit with slightly uptilted eyes beneath wing-like brows and framed by long dark lashes. Beautifully modelled cheekbones and a small delicately chiselled nose added to the distinction of that face, tender, faintly smiling lips and the dreamy expression in her eyes, an air of mystery. Her hair, dark and abundant, was dressed pompadour fashion in the silver-framed studio portraits taken, most likely, at His Majesty's request when their love affair was at its height. Portraits which had possibly graced the drawing room at Driftwood and Sarah's bedroom here at 'Tara' until, plagued by the infirmities of age and failing health, no longer able to bear the sight of herself in a mirror or the perfection of face and form that had once been hers, she had given instructions to have them cleared away once and for all, along with a dozen or so photograph albums contained in the chest. Albums which Caroline intended taking home with her to examine more closely. Now was neither the time nor the place. She was far too tired, in need of a hot bath, a bite to eat and an early night.

Tired as she was, sleep would not come.

Switching on her bedside radio, she listened to the shipping forecast, the National Anthem, then turned to Radio Three in the hope of hearing a Chopin nocturne or Elgar's *Enigma Variations,* something soothing to lull her into a state of forgetfulness of her immediate problems, which seemed suddenly to have crowded in on her in the loneliness of the semi-darkened room.

But the music was not to her taste nor in accordance with her present need of comfort and reassurance following a day which had gone horribly wrong.

Try as she might, she could not forget the way Cam McCauley had turned his back on her in the bar of the Mallyan Spout Hotel. Did he really hate her so much that he couldn't even bear to look at her, much less be civil to her? Probably not, considering the dressing down she had given him at their last meeting.

To add to her troubles, the builders were not getting on as quickly as she had hoped at 'Tara'. And there was another irritant. She must give her future home a proper name. But what? 'Villa St Just'? 'Crossroads'? 'Ich Dien'? 'Dunroaming'? All quite ridiculous, of course. But how about 'Driftwood House'?

Driftwood! Closing her eyes, Caroline recalled the steady, insistent beat of the

271

sea on the shore during her brief stay at that summertime residence which she had come to love more than any other place on earth, which would forever remain a part of her own self and being.

How strange, she thought, that first day she had stood looking down at the cottage, thinking that it looked a bit like Noah's Ark washed up by the sea and stranded on a ledge of rock beyond the reach of the tide, how little she had known then how much it would come to mean to her. If only she might go back in time, back to Driftwood. But there could be no return to the past, except in memory.

She fell asleep eventually to the sound of imaginary waves running in on the shore of a sandy cove beneath a heaven thick with stars.

Next day she went to the saleroom to pay for the items bought at the Grange, and made arrangements to have them put into store for the time being. This done, she drove to 'Driftwood House' to meet Guy Fenton, the general manager of the firm she had employed to take charge of the work in hand, who told her reassuringly that all was going according to plan.

'Really? You could have fooled me!'

'Well, I admit we have hit certain snags regarding deliveries,' he said smoothly, 'all of which have now been ironed out, I'm pleased to say.'

They were in the kitchen at the time. Thankfully, the structural alterations had been completed, the labyrinthine passages and various box-like larders done away with to create more floorspace. Moreover, the tiling had been completed and power points installed to serve the deep-freeze units and the split-level cooker she had ordered, plus the microwave, dishwasher and the washing-machine, when they arrived on the scene.

'I understand your feelings of frustration that the work has been hindered to some extent by circumstances beyond my control,' Fenton explained apologetically, 'but the plumbing has been dealt with satisfactorily, and I can safely say that the sink unit will be in place later today.'

'Yes, of course, Mr Fenton. I'm sorry I spoke so abruptly. I'm sure that you are doing your best to iron out the—snags.'

He said, feeling sorry for the woman, 'Things are not as bad as they may seem to you right now. The roof repairers should be out of your hair by Monday at the latest, and I've hired extra decorators to make certain everything's finished on time. The kitchen units will be fitted on Monday, and the floor tiles laid immediately afterwards.'

'Thank you,' Caroline responded gratefully. 'Then I'll be able to have the carpets laid, the curtains hung and start moving in the furniture.'

'It's a grand house,' Fenton remarked thoughtfully. 'It'll make a fine hotel once it's finished.'

'Hotel?' she looked at him in amazement. 'Whatever gave you that idea?'

'Er, a natural assumption, I suppose, in view of the kitchen modernisation,' Fenton said, aware of his gaffe, speaking cheerfully to minimise his mistake. 'It's really remarkable what a difference the structural alterations have made in creating so much space.' He was waffling, and he knew it. 'It simply occurred to me that, on completion, it would stand comparison with that of a first class hotel.'

Caroline smiled. 'Don't worry, Mr Fenton,' she said lightly. 'I just happen to prefer cooking in a spacious atmosphere, so I really needed to get rid of all those passageways and larders, thought I love the rest of the house just the way it is.'

For a split second, Fenton entertained the notion that his employer intended living in the house alone. But that was ridiculous. A woman of her age was bound to have family connections, sons and daughters at university, most likely, who would crowd in on her during vacations, possibly even a husband tucked away in the background, an Army officer, most probably, or a diplomat on overseas duties.

Yes, that was the obvious answer, Fenton concluded to his own satisfaction, and yet ... bidding goodbye to Caroline Fraser, getting into his car and driving away from the house, he wondered why the gut feeling persisted that he was wrong in every respect: that his client had every intention of living in that strange mansion entirely alone. If so, she must be either mad or eccentric.

But his common sense told him she was neither, simply a wealthy, middle-aged, lonely lady in search of a purpose in life.

She had saved the albums to look at later that day. She would have lunch in town, then visit a specialist lighting shop on the South Cliff in search of table lamps and shades. 'Tara' was beginning to come together now. 'Tara', the name had stuck, Caroline realised, smiling. In any case, there could never be another Driftwood. Perhaps she should plant cottonwood trees in the garden? Which reminded her, she needed to get in touch with the firm she had earmarked to bring the garden under control.

She had not at first realised the extent of the grounds until, on a voyage of discovery one day, she found out that the wilderness of overgrown trees and steep paths leading down to the valley below and bordered by a high brick wall, was part of the estate. She had made a surprising discovery that day, a metal tripod similar to the one on the verandah at Driftwood.

Pondering the significance of the objects, this one, she'd noticed, had been set on a rockery in the centre of a small, once ornamental pool now thick with decayed lily-pads static in scummy, weed infested water.

Her visit to the lighting shop paid dividends in the shape of four elegant table-lamps, the bases, of Chinese origin, richly patterned in glowing colours, surmounted with hand-made, rose pink silk shades which would have cost twice the price in Harrods. The tall, quietly spoken owner of the shop had been more than helpful and kind in allowing her time to pick and choose what she wanted with no feeling of pressure, making her visit to his shop a pleasure, so that she had also purchased from him two gilt-framed mirrors and, because she couldn't resist it, a child's nursery lamp resembling Aladdin's Cave, all of which he would deliver to 'Tara' when the house was ready to receive them.

Homeward bound to the bolt-hole, on a

sudden, unaccountable impulse, she called in at the 'We Aim to Please' agency for a word with her friend, Lara Westwood. A social call, nothing more, or so Caroline had imagined until, staring up at her, 'Oh, I'm so sorry, Mrs Fraser,' Lara blurted dramatically. 'I've just had word from the Farmers that friends of theirs are interested in buying your flat, and they'll be coming to take a look at it over the weekend, if that's convenient.'

Caroline's heart sank. Words could not express how much the bolt-hole had come to mean to her during her brief tenancy.

'Have you any idea when these people will be arriving?' she asked Lara. 'Over the weekend seems a bit vague.'

'I'll give Mr Farmer a ring and ask him.' Lara picked up the phone, prodded the numbers and waited. 'Oh, is that you, Mr Farmer? The Agency here. Lara Westwood speaking. Mrs Fraser is in the office ... Yes, of course, I'll put her on ... He wants to talk to you,' she mouthed, handing Caroline the telephone.

'Hello, Mr Farmer ... Yes, Miss West-wood told me. I just wondered when ... Oh, I see. How disappointing for you ... No, not at all, as a matter of fact I feel relieved,' drawing in a deep breath, 'you see, I've grown attached to the place ... Oh, how kind of you to say so. My pleasure, believe me. I believe in taking care of other people's belongings ... Yes, I can understand your feelings ... No, I don't think you are being too sentimental, I'd feel the same way myself; after all, she was your mother.'

Lara was listening intently to this one-sided conversation, attempting to catch the drift of what was being said on the other end of the line. Her eyebrows shot up as Caroline continued, 'The truth is, Mr Farmer, if you are agreeable, that is, I am prepared to make you a firm offer for your property, the contents to remain in situ until you and your family have had time to think things over, if that makes sense ... Oh please, no thanks necessary, I assure you ... You really mean it? ... Yes, of course. Shall we say tomorrow afternoon at two-thirty? ... Oh good. Until tomorrow then? Goodbye, Mr Farmer.'

'My God,' Lara said admiringly, 'you certainly believe in taking the bull by the horns, don't you? What happened to the "friends" by the way?'

Caroline laughed, 'A case of male domination, I gather. Mrs Friend fancied a change of scenery, Mr Friend had different ideas. Guess who won?'

'You buy property like most women buy lipsticks,' Lara commented wryly. 'Lord, what it must be like to be rich! I envy you, Mrs Fraser, I really do!'

'Then *don't!* Money doesn't necessarily mean happiness, you know.'

'P'rhaps not, but I bet it makes misery a helluva lot easier to bear,' Lara said mournfully. 'Not that I'm ever likely to find out!'

Returning to the bolt-hole, crossing the threshold, what on earth had possessed her? Caroline thought guiltily, wondering what Jon Carradine's reaction would be when she confessed to having let her heart rule her head once more? At the rate she was going, there'd be next to nothing left for The Battersea Dogs' Home, and yet a sense of quiet happiness invaded her heart with the realisation that no way could she have borne to part with this little haven of peace she had discovered at the heartbeat of Scarborough, as the custodian of an old lady's treasured belongings. Just an ordinary old lady, not the former mistress of a king; possibly far happier than Sarah had ever been during her lifetime.

Going through to the kitchen, Caroline made herself a sandwich and a cup of coffee, then, returning to the sitting room, she switched on the fire and the standard lamp and opened the photograph albums.

Chapter Seventeen

Turning the pages, Caroline experienced the strange sensation of having entered a different dimension, a bygone era. There were photographs of working class people about their daily lives: a plump, smiling woman sitting near a cottage door, shelling peas into an earthenware bowl on her lap; an old man in a striped, open necked shirt, smoking a clay pipe; barefoot children in an orchard, picking apples; the same children playing on the sands, the girls wearing sunbonnets; photos of the two girls, arms about each other's waists, near the sea's edge, captioned 'MEG AND SALLY, TALLAND BAY', in neatly printed capital letters.

There were pictures of hay-wains coming in from the fields, men in shirt-sleeves resting from their labours near a farm gate, grinning at the camera, bait-boxes and tea-cans scattered near them on the grass: scenes depicting rural life in an age far removed from modern farming equipment, when shire-horses pulled the tractors, seed was hand sown, and milking machinery was unheard of.

The girls, Meg and Sally, featured in many of the photographs, and they seemed inseparable, of the same age, one tall, slender and dark-haired, the other fair-haired, slightly shorter and much plumper than her friend, or possibly her sister?

Suddenly, with a frisson of excitement, Caroline knew the identity of the two girls. Of course, Meg and Sally, derivatives of the names Margaret and Sarah! Margaret Roberts and Sara St Just! And the place was Cornwall. Talland Bay was in Cornwall, a stone's throw away from Polperro! She had always suspected that St Just was a Cornish name. Now she was sure.

So Margaret Roberts and Sara St Just had grown up together, remained together throughout their lives, grown old together, died within days of each other and been laid to rest side by side? Truly, 'In death they were not divided,' as suggested by the inscription on Margaret's gravestone, for the obvious reason that poor Margaret could not go on living without her lifelong companion and friend, and had died of a broken heart.

Closing the first album, switching off the fire and the lamp, Caroline went to bed to face another restless night.

Something was wrong somewhere, but she couldn't think what. It was just a feeling she had of bad news in the offing, a presentiment of danger in some shape or other, to do with the divorce proceedings, perhaps?'

Staring up at the ceiling, unable to sleep, she reviewed the components of her life so far; her happy, uncomplicated childhood in the bosom of a loving, small family circle; her hasty, unsuccessful marriage to the charismatic Felix Fraser who had married her not for love, but money—her initial inheritance on the death of her beloved Grandma Heritage spent underwriting her husband's ambition to become a world famous author.

He had succeeded in his ambition, but never had he given a moment's thought to her contribution to his success; had never held her in his arms or kissed her as if he meant it; had simply climbed his way up to fame and fortune with a total disregard of her own happiness or wellbeing, indulging in various minor flings along the way. Then his major sexual encounter with Francesca Delgado, by which time he had insisted on living in some considerable style in the Eaton Square mansion which she, Caroline, had seen all along as a millstone round the necks of other than the seriously rich people of the world.

And yet she had felt obliged to plough as much cash as she could reasonably afford into that house, for the simple reason that, prior to his blatant affair with Francesca, she had still loved him.

Then had come Driftwood, a new concept of life based on her need to escape from the heartbreak and humiliation of the past, a return to a much simpler, far more rewarding way of life: a new-found love with a man in whose arms she had discovered the true meaning of love, a happiness she had never known before. A love destined to live on in her heart.

If only it were that simple. Now she was faced with a bitter legal battle to rid herself of the financial and emotional entanglements of a marriage which, had she possessed more wisdom, would never have taken place at all. Her father had tried to warn her, she remembered—to no avail. Now she was paying the price of her folly, and she had no one to blame but herself.

A letter from Basil Pryde, next morning, confirmed her forebodings of the night before. Felix was about to contest the divorce on the grounds of her adultery; demand full financial compensation in respect of the Mercedes and various gifts of jewellery he had bestowed on her prior to her unwarranted desertion, plus the lump sum of £500,000 in respect of the stress and anxiety her actions had caused him.

Pryde went on to say that the divorce hearing had been fixed a month hence, mentioning the date, time and place, and he strongly advised her to be present at the hearing which he himself would, of course, defend to the best of his ability; pointing out that her presence in court would add weight to his defence.

So it had come to this, Caroline thought despairingly, a bitter, acrimonious, well-publicised, financially-motivated struggle between herself and Felix, because this was what it boiled down to in the long run: her husband's greed for money. In which case, why not give in gracefully? What had she to gain apart from more humiliation and heartbreak in even attempting to defend herself against a man hell-bent on personal gain, and something more besides—even more disturbing—revenge?

Revenge! Yes, of course, Caroline realised, pursuing this new line of thought which had never occurred to her before. Felix had married her not merely disliking but loathing her intensely. Why else would he have treated her so badly?

The answer came as clear as day: because he had always seen her as an encumbrance rather than an adornment, a plain woman incapable of arousing his ardour—even in bed on their wedding night.

And she had lived through the years of their marriage as a kind of whipping-boy, unable ever to please him no matter how hard she tried—except in matters pertaining to money, when she had bought him, for instance, his first computer, his gold Rolex watch, pearl cufflinks and the surprise birthday present of a trip to Italy aboard the Orient Express.

She knew now, to her cost, that money cannot buy happiness, and she had learned that lesson the hard way. So why cling to her inheritance so devoutly? What had she to lose that had not already been lost beyond recall? Her affair with Peter Augustine had had nothing to do with money, but love. Love, the richest gift of all; the pearl beyond price.

And so, she thought, why fight? Why even attempt to defend herself at the divorce court hearing? If Felix wanted money and revenge so badly, why not give in to his demands? After two sleepless nights, she was past caring.

She would write to Basil Pryde, telling him that, after due consideration, she had reached the decision not to defend her husband's divorce action against her, with one proviso, that he would return to her her mother's wedding ring and her Grandmother Heritage's rocking-chair. Not much to ask, in view of all else,

Caroline thought wearily. Surely not even her money-crazed husband would object to parting with items worth less than nothing in his estimation?

Tired and stressed, she scarcely knew what to do, what to think anymore. So best let someone she trusted do the thinking for her. She would ring Jon Carradine first thing on Monday morning. In the meanwhile, she had her meeting with Mr Farmer to come. Had she jumped the gun in saying she wished to make an offer for the bolt-hole? Would Jon consider she had acted unwisely in saddling herself with two homes in the same town?

She had acted impulsively once more, just as she had done the day she left London to drive north to Yorkshire, the day she had decided to buy 'Tara'; when she had written to Basil Pryde telling him to go ahead with her divorce action against Felix, and when she had made Sam Cooper a gift of the Mercedes, her impulses engendered by a new-born longing for freedom after the years she had spent in the captivity of a soul-destroying marriage. Was she about to give up that freedom so easily? It was up to her to decide whether to fight on or give in to emotional blackmail.

Squaring her shoulders, she went through to the bathroom to shower, then to the kitchen to make toast and coffee, finally to the bedroom to dress, apply her make-up and brush her now shoulder-length hair into a french plait.

Looking at herself objectively in the dressing-table mirror, she wondered if, attending the divorce hearing, coming face to face with Felix again, he would recognise the 'new look' Caroline as the timid sparrow of a woman he had last set eyes on.

Refreshed, Caroline walked into town to buy food for the weekend and fresh flowers for Gladys Farmer's vases.

She took to Mrs Farmer's son, Harold, on sight. A man in his sixties, quietly spoken, neatly dressed in a brown suit, collar and tie, she invited him in to sit near the fire, understanding his emotional response at his return to his mother's home, the glint of tears in his eyes.

Pretending not to notice, excusing herself, she went through to the kitchen to make a pot of tea. When she returned with the tray, he was standing near the sideboard admiring a vase of pink and white carnations.

'Carnations were my Mum's favourite flowers,' he said mistily. 'Thank you, Mrs Fraser, for the care you've taken of the flat, for keeping everything so spotless, just the way she used to.'

The interview went well but slowly at first, with Harold far more interested in reminiscing about his mother than discussing matters pertaining to the sale of the property. He had drunk two cups of tea, and Caroline had made a fresh pot before he plucked up enough courage to mention money. A nice, unassuming man, she had the feeling he'd probably give the place away, gift-wrapped, rather than cause offence by placing too great a value on it. Then it had been up to her to make what she believed to be a realistic offer which, perspiring profusely from the heat of the fire, he accepted at once, with the air of one who, expecting nothing, had been offered twice as much.

'Well, if you're *really* sure,' he reiterated for the third time as she ushered him towards the front door, 'my solicitors will be in touch with you in due course. Meanwhile, thanks again, Mrs Fraser, for your kindness and generosity. It's been a pleasure meeting a really nice lady such as yourself, with her heart in the right place.'

When he had gone, returning to the sitting room, Caroline sat down for a while to draw breath, then, switching on the standard lamp as evening shadows invaded the room, she opened the second photograph album. The here and now ceased suddenly to exist as she found herself caught up in a time-warp of photographs depicting lives of the long dead and forgotten people of a different age, in which they had loved and laughd and smiled at the camera, as if life as they knew it then would last forever. In particular, the two girls, Meg Roberts and Sally St Just: grown from awkward schoolgirls into comely, attractive young women.

But the setting was different and so was the clothing. In several of the photographs they were wearing what appeared to be maids' uniforms, black skirts, high-necked blouses, starched aprons and mob caps, along with other girls dressed in similar outfits, standing self-consciously, hands folded across their skirts, looking prim and proper.

So Margaret and Sarah had gone into service, as parlour-maids presumably? Nothing unusual in that, Caroline thought. Leaving school, they would need to find work to help support their families, which would have also meant leaving home at an early age to find employment with the gentry families of Cornwall, as house or nursery-maids, tweenies, skivvies or dairy-maids, depending on their aptitude for the work involved, their appearance and school attendance records.

Poor Meg and Sally, Caroline thought tenderly, how homesick they must have felt leaving home for the first time to face a new way of life, their few belongings strapped into boxes and hefted aboard a farm-cart, most likely. At least they had remained together, a crumb of comfort for both of them, and their loved ones.

Then, turning the pages, Caroline came across the neatly printed caption: 'Richmond Park'.

Richmond Park? But this seemed incredible! Richmond Park was near London. She had been there many times with her parents, on picnics, as a child, and there had been something special about it, something mysterious and vaguely exciting. If only she could remember what. Suddenly, she knew! There was a magnificent Georgian mansion set somewhere in that park which, her mother had told her, had once been the home of the Prince of Wales, the future Monarch, King Edward VII, following the death of his illustrious mother, Queen Victoria, Empress of India.

Immediately, Caroline, aged about seven at the time, had begged to look at the house in the park. Now she clearly recalled her mother's words: 'I'm afraid that's not possible, darling.'

'Why not? Why isn't it?' hopping impatiently from one foot to the other.

'Because the house is not open to the public, more's the pity.'

'Mummy! What is "the public"?'

'You are, I am, so is Mummy,' her father explained laughingly, 'more generally known as "commoners", and the rule book has it that commoners may not rub shoulders with kings. The result may well prove disastrous!'

She hadn't a clue what he meant at the time. She knew now. Sarah St Just had learned that lesson the hard way, when a commoner, albeit a beautiful commoner, had caught the eye of a future king at that Georgian mansion in Richmond Park. She had gone to work there, aged fifteen at the most, shortly after the eighteen-year-old Prince of Wales had been granted his own establishment, it being the earnest hope of his father, Prince Albert, that his son's removal from the fleshpots of London would bring about a much desired improvement in his generally slack demeanour so far as affairs of the heart were concerned.

So Sarah and Edward's affair had started as long ago as that, Caroline concluded, when a foolish young prince had looked at a commoner and fallen head over heels in love with her? Obviously neither of them had been aware of her father's eponymous 'rule book' at the time, and would not have cared even if they had.

But that was the way with love. Live for today with no thought of tomorrow. How could it have been otherwise when a bored, lonely young man had beheld a face as lovely as Sarah St Just's? In bed together, would it really have mattered which was royal, which the commoner?

But it *had* mattered in the long run.

In bed later that night, it occurred to Caroline that she had not yet opened the fourth chest.

Tomorrow was Sunday, a day of rest for the workmen. She would sleep late, read the Sunday papers, cook herself a bacon and egg brunch, then go to 'Tara' and delve into the contents of chest number four, which, she imagined, would contain nothing more than discarded bed-linen; sheets, blankets and pillowcases, moth-eaten and discoloured.

She was wrong. The chest contained clothing; dresses, hats and underwear which Caroline knew instinctively had belonged to Margaret Roberts, just ordinary garments, in no way spectacular or flamboyant, but plain, almost dowdy, in decided contrast to those belonging to Sarah.

Beneath the layers of garments, at the bottom of the chest, lay several books in brown-paper jackets; recipe books, perhaps, or household account books of the kind kept by practical housekeepers of that era. And Margaret had been a very practical, down-to-earth person, Caroline guessed, deeply aware of her responsibilities towards her lifelong friend and companion.

But these were not recipe nor household account books. They were diaries! Margaret's diaries! Painstakingly kept records of an age long gone and forgotten, memories set down in black and white.

Sarah had also kept diaries, meant for her eyes only. Caroline harboured the strange notion that Margaret, on the other hand, had meant her own diaries to be discovered and read some day, as if stretching out a hand beyond the grave in the hope of understanding or forgiveness.

Chapter Eighteen

'We both fell fast asleep towards the end of the journey,' Margaret had written in her neat, copperplate handwriting, 'so tired and worn out we clung together on the back seat of the carriage for comfort. Besides, we were very hungry, having eaten the pasties and apples out mothers had packed for us, at midday, when the horses stopped for a rest and the driver got down to 'wet his whistle', whatever that means.

'Sally said it meant that he wanted a drink of beer, and she, for one, could do with a glass of lemonade. I had all on to stop her getting out of the coach to follow the driver into the public house, saying it wasn't ladylike, and we'd best make do with the bottle of cold tea in our bass bag.

'But that wasn't good enough for Sally. If lemonade was what she wanted, lemonade she would have! I knew it was just Sally's way of pretending not to be scared of what lies ahead of us, but her pretence didn't last long. She was just as miserable and homesick as I was deep inside, wishing the carriage would turn round and take us back to where we belong.

'I'm writing this near midnight, by the light of a candle in the attic room we are sharing. Sally's already fast asleep in the other bed. My own eyes are heavy with sleep, but my brain is still wide awake, thinking of this strange new place we've come to, so far away from home. A great and magnificent house, by what I've seen of it so far, set in acres of parkland, with lighted windows shining into the darkness of a summer night.

'Shall we be happy here, Sally and I? I do hope so, and I think it likely, since we were kindly received by a tall lady in black who gave us a meal of chicken pie and mashed potatoes before showing us upstairs to our room and bidding us to report to her at six o'clock tomorrow morning to be given our uniforms and a list of duties. So I'd best try to sleep now, otherwise I may fail in those duties, whatever they may be. Meanwhile, I pray, may God bless Mother and Father, Grandpa Roberts, my brother Ted, sister Emily, and my dear friend Sally St Just. Amen.'

Reading on, Caroline gleaned that the two girls had been recommended to the Royal Household by a Cornish nobleman, an acquaintance of the village schoolmistress, whose glowing reports on the aptitude and hard work of her two star pupils had led to a discussion on their prospects of future employment when they left school.

The squire, Sir Charles Trevelyan, a member of the House of Commons, a man of some authority and distinction with friends in high places, had promised to give the matter some thought.

He must have been aware at the time that the Prince of Wales had been awarded his own establishment in Richmond Park, and girls of good character would be required as house-maids to work under the auspices of an upper echelon of servants, hand-picked by Prince Albert, from trusted members of staff at Windsor Castle.

So fate had decreed that two bright pupils from a village school in Cornwall had been chosen to begin their working lives in the service of Albert Edward, Prince of Wales, known to his family as Bertie, the bane of his parents' lives, who, at the early age of eighteen, had already shocked their sense of propriety by his profligate attitude to life, his propensity for wine, women and song, lack of moral fibre and general laxity in matters pertaining to his future role in life as Heir Apparent to the throne of his mother, Queen Victoria.

Not that two innocent young girls on their way to Richmond Park in a hired coach one July day in the year 1859, would have had an inkling of what the future held in store for them apart from hard work in unfamiliar surroundings, in a world as far removed from the old familiar pattern of life as the moon from the sun.

Viewed through Margart Roberts' diaries, Caroline realised how difficult it must have been for her and Sarah to adjust to their new regime, the sheer drudgery entailed in rising at dawn to clear away the ashes of yesterday's fires from the grates, to scour the hearths, bring in kindling and coals from the fuel-stores in the yard to relight new fires in readiness for the day ahead to ensure the comfort of the prince and his entourage, who might wish to warm their backsides even at the height of summer: the carrying of cans of hot shaving water to their rooms, after which their breakfasts of bacon, eggs, sausages, devilled kidneys and kedgeree, would be served by the footmen from the silver chafing dishes on the dining-room sideboard.

'They are unpleasant men on the whole,' Margaret had written, 'very smug and self-satisfied, especially Colonel Bruce, who treats the prince as a tutor would treat a schoolboy. As for the prince himself, he's very stout for his age, and not very handsome in my opinion, with bulging eyes, although his hair is quite thick and wavy. Not that I've seen him all that often, except on his way downstairs to the dining room, or in the stable-yard mounting his favourite horse with the aid of the groom—his legs being on the short side.

'Truth to tell, I feel a bit sorry for the poor young man, without a soul to call his own, though I refuse to listen to gossip about him in the servants' hall, which has it that Colonel Bruce and his equerries are here to keep an eye on the prince, to teach him protocol and so on: plus ribald remarks about his inability to keep his trouser buttons properly fastened.

'But this is none of my business. I came here to work, not to worry my head about my employer. In any case, when evening comes, after supper in the servants' hall, I'm too tired to do anything more than write up my diary, blow out my candle, and go to sleep!'

Intrigued by the wealth of detail encapsulated in the closely written pages, reading between the lines, Caroline realised the differing personalities of the two girls. Margaret emerged as the more intelligent, the quiet one, the thinker, the plodder, Sarah the sharper, the less conscientious, the more wayward of the two.

Caroline could see why. Sarah reminded her of a proud, high-stepping filly, Margaret a patient, docile cart-horse. Or was that too cruel a comparison? If so, she didn't mean to be cruel, just realistic. Sarah was beautiful, Margaret plain; Sarah ambitious, Margaret content with her lot, and it was these differences between them that had marked their passage through life as mistress and servant.

Sarah would have needed a confidante, Caroline realised, someone she could trust implicitly, a shoulder to cry on in times of trouble, an uncritical, undemanding presence in her life, who really loved her and would stand by her through thick and thin, a role infinitely suited to her lifelong friend and companion, Margaret Roberts the compassionate, of the simple, warm, understanding heart, who had written in the autumn of 1859:

'Unable to sleep at all last night. Sarah's bed remained unslept in until the early hours of the morning. I asked her where she had been, when she finally came upstairs to our room, and she said she had been to a supper party at the house, to which she had been invited by no lesser person than the Prince of Wales himself, in the absence of Colonel Bruce and his equerries.

'Deeply shocked, I asked Sarah if she

had had supper alone with the prince, to which she replied, "No, of course not. There were lots of other people present, personal friends of his from London; gentry folk, real ladies and gentlemen! Oh, don't look so cross, Meg! I was there to help serve the supper, not to partake of it, though the prince took the trouble to speak to me more than once, and he knew my name and where I was from."

'I told Sarah that I wasn't cross, just worried for her welfare when she hadn't come to bed at her usual time. Why hadn't she told me she would be out late, that she'd been invited to serve supper in the prince's private apartment?

'"The trouble with you, Meg," she said, undressing and getting into bed, "is you want all your 't's crossed and every comma in the right place! The fact is, I enjoyed tonight more than I've ever enjoyed anything in my life before; meeting all those fine people, serving all that wonderful food—quails' eggs in aspic, smoked salmon, caviare, rich cakes and pastries bursting with cream fresh from the dairy. Besides which, the prince was so easy and pleasant to talk to, I felt quite at ease with him, not a bit like a servant."'

So that was how the affair had begun,

Caroline thought, closing the first of Margaret Roberts' diaries. A story reminiscent of King Cophetua and the Beggar Maid.

In the fullness of time, Sarah's nocturnal visits to the prince's private apartments had become more frequent, to Margaret's distress.

In vain she had warned her friend against the folly of becoming too involved with His Royal Highness, to which the red-haired Sarah had retorted touchily that it wasn't her fault she'd been chosen to help serve the food at the prince's private functions, when his friends from London were invited to attend supper parties in the absence of his stuffy old tutors.

His London friends were young and gay, fun to be with, there were charades, musical interludes, informal dancing, wine flowing like water, magnificent flower arrangements, discreet lighting, sparkling crystal, silver cutlery, monogrammed napery in gleaming napkin rings engraved with the Prince of Wales' feathers.

At Christmas 1860, the prince had given Sarah a similar ring engraved with the initials S.S.J.

In the new year, Sarah had moved out of the room in the annexe she had shared with Meg, to more prestigious servants' quarters on the top floor of the royal residence across the park, to a room of her own. This was an accolade awarded only to favourite members of the prince's personal staff, not including his housekeeper, chef, major-domo and valet, who occupied grace and favour apartments in a separate wing of the house, as befitted their exalted station in life or, as Margaret Roberts had observed wryly in her diary, 'to keep them out of harm's way when the prince wishes to be alone with one or other of his lady friends.

'My main concern is for Sarah, alone in that room of hers across the park. My constant worry is that the prince, with his liking for pretty women, may one night force his attentions on Sally, who powerless to resist his advances, might well be forced to appease a disgusting sexual appetite more in keeping with a beast of the field than that of a man born to be king.'

Obviously there had been no love lost between Margaret Roberts and her future sovereign at that stage or afterwards, Caroline realised, reaching the point in the third diary when, in the summer of 1861, Sarah had admitted in desperation to Margaret that she and the prince had fallen deeply in love, that she was expecting his child, and begged Meg to stand by her in her hour of need. She needed Meg to travel with her to Yorkshire, where Edward had found her a place to stay with friends of his until he had made more permanent arrangements on her behalf, with one proviso: that the child she was carrying must be aborted as soon as possible, otherwise he would deny all knowledge of the affair and refuse her access to his presence ever again. The choice was hers entirely. He would, of course, pay for the operation at a hospital of his choosing, which she must enter under an assumed name for obvious reasons.

And so Sarah had had her child aborted under the assumed name of Margaret Roberts, who had been at hand throughout the ordeal to comfort and protect poor Sally St Just, the lovely, wayward girl she loved dearly as a sister, whose side she was destined never to leave again in this world; the keeper of a secret which, had it been made public, might well have shaken the monarchy to its foundations and brought into question Edward's fitness to fulfil his destiny.

Margaret wrote: 'Sally has been desperately ill and unhappy. There was no question of our returning to Cornwall following the abortion. The prince forbade it absolutely. We were forced to remain in lodgings in a suburb of London until arrangements had been made for us to travel north to Yorkshire.

'Sally had got it into her head that we would stay in some grand house or other, she as an honoured guest of HRH, myself in my assumed role as her personal maid-servant/companion. No such good fortune attended us. We were sent to stay at an isolated farmhouse on the Whitby Moors, a rough, stone-built dwelling in the back of beyond, tenanted by a churlish sheep-farmer and his uncommunicative wife, who gave no sign of knowing who we were, the reason for our visit or its duration.

'We were given whitewashed rooms, chilly and inadequately furnished, plainly cooked food consisting mainly of eggs, home-cured bacon, rabbit pies, stewed lamb, thickly sliced vegetables, and steamed suet puddings, served at the kitchen table in the presence of the farmer and his wife, whose silence drove Sally to the brink of despair on more than one occasion.

'"It's no use, Meg," she wept, clinging to me for comfort, "I shall go mad if I stay here much longer! Oh, why doesn't Bertie send me a message? He knows how much I love him, and he said he loved me. How could he have sent me to this awful place to eat my heart out wondering if he really meant what he said?"

'I begged her to be patient. What else could I have done in the circumstances? I felt, at least, that the strong moorland air and the plain but wholesome food on our plates had put colour in her cheeks and flesh on her bones. Besides which, I had the feeling that the farmer and his wife had been well paid for their silence, that they were obeying strict orders from on high, the owner of their farm most likely, and the acres of land surrounding it.'

Weeks had passed, apparently, during which Sarah had had no word from her lover. Margaret had described in detail those weeks, during which Sally had grown increasingly moody and low-spirited with nothing to do except stare out of her bedroom window, reliving, in memory, those passionate, forbidden hours of bliss which had led to her downfall.

It was then that Margaret had encouraged her to set down her feelings on paper in the form of a journal, as she herself had done. Sarah had seemed dubious at first, afraid that someone would read what she had written, extracting a promise from Meg that, should anything untoward happen to her, she would burn the journal unread.

Meanwhile, Meg had circumvented boredom by the simple expedient of helping
the farmer's wife in the kitchen, peeling
potatoes, preparing the vegetables, learning
how to skin a rabbit, scouring pots and
pans, lending the woman a hand on
washdays to poss the clothes in the dolly-
tub and hang them on the washing-line in
the garden afterwards, going down to the
hen-roost, basket in hand, to collect the
eggs, gradually breaking down the woman's
initial hostility towards her to the extent
that she had confessed the reason for that
hostility.

'It were t'maister's notion, not mine, to
tek in lodgers,' she'd explained. 'I tould
'im, plain an' simple, I wanted nowt to do
wi' lookin' after strangers, that I had all on
lookin' after us-selves, but t'maister said
'e'd been given orders from 'Is Lordship's
agent, no less, to do a 'e was tould, an' for
me an' 'im to keep us mouths shut tight
about the—arrangements.'

The owner of the moorland farm,
Margaret had learned, was no less a
personage than Lord Londesborough, a
close friend and confidant of the Prince
of Wales.

Then it had been the turn of the farmer's
wife to ask questions, none of which
Meg had answered to her satisfaction.
Indeed, with an ingenuity which delighted

306

Caroline, reading that particular entry, she had told the farmer's wife that her 'mistress', Miss St Just, on the verge of a nervous breakdown, had been advised by her London physician to take a long holiday in the country, somewhere quiet, off the beaten track, with lots of fresh air and good food to build up her constitution, and 'madam' had been fortunate indeed in trusting her physician to pull the right strings in finding her the perfect place to aid her recovery.

'Oh, is that all?' The farmer's wife had seemed disappointed. 'An' there was we, t'maister an' me, thinkin' there was summat queer goin' on. What I mean is, some kind of scandal or t'other as needed hushin' up.' She continued, 'We could see at once that the young lady was a cut above the rest of us, with 'er fine clothes an' all. Truth to tell, we'd got it into us heads she was—in the family way. Well, we was wrong about that.' Avidly, 'So what caused 'er nervous breakdown? A broken engagement?'

'How well you understand such matters, Mrs Tempest. Now, if you'll hand me that basket, I'll collect the eggs.'

A fortnight later, a letter had arrived at the farm requesting Sarah's presence at a solicitor's office in Whitby the following week. A carriage would be sent to convey herself, Margaret and their luggage to a hotel, where they would stay overnight prior to Sarah's meeting with a Mr Aylott, the personal representative of a London-based firm of lawyers acting on behalf of their client Henry Brown.

Aglow with excitement, Sarah had begun packing at once.

'Just think of it, Meg,' she cried ecstatically, 'staying in a hotel after this hovel! I'll be able to bathe properly in hot running water, sleep in a soft bed, have breakfast brought to my room, my hair attended to! I knew all along that darling Bertie hadn't forgotten about me! I just *knew* it!'

Had the expression, 'You could have fooled me,' been in vogue at the time, Caroline felt certain that Margaret would have used it, having endured weeks of Sarah's tears and tantrums, her boredom and bitter complaints about everything under the sun.

But Margaret's love for the wayward Sarah knew no bounds. She had written: 'I pray there is good news in store for Sally, that she is right in thinking the best of "B". The poor girl has suffered a great deal lately through no fault of her own, including the fact that she was born beautiful—a burden rather than a blessing at times, I imagine. A burden which I, thank God, shall never be called upon to shoulder.'

Meg's plumpness and plain way of dressing, plus her proprietorial air towards Sally, must have imparted an impression of greater maturity, Caroline thought. Perhaps this was the impression Meg wished to impart, so that no one would question the mistress-companion relationship she had concocted to safeguard her friend's reputation at a time when a young lady travelling alone and unchaperoned was unthinkable.

Caroline's heart lifted and warmed when she read the outcome of Sarah's meeting with Mr Aylott.

'We were taken to a clifftop overlooking the sea near a place called Robin Hood's Bay. Dismounting from Mr Aylott's carriage, we walked down a steep path to a little house set on a ledge of rock, with steps leading to a sandy cove with the tide running in on the shore and seabirds wheeling overhead.

'The house reminded me of pictures I've seen of Swiss chalets, neat and pretty, with an odd kind of turret room with a little wooden balcony above the sea-facing verandah. I fell in love with it at first sight.

'Inside the house, all was immaculate, beautifully furnished in the best of taste down to the last detail. There were richly-patterned carpets, velvet curtains, sofas and armchairs, gilt-framed watercolours, polished satinwood and rosewood tables, elegant dining-room furniture; silver epergnes and cut-crystal decanters.

'In the first floor rooms, solid mahogany bedroom suites, brass bedsteads, soft feather mattresses, silk sheets and pillow-cases, satin eiderdowns and lace bed-spreads. On the same landing, a bathroom with gold taps, complete with flagons of perfume and tablets of sandalwood soap.

'The turret room above, which Mr Aylott referred to as "the servants' quarters", was not so richly furnished. There were two single brass bedsteads with flock mattresses, a marble-topped washstand with a soap-dish, ewer and basin, and a chamber-pot in the cupboard below. The beds had cotton sheets and pillowcases. Not that I minded. Cotton's what I'm used to, not silk. Besides which, I shall love sleeping alone in that oddly-shaped room and standing on the balcony at night to look up at the stars.

'But it was the kitchen I liked best of all, with its rows of copper pans and the built-in dresser filled with shelves of pretty china; a well-scrubbed central table, store

310

cupboards, deep stone sink and draining-boards, and the cooking-range with its many side ovens, roasting-spit and hobs. Last but not least, the oak rocking-chair near the hearth, where I shall sit and rock and put my feet up on the fender if I feel like it.

'I harbour no delusions about the purpose of this place, this house, built as a "love nest" by B whenever he cares to visit Sally, or the role I shall be called upon to play, as cook and servant, when he arrives incognito, expecting the best of everything by way of service, food and wine for himself and his "hanger's on" his personal valet and private secretary, no doubt, and their lady friends, only too willing to turn a blind eye to their master's machinations.

'But perhaps I am letting my imagination run away with me? Who knows? Who can tell what the future may hold for Sally and me? She seems happy now at any rate, over the moon about the hotel, the beach house, Mr Aylott and his fine carriage. She dined alone with him at the hotel "to discuss business matters", she said lightheartedly, twirling in front of her bedroom mirror to admire her reflection; full of tomorrow's drive to Scarborough to view the town property the mysterious "Mr Brown" has bought for her.

'"I'm to have a carriage of my own," she said, "and servants—a cook housekeeper, footman, parlour maids, coachman—a quarterly dress allowance! Oh, Meg, isn't it all exciting? Just think, nothing at all to worry about from now on! Bertie, or should I say 'Mr Brown', will settle the household accounts, pay the servants' wages and so on, and I'm to choose exactly what I like to eat and drink, the best of everything, though I mustn't invite people to take tea with me, to visit the house or dine there without his permission, which is stuffy of him, don't you think?"

'Poor Sally. She hasn't got it into her head that there's a price to be paid for women in her situation, rather like that of a bird of paradise in an aviary, allowed to flutter its wings, but never to fly any distance. As for myself, how shall I fill my time sharing that aviary?

'My deepest pleasure lies in the preparation and cooking of good plain food, a skill taught me by my mother, along with washing and ironing, the simple everyday tasks which make a house into a home. How will this be possible with a cook-housekeeper in charge of the town house?

'My hope lies in the beach house, "Driftwood"—a lovely name for a lovely place—where, during the summertime, when Sally and I are alone there together, I shall be free to cook, wash and iron, clean and polish to my heart's content ...'

Chapter Nineteen

To Sarah's distress, events overshadowing her lover's life had prevented his visiting either Driftwood or the town house. At least this was what she had chosen to believe. His father, Prince Albert, had died suddenly, necessitating Edward's return to Windsor to support his grief-stricken mother.

Margaret's role had been to comfort and support Sarah, despite her own misgivings that the prince, having discharged certain obligations towards his former mistress, had gladly washed his hands of her. Not that she had dared give voice to that privately held opinion in view of Sarah's quixotic mood-swings from shining hope to black despair, and vice versa, awaiting letters or messages from her lover destined never to arrive on her doorstep.

'He could at least write to me; tell me he still loves me,' Sarah had sobbed hysterically.

But Margaret, in her wisdom, had known that no such damning confession would ever be penned by a man intent on glossing over a past indiscretion as quickly and as quietly as possible. She doubted if he even remembered his brief physical relationship with a servant girl in the spring of 1861. In any event, he had rewarded her handsomely for "services rendered", and that was the end of the matter so far as he was concerned, Meg surmised.

At Driftwood, she had encouraged Sara to take full advantage of the sea air, to sit on the verandah or walk along the beach to the breakwater and back, whilst she, Meg, saw to the cooking and cleaning.

Twice weekly, the coachman would arrive with the fresh meat, fish, bread and vegetables Meg had ordered at his last visit, plus the many luxury items Sarah had added to the list—wine, pâté de fois gras, peaches in brandy, hothouse grapes, chicken in aspic, and specially ground coffee, 'just in case the prince should turn up unexpectedly,' Meg had written.

'It breaks my heart to see her in this state. A pretty lass like her should be enjoying life, not waiting for something that will never happen.

'If only she would realise, as I do, that the affair is over. But how can I tell her so? The state she's in, she wouldn't even listen, and who am I to add to her misery?

'I wish we could go back to Cornwall where we belong, that we had never been sent to Richmond Park. One thing I've learned, that all the money in the world doesn't bring happiness.

'I never cared much for the prince, now I hate him for the harm he has caused Sally. He must have known that setting her up in her own establishment, giving her money to burn, would lead her to believe that he still cared for her, still wanted her. But caring and wanting are two different things entirely. All he wanted was to get rid of her, in my opinion, as quickly and as quietly as possible; the town house and Driftwood, the carriage, servants and the money were meant to ensure her silence.

'His mistake lay in thinking that Sally cared as little for him as he did for her.'

Worse was to come. Edward's betrothal and marriage to Princess Alexandra of Denmark, had driven Sarah to the brink of despair.

'How could he have done such a thing?' she wept, reading accounts of Alexandra's triumphal entry into the City of London at dusk on the eve of their engagement, seated beside Edward. They drove across London Bridge, illuminated with charcoal-burners flaring brightly against the night sky, to the rapturous cheers of the onlookers thronging the pavements to catch their first glimpse of a future Queen of England.

'How could he have done such a thing

when it's me he really loves?'

'No use upsetting yourself, Sally. You know as well as I do that such matters are arranged by the heads of State, for political reasons. Edward was bound to marry sooner or later. I daresay he had little or no choice other than to propose marriage to the one they had picked out as being the most suitable bride for him. I don't suppose that love enters into a marriage of convenience.'

Poor Margaret, Caroline thought, how desperately hard she had tried to keep Sally on an even keel throughout the celebrations attendant on the wedding of Edward and Princess Alexandra in 1863, realising, as she obviously had done, the delicately balanced state of her friend's mind, her difficulty in differentiating between dreams and reality at times, linked to her obsessive belief that Edward would come back to her one day to pick up the threads of their interrupted love affair.

Meg had done all in her power to persuade Sally to spend some time with her in Cornwall when she had decided to go home for a while to visit her family, but Sally would not hear of it. She must stay in Scarborough in the event of unexpected guests arriving on her doorstep.

Nothing would change her mind. Meg must go if she wanted to, and she would pay for the journey and the necessary accommodation en route. And Meg mustn't worry about her, the servants would take care of her. A hard decision for Margaret to make, but she had not set eyes on her family since she left home for Richmond Park six years ago, and her heart yearned for them.

How to explain Sally's absence and their present circumstances were hurdles she would have to cross when she came to them. To tell lies was not in her nature. Sally had begged her to say they had found good situations in a wealthy household, and leave it at that. Easier said than done, Meg thought, making no promises she could not keep.

Sally had clung to her at the last moment. 'You *will* come back to me, won't you, Meg?' she pleaded. 'I'll feel lost without you!'

'Of course I will!' This was a promise Margaret knew she could keep. She would feel equally lost without Sally. At the same time, she longed for a break from the stultifying atmosphere of the town house, which she had come to regard as a prison without bars.

Now Caroline felt rather like a child who, visiting a chocolate factory, had eaten too many sweets. She must read the rest of the diaries at a later date when her head felt clearer, when she had breathed fresh air into her lungs, and come to grips with the present rather than the past.

In the kitchen, making coffee, the doorbell rang suddenly. Who on earth? she wondered. The time was six o'clock, daylight was fading. Still held in the sway of the diaries, strung, as Sarah St Just had once been, in the hinterland between dreams and reality, 'Yes, who is it?' she asked bemusedly, unable to focus clearly on the features of the woman on the doorstep.

Then the woman spoke in a familiar Scottish accent, and Caroline, between laughter and tears, hugged delightedly her friend and former housekeeper, Ginny Gordon, close to her heart, then drew her into the warmth of the firelit sitting room, so pleased to see her that she could scarcely bear to let go of her hands. Dear, down-to-earth Virginia Gordon, the last person on earth she had expected to see.

Returning to the kitchen, Caroline finished making the coffee, rustled up a plate of ham sandwiches for her unexpected visitor, and carried the tray through to the other room, eager to know what had brought Ginny to Scarborough, of all places, at this time of year, remembering that she had usually plumped for time off in September to visit her family in Edinburgh.

'I'm nae on holiday this time,' Ginny said, helping herself to a sandwich. 'I've left London for good and all; found myself a job as cook-housekeeper to a Scottish laird and his family at their estate near Crianlarich, starting there in a fortnight from now. Meanwhile, I'll stay with my ain folk in Edinburgh tae recover from what I've been through lately wi' that bluidy artist woman ruling the roost; nit-picking from morning to night, giving herself airs and graces, and *him,*' she meant Felix, 'on the verge of bankruptcy through his own stupid fault—'

'*Bankruptcy?*' Caroline frowned. 'But I don't understand. *Why?* Why has this happened?'

'So far as I can make out,' Ginny explained, 'because his last novel failed to come up to expectation, and his latest was turned down flat by his publishers as being not good enough to warrant a six-figure advance in view of the removal of his name from the top ten list of bestselling authors.' She sighed deeply, 'I guess his mind hasn't been on his work lately, and I can understand why. Need I say more?'

'No, I guess not,' Caroline replied, sick at heart that her husband's affair with Francesca had been in no way inspirational so far as his writing career was concerned, rather the opposite. Somewhere along the way, coinciding roughly with the start of the affair, Felix had forfeited the power of his writing for the softer option of sexual fulfilment in the arms of his lover.

And so, perhaps throughout the years of his marriage to a woman he did not love, the unremitting hostility and tension between herself and Felix had been the burr under his saddle? The sharp edge he had needed to add punch to his prose?

In a state of nervous tension, needing to talk, Ginny painted a verbal picture of events leading up to the handing in of her notice. 'I'd reached the end of my tether,' she said dramatically. 'Flesh and bluid could stand nae more, and I told her so in no uncertain terms that Sunday morning she swanned into the kitchen tae tell me there'd be six extra for lunch and dinner, an' expecting me tae provide for them at the drop of a hat.

'Twelve extra meals, I ask you! I told her she was asking the impossible—'

'Francesca, you mean?' Caroline asked.

'Of course Francesca, who else? "Why impossible?" she wanted to know in that offensive way of hers. "What's wrong with the deep-freeze?" "Nothing," I said, "except that it's empty, and has been for some time now." Well, that started the ball rolling. I saw red when she called me a poor excuse for a housekeeper not

321

to have re-stocked the freezer, wanting to know why not. So I told her.'

Ginny smiled grimly. 'My dander was up, and I let rip! Food costs money, I told her, and bills need paying, as simple as that! The freezer was empty because the frozen food firm I dealt with had refused further credit until the last two bills had been settled, and the payment of bills wasn't my province, never had been nor ever would be. Then I said I'd had it up to here with her—and *him*—and they could whistle down the wind for their Sunday lunch and dinner, since I wouldn't be there to cook it.

'The fact is, I was so angry I scarcely remember all the other things I said to her. A "poor excuse" for a housekeeper, indeed! Of all the nerve! I think I called her a poor excuse for a human being; him a jumped-up nobody with delusions of grandeur: the pair of them, lumped together, with half a brain between them, if that!

'Faugh! I could have strangled the stupid thing with my bare hands, the way she stood there mouthing something about forfeiting my wages if I left without notice.

'"Wages? What wages?" I asked her, point blank. "I haven't had any wages for the past three weeks! But I'm not leaving without them, so make no mistake about that, my lady! Otherwise, I'll take you to court!" Then I took off my overall, threw it down on the table, marched upstairs to pack my things, and, well, here I am!'

'And did you get your wages?' Caroline asked bemusedly.

'Oh aye, but I didn't really care all that much. All I cared about was getting away from that house as quickly as possible.'

Caroline knew the feeling.

Ginny continued, 'Thank God I'd had the sense to apply for another job when I realised the seriousness of the situation facing me in London. You see, even the other tradesmen were growing restless over the non-payment of bills. Besides which, things weren't all sweetness and light between Felix and Francesca. Far from ... sorry, I shouldn't be telling you all this.'

'No. Please go on!' Caroline said quietly.

'Very well, then, if you insist, but it's not a very pretty picture, I'm afraid. They had started quarrelling intensely from morning to night, saying dreadful things to each other, not bothering to lower their voices. The rows were mainly about money, I gathered, or the lack of it.

'Felix, it appeared, had taken for granted that he would have access to her money, that she would stump up the wherewithal for a trip to Tuscany in the new year, and I know for a fact that he wanted her to sell her villa near Florence and plough the proceeds into Eaton Square. Francesca wouldn't hear of it. Can't say I blame her.' Ginny sighed deeply. 'So what did the silly idiot do then? He bought her a sapphire and diamond necklace, and threw a champagne supper party at the Savoy, in her honour, I ask you!'

Mrs Gordon continued, 'The writing was on the wall and had been for some time, but Felix hadn't the sense to see it. He just went on spending like there was no tomorrow, even after his latest manuscript had been turned down flat by his publishers, which he regarded as a temporary hiccup, no doubt, certain of his ability to talk his bank manager into extending his overdraft facilities. But his luck had run out all of a sudden, and it gives me no pleasure to say so, Mrs Fraser, believe me.

'Frankly, I felt sorry for the man. I still do in a funny kind of way. What I mean is, all that talent gone to waste because of a misbegotten, so-called love affair with a woman who didn't really give a damn about him, the way that *you* did, remember?

'Not that I blamed you for leaving him when you knew about his relationship with Francesca; the fact remains that he went to pieces without you.

'That day he returned from America, for instance, and I told him you'd gone away leaving no forwarding address, I've never seen a man so upset, so angry—so bewildered.

'One thing he said that morning, which has stayed in my mind ever since. He said, "But she *can't* have left me! She's my *wife*, for God's sake!"'

Caroline said softly, 'In what way did he go to pieces without me?'

Ginny replied thoughtfully, 'It's hard to say why, exactly, except that you'd always been there, before, to ...'

'To act as his whipping boy, you mean?' Caroline asked quietly, 'to bear the brunt of his displeasure? Well, yes, I can see why he might have gone to pieces without someone else to blame for his own shortcomings.'

'There was more to it than that,' Ginny said slowly, feeling for the right words to express her exact meaning. 'My belief is that he knew deep down that he couldn't do without you, that he certainly couldn't *write* without you.'

'Despite the fact that he never really loved me?' Caroline murmured wearily, uttering the truth as she saw it, remembering her wedding night, the brief, unsatisfactory coupling after which Felix had turned his back on her to fall fast asleep, whilst she had remained wide awake, staring up at the ceiling, her face wet with tears.

'There are different ways of loving,' Ginny said unexpectedly. 'I think that Felix has lived to regret his liaison with Francesca Delgado, that it's all over, bar the shouting.

'Truth to tell, that's why I came here today. Oh, I wanted to see you again, of course I did. We were such good friends, and, hopefully will always remain so. It simply occurred to me that you should be made aware of current events. After all, the Eaton Square house was your home, too, Felix is still your husband; the Delgado woman will soon be on her way back to her villa in Tuscany, and so ...'

'You think that I should return to London, is that it?' Caroline asked tautly. 'To do what, exactly? Forgive my husband his trespasses? Settle his debts? Save a sinking ship from disaster? Oh, I really don't think so.'

'It's all that you put into your marriage and what you stand to lose if you let things slide,' Ginny said forthrightly. 'I know it's none of my business, but I hate to think of you being cheated more than you have already, with no say in the matter.

'The mistake you made all along, if you'll forgive my saying so, lay in thinking

326

that Felix was the clever one—'

'Felix *is* clever,' Caroline interrupted. 'I knew that the first time we met. That was why I fell in love with him. I realised at once his potential for success as a writer, given the necessary help and encouragement.'

Ginny nodded. 'Fair enough. So you booted him up the ladder of success; catered to his every whim, acted as his whipping boy? Your own words, remember? And what happened as a result? He treated you like dirt and you let him—until you had guts enough to leave him, to realise your own potential, to say, this far and nae further! Am I right?

'They say the onlooker sees most of the game, and what *I* saw made my blood boil, at times. My heart rejoiced that morning he came home from America to find you'd flown the coop! And, yes, ma wee bully, thought I, not so sure of yourself now, are ye, with no one but yourself, to blame for your misfortune?'

'I'd rather not discuss it any more, if you don't mind,' Caroline said shakily, 'I'm not thinking straight, at the moment.'

Rising to her feet, attempting a smile, a lightheartedness she did not feel deep inside, clearing away the coffee cups and the empty sandwich plates, 'You must stay the night,' she said. 'I have a tiny spare room, but the bed's not aired. I'll switch on the electric blanket, cook you a decent meal—'

'No. Thanks, but that won't be necessary. I've already booked a room for the night at the Royal Hotel. I'll be away to Scotland first thing in the morning.'

Ginny added wistfully, 'I'm sorry if my visit has upset you. That was the last thing on my mind. I just wanted to see you again.'

'I know,' Caroline said, 'and I'm glad you came. Good luck with your new job, and you will keep in touch?'

'Yes, of course,' Ginny promised, turning back to wave and smile at Caroline on her way to her car.

When she had gone, returning to the sitting room, Caroline thought long and hard about her future role in life. The answer seemed clear cut and inevitable, as perhaps it had been all along.

Part Three

Part Three

Chapter Twenty

The new house, though small, possessed both charm and character. The kitchen opened on to a patio, a well-matured walled garden, and what Caroline thought of as 'the doll's house', a two-up, two-down stone cottage, tucked away amongst trees at the far end of the garden, which Felix termed 'the studio', and regarded as his own special and private sanctum.

There he had installed a computer, fax machine, filing cabinets, desk, swivel chair and bookshelves, telephone and answer-machine, a stereo-system, divan bed, microwave oven, refrigerator, kitchen table and chairs, crockery and cutlery, his spare shaving gear, bath-towels and bath-robe: indicative of his desire for independence should he wish to work or sleep late; no questions asked as he came to grips with a new novel.

And so, in a sense, they were still living separate lives, Caroline realised, and perhaps it was better so. Felix had not taken kindly to the sale of the Eaton Square house at her instigation, to remove the spectre of bankruptcy hovering over him like a bird of prey.

This had been the last thing on earth she had wanted to happen to him; the slur, the indignity of a writer of her husband's calibre being called upon to face detailed public scrutiny of his financial affairs. The media would have a field day. More importantly, Felix might never again hit the ground running as a bestselling author with soaring sales figures, TV and film contracts, to prove his success, had she not intervened on his behalf.

Following Ginny Gordon's visit to the bolt-hole, Caroline had realised, that, despite Felix's mistreatment of her, his affair with Francesca Delgado, his cavalier attitude towards money, his greed for the good things of life, he was still her husband, the man she had married for better or worse: that it was up to her to help him back to the road of success in any way possible. Even to the detriment of her own happiness.

She had put Tara up for sale. The house in its present condition, inclusive of the carpets, curtains and fittings she had chosen with such care and with so much pleasure, would sell well, Fenton assured her, puzzled by his client's change of heart after all the hard work and effort involved in the alterations.

'I shan't be needing it now,' was all she

said by way of explanation.

Jon Carradine's attitude had been that of shocked disapproval when she told him of her intentions. 'Have you a death wish, Caroline?' he demanded when she spoke to him on the telephone. 'You might at least have consulted me first. Can't you see what you're letting yourself in for? All Felix ever wanted from you is your money. Now you're about to hand it to him on a plate! But what about *your* life, your future, your own happiness?'

'That's just it,' she said wearily. 'I can't see a future ahead of me until the past has been laid to rest.'

'So how soon are you coming to London?'

'Next week,' she told him, 'to see Felix's bank manager. You will come with me, won't you? I need to find out the extent of the damage ...'

'You mean the extent of the mess Felix has landed himself in?'

'Yes, and what needs to be done to sort it out.'

'The Eaton Square house will have to be sold, to start with,' Jon said forcibly.

'I know, but I doubt it can be sold without my consent. I'm sorry, Jon. I know you're angry with me, but please don't be. I just want to do what is best for all concerned.'

'Especially Felix? Oh, I'm sorry, Caroline, I shouldn't have said that. Forgive me? Look, my dear, let me know when you'll be here. I'll meet you. We'll have lunch together, and take it from there, shall we?'

'Yes. Thanks, Jon. I'll be in touch.'

Later, Jon sat at home in his penthouse flat, nursing a glass of whisky and soda, pondering the mystery of love, thinking of Caroline, remembering Ramona; how different things might have been for both himself and Caroline, he thought, had not Peter Augustine died in that plane crash, had Ramona survived the birth of their baby.

How little one really knew of other people's lives or motivation so far as love was concerned, the entanglement of heartstrings leading back to some shining moment of never-to-be-forgotten joy, however distant or remote that moment now seemed. In which case, what right had he to criticise Caroline's desire to help Felix out of the hole he had dug for himself? The man, after all, was her husband; Caroline was a kind, caring, conscientious woman who, on her wedding day, perhaps, had seen him as a knight in shining armour? Just as he, on his wedding day, had seen Ramona as a goddess clothed in light; a happy, healthy human being with whom he had anticipated spending the rest of his life.

Would Caroline have been happy with Peter? he wondered. Impossible to tell. One started out with such high hopes where love was concerned. Every person needed someone to care for, to lean on, to trust. Growing older, companionship outweighed passion, that 'first, fine careless rapture' which happened only once in a lifetime—if one was lucky enough to have known it at all.

Deep in thought, he wondered if he and Caroline would be happy together if, perchance, they decided to settle for second best; if tenderness, warmth, companionship, would be enough to replace the passionate intensity of a deeply fulfilling physical love affair?

Sir Paul Sergeant, head of the City of London Bank, an elderly, astute man on the verge of retirement, a lifelong friend of Caroline's father, John Heritage, had greeted her and Jon Carradine warmly yet gravely when they entered his office. He knew the reason for their visit, and obviously did not relish the coming interview; the revelation of unpalatable facts concerning the enforced sale of the Eaton Square property, impossible without

Caroline's consent.

'You have my consent, Sir Paul,' Caroline said clearly and succinctly. 'That's why I am here: to do all in my power to raise collateral on my husband's behalf to settle his overdraft and help him to make a fresh start. He really is a talented writer, you know. He's just had a run of bad luck, recently ...'

Caroline was speaking the truth as she saw it. Given a second chance, the threat of debt and bankruptcy removed, and now that Francesca had returned to her villa in Tuscany, Felix, she truly believed, with herself by his side to help and support him, would resume his role in the top ten.

And so she had given her written consent to the sale of the Eaton Square house, and its contents, with a few exceptions—her father's paintings, her mother's wedding ring, her grandmother's rocking-chair. She had then offered the deeds of Tara as further collateral and signed a promissary note stating that monies from the sale of her Scarborough property would be paid directly to the London Bank.

Finally, she had signed a personal cheque for ten thousand pounds which she handed across the desk to Sir Paul, with the words; 'Please, tell me, have I done enough? If not, I'll do more.'

Jon's heart bled for her at that moment.

Sir Paul said gently, 'You've done more than enough, Mrs Fraser. I simply hope that your husband will appreciate your efforts on his behalf. He must be made aware, of course, that the sale of the Eaton Square property is unavoidable in the present circumstances.' A discreet cough, then, 'You have my sympathy, Mrs Fraser—Caroline. Parting with a well-loved home cannot be easy for any woman, I imagine.'

'You are wrong, Sir Paul,' Caroline said quietly. 'I never wanted that house in the first place. And that's all it was to me, a house, never a home. Frankly, I never want to set foot in it again for as long as I live!'

The resumation of their marriage had not been easy for herself or Felix. Not that Caroline had imagined for one moment that it would be, in view of the wealth of misunderstanding between them. Felix's pride had been stung at the sale of the Eaton Square house, at the lack of money to squander on the good things of life. His dependence on his wife's largesse for the clothes he wore, the food he ate, the stupid box of a house she'd bought on the outskirts of Hampstead, the feeling he had of being watched over every minute of the day and night had irked him past bearing, until he had moved into the cottage at the end of the garden to get away from her—his thorn-in-the-flesh wife Caroline ... so very different, so far removed from the love of his life, Francesca ...

He had begun to write again as a matter of urgency, of necessity, of an inborn determination to claw his way back to the ranks of bestselling authors, to prove to the world and to his ninny of a wife, that he was still a force to be reckoned with, not realising that anger and frustration, not the silken dalliance of soft lips and long dark hair, had acted as the burr beneath his saddle; that what he had always needed to fire his imagination as a writer of psychological thrillers was the presence of a whipping boy in his life.

And yet he had to admit reluctantly to himself that Caroline had changed a great deal during the past months. The term 'ninny' was no longer applicable. She no longer went out of her way to please him—not that she ever had pleased him—and her efforts to do so had irritated him past bearing.

Resentment now hinged upon her controlling influence concerning money. His fall from grace in the publishing world had been a bitter pill to swallow. He missed being king of the castle, the lavish entertaining involved at the height of his career, his crowd of hangers on who had suddenly drifted away from him—rats deserting a sinking ship—as even Francesca had done in the long run.

Theirs had been a passionate yet uneasy relationship from the beginning. Her forceful, dominant personality had outmatched his own at times, engendering explosive quarrels when fire met steel.

Francesca, he'd discovered, had a cruel streak, belied by the loveliness of her face and her deceptively cool and charming façade in the presence of the press, the paparazzi, at television interviews, champagne receptions held in her honour, at dinner parties when, as the centre of attention, she had kept well hidden the less appealing side of her person.

In short, Francesca purred like a kitten in the limelight, when things were going her way: clawed like an alleycat and fought like a tigress when they were not. Fiercely independent, a successful artist in her own right, she had poured scorn on her lover's failure as a writer when his latest book had been turned down flat by his publishers; refusing utterly to shore up his rapidly dwindling finances with her own money; reminding him constantly of her own success; refusing, at times, to even sleep with him in the wake of one or other of their more spectacular quarrels, often in the early hours of the morning when they had both drunk more than was good for them, and the house in Eaton Square had rung to the sound of their upraised voices in the far from silent watches of the night.

Now, ensconced in his studio, Felix battled towards the completion of a potential bestseller, soured by rejection, inwardly railing against his wife's reappearance in his life as his keeper. Resentful of her control over him, financially speaking, he could not come to terms with the fact that he had, somehow, lost control over her.

Curiously, at the heart of his resentment lay a dull feeling of jealousy over her affair with Peter Augustine, never mentioned between them or discussed, as so many other important issues had been pushed into the background by Felix. He meted out the silent treatment as a form of punishment, an attitude of mind stating more clearly than words his intention to keep his wife at arm's length in future—an unhappy situation which Caroline accepted as a less harrowing alternative than the old bullying tactics of his which had once made her life a misery.

Left alone for much of the time now that Felix was virtually living in the garden cottage, she had fallen into her own routine of early rising, breakfasting alone on the patio if the weather was warm, shopping, cooking, cleaning, visiting the library, writing letters to the Coopers, Reg Rossiter and Lara Westwood.

Occasionally she would travel to the City by tube to lunch with Jon Carradine; go to a matinée or a concert, window shop or simply sit alone in Hyde Park trying to make sense of her life; longing for something, she scarcely knew what, which she had lost somewhere along the way, a dream never realised, always tantalisingly out of reach, beyond her power either to hold or recapture. And then she would think of Driftwood; hear in memory the sound of the sea washing in on the shore; see, in her mind's eye, the view from the turret room balcony, seabirds wheeling wild and free in the immensity of a sunlit Indian summer sky.

'Caroline, my dear, you cannot go on like this,' Jon said one day over lunch. 'I can see you're not happy, and you should be. You are missing out on time that will never come again, and why? For what reason? You've done your best for Felix. He's writing again, you say? I can't understand why you felt it necessary to set up house with him. After all, you still have the bolt-hole. You could go back there tomorrow, take up the threads of your old life once more.'

'Perhaps I shall, one of these days, but not yet. Not until Felix has finished his book, until he is back on his feet again, earning a living. I'm sorry, Jon, but that's the way it is.'

'And then what? Think about it, Caroline. What if this new book of his doesn't make the grade? What if he's finished, burnt out as a writer?'

'Then I'll stay with him till he does make the grade.' She smiled wistfully. 'You mustn't worry too much about me, Jon. I'm not really unhappy. This way, at least I have a purpose in life.'

'Yes, but what about—love?'

'Love?' She looked at Jon uncomprehendingly across the table, frowning slightly, as if he had uttered the word in a foreign language. 'What about it?'

He said in a low voice, 'I have no right to ask, but please tell me. Are you still in love with your husband?'

She paused a while before answering, then, 'No,' she replied, 'not now. Not any more.' Speaking softly, 'There's nothing left to love, you see. Just the shell of the man I married. All I feel for him now is—pity. Clearly, all he feels for me now, all he has ever felt for me is contempt. It took a long time to realise, to come to terms with the fact all he has ever felt for me is contempt.' Tears filled her eyes. 'The hardest thing to live with is ill-concealed irritation born of contempt, and I should know.' She brushed away the tears, 'It took a brief love affair with a kind, gentle, sensitive human being to make me aware of all I had been blind to before I met Peter Augustine.'

'I see. So, forgive me if I'm wrong, what you are saying is that you are prepared to stay with a man you don't love, who has never loved you, as a matter of conscience?'

'Well, yes, I suppose I am,' she admitted.

'And if the new book is successful, what will you do then?' Jon probed gently.

Her answer came clear cut and simple. 'Then I'll go back to the bolt-hole, start that restaurant I told you about, leave Felix to his own devices. I doubt he'll even notice I've gone until he's hungry. I shan't even say goodbye to him, just leave him a note, and a casserole in the fridge, plus the deeds of the house and a pile of clean shirts on the kitchen table.' She smiled. 'A consummation devoutly to be wished, wouldn't you say?'

Jon Carradine knew that he had never liked and admired Caroline Fraser more than he did at that moment. But liking was not love, and never would be. The spark was missing from their relationship. He knew that now, beyond a shadow of doubt. But he would always remain a part of her life. Saying goodbye to her on a London Underground platform, awaiting the arrival of the tube train to Hampstead, Carradine knew that, even had he proposed marriage to Caroline, she would have said no; for the simple and very good reason that she was not in love with him either.

Chapter Twenty-One

Caroline rang Maudie Cooper on the last day of August, late in the evening, when she knew supper would be over and the washing up done. When Maudie answered the phone, Caroline said simply: 'It's over at last! I'm—coming home!'

'Oh, my dear! That's the best news I've had in ages! When? When are you coming?'

'Tomorrow. The first of September.'

'Then his lordship's book has been accepted?'

'Yes, praise be to God!'

'And have you told him you're leaving?'

'No, I don't want a confrontation. I'm all packed ready to leave just as I planned. I'll leave first thing in the morning to avoid the heavy traffic, the way I did last September. Strange, isn't it, the way things work out in the long run? I have the feeling, somehow, that the wheel of life has turned full circle, that I have lived through all this before.'

Maudie said quietly, 'I know what you mean, but it's a bit different this time, isn't it? You hadn't a clue where you were heading for last September. This time you're coming home, to people who care about you.' She added briskly, 'Now just say if the idea doesn't appeal to you, and I shan't take offence if you say no, but why not break your journey, stay here overnight? You'll be flaked out, I daresay, in need of a bath, a bite to eat and a good night's sleep. Well, what do you think?'

'I think it's a marvellous idea! Thanks, Maudie.'

'Right then, we'll expect you when we see you! You just drive carefully, that's all. Well, goodnight, love, and God bless —until tomorrow ...'

Until tomorrow, Caroline thought, sitting down at the kitchen table to write the letter she would leave for Felix to discover after she had gone—a letter she had composed in her mind over and over again for some time now—which, nevertheless, was harder to write, now the time had come to set pen to paper, than she had anticipated. It was a letter destined never to be written.

Felix had come across from his studio in search of coffee. He was wearing a bathrobe, his hair was damp, brushed back from his high forehead. He looked gaunt, tired. The hard, concentrated work of the summer had taken its toll. He appeared as he used to in his journalist days of meat pies and beer lunches, his lean and hungry years before he'd had a Rolex watch or a pair of Gucci shoes to his name.

'What are you doing?' he asked abruptly.

'Trying to write a letter,' Caroline said, putting down the pen. 'There's no need now. You've saved me the trouble.'

'I don't get it. What the hell are you on about?'

'The letter was meant for you,' she stood up, 'to tell you I'm leaving first thing in the morning, going back to Yorkshire where I belong.'

Gathering her thoughts, she continued, 'I was going to say how glad I am that your new book has been accepted, to explain that this is what I had hoped for all along, the reason why I consented to the sale of the Eaton Square house, for your sake, to give you—or rather to make possible a new start—'

'Not even bothering to ask how *I* felt about it?' he interrupted bitterly. 'Tell me, how did *you* feel at the time? No, don't tell me, let me guess! Holier than thou, to put it mildly, a bloody Lady Bountiful clutching the purse-strings in her hot little hands, as usual.'

'You couldn't begin to understand my feelings in a thousand years,' Caroline said quietly. 'How could you? You never even tried. All that held us together was those purse-strings you pretend to despise so much, that was why you married me in the first place. It didn't occur to me for some considerable time that you despised me too. But I don't care any more what you think of me.

'I'm leaving now you are back on your feet. What you make of your life from now on is your own business, not mine. The deeds of this house are in your name. My parting gift to you, to sell or to hang onto as you see fit. We'll agree to a divorce by mutual consent, I hope? Far less messy that way, don't you think?'

Felix laughed unpleasantly, unmirthfully. 'So you have everything worked out pat, I see, in that astute, cunning little mind of yours?'

Regarding him thoughtfully, 'Do you know,' Caroline said, tongue-in-cheek, 'that's the nicest compliment you could have paid me, in view of the times you have called me a brainless idiot, remember?'

'You've changed,' he said dourly.

Caroline smiled wistfully. 'You haven't! Well, goodbye, Felix, and—good luck!'

Turning away, she walked out of the room, closing the door on her life with Felix firmly behind her for good with no regrets—except one.

If only he had spoken a kind word to her before the closing of the door, had told her he'd miss her, asked about her plans for the future, apologised, however awkwardly, for his past sins of omission. But no. Walking slowly upstairs, she heard the click of the patio door, signalling his return to his studio. Close to tears, she remembered that he hadn't even bothered to say goodbye to her.

Maudie welcomed her with open arms. 'Come in and sit down, love,' she fussed. 'You look all in. I'll put the kettle on for a nice hot cup of tea. Sam will be home soon to lend a hand with your luggage, then you'd best pop upstairs for a bit of a rest before supper.'

'Oh, Maudie,' Caroline murmured weakly, 'if you only knew how glad I am to be back.'

'Go on, lass,' Maudie advised sympathetically, 'have a good cry if you feel like it, it'll do you good. No use bottling things up, in my opinion. Here, take my hanky, whilst I make the tea.'

Later, upstairs in her room, Caroline recalled her early departure from Hampstead, the increasing heat of the day as the journey wore on, her intense feeling of loneliness, as if she was halfway between two worlds—the past and the future—not knowing to which she rightly belonged, if either; missing Peter so dreadfully she could scarcely bear the thought of a future without him. A state of mind engendered by her final confrontation with Felix, she realised, which would never have happened had he not returned to the house when he did.

She had so much love to give. But to whom? For a brief moment in time she had imagined that someone might be Jon Carradine, a man she liked and trusted implicity. But somehow the body language, the vital spark had been missing from their relationship, even when they had dined together and touched hands across the table.

And yet, God help her, when Felix had walked into the kitchen last night, his hair damp from the shower, wearing his old bathrobe, she had experienced, momentarily, a strange desire to be held by him, loved by him as she had done long ago on their wedding night—to no avail. She knew now that one could not manufacture love from thin air, that it either existed or it did not, that no power on earth could ever draw fire from a pyramid of damp kindling.

Recovered from her journey, refreshed after a warm shower, she went downstairs to supper. Jake and Zach welcomed her as a favourite aunt. Sam, whom she had seen earlier when he had carried her luggage upstairs, beamed from the head of the table as he carved ample slices from a shoulder of cold roast lamb.

Maudie had provided new potatoes and salad, home-made barm cakes, apple pie and cream. Eating hungrily, the boys wanted to know how the Mini was standing up to wear and tear. 'Better than us, I hope,' Jake laughed. 'Lumping furniture in this heat is no joke, believe me. That there repository is very nearly empty at the moment, but it won't be for long. We'll have loads of new stuff coming in next week.'

The repository, Caroline thought, remembering the Driftwood storage bay, wondering if that was now empty, if Cam McCauley had opened his antiques shop, had sold the contents of Sarah's cottage at a handsome profit?

Preferring not to think too deeply about that, 'How are Reg and Mrs Rossiter?' she asked.

Zach snorted. 'Ha! If Reg ain't careful he'll end up on the shelf!'

'Don't talk soft,' Jake chortled, 'only women end up on shelves. They're called "old maids".'

'Yeah. That's what I meant, daft-head. 'Spect Reg grew that beard of his to remind his ma he's a fella, not a lass!'

351

'That's enough, you two,' Sam said sharply. 'My lady doesn't want to listen to that kind of talk!'

'Sorry, Pa,' Zach said. 'It's just that poor old Reg hasn't much of a life with his mother breathing down his neck the way she does. He'll never get married and settle down in a place of his own if *she* has owt to do with it! He hasn't even got a steady girlfriend yet.'

'That has nothing to do with you,' Maudie reminded him. 'Reg is a good son to his mother, think on.'

'Okay, Ma, we get the message,' Jake laughed, 'just as long as you don't stop us getting wed when the time comes.'

'Stop you? I'll be glad to see the back of you!' Maudie retorted, enjoying the joke, 'Not that any lass in her right mind would want you!'

'By the way, Ma,' Zach asked, 'have you told Caroline about Gloria?' Not waiting for a reply, he continued, 'Fancy old Cam becoming a father at his age. Not that he seems over the moon about it, but then, Cam's never over the moon about anything, is he, the crusty devil!'

'You mean—Gloria's going to have a baby?' Caroline looked to Maudie for confirmation of the fact.

'Not going to have, she's already had it. A girl, born the last week in July,' Maudie said. 'It came as a bit of a surprise, really, didn't it, Sam? What I mean is, we all thought that Gloria would go back to her husband sooner or later, but she didn't. She stayed on at Gull Cottage with Cam.'

'I see.' Caroline attempted a smile. 'Well, I'm glad things worked out well for them in the end.'

After supper, when the boys had gone down to the pub for a game of darts, and Sam was in the garage tinkering with the Mercedes, 'I'm sorry you had to sell your house in Scarborough,' Maudie said. 'That must have been a wrench for you after all the carry-on over the alterations and suchlike.'

'It was, but I had no alternative. I had to be realistic. I knew Felix was in deep financial trouble, that a great deal of money would be needed to clear his overdraft and give him a new start in life.

'I realised from the outset that the London house would have to go too, that the proceeds from the sale of both properties might not be enough to cover his debts, and I was right, although the sale of the contents of the Eaton Square house just tipped the balance in our favour.'

'What beats me,' said Maudie, who had

353

never been in debt in her life, 'is why you went on living with him the way you did.'

Caroline smiled wistfully, 'I *had* to, for his sake, to make certain he got on with his writing. I just felt that, given the right circumstances, he would get back into his stride. I can't explain exactly how I felt, a bit like a mother wanting the best for her child, I imagine, expecting nothing in return, neither gratitude nor love. Well, as the saying goes, "blessed are they that expecteth nothing", or words to that effect. I simply clung to the belief that one day, God willing, I'd be free to come home once more.'

'Having done your duty?' Maudie suggested quietly.

'Well yes, something like that,' Caroline admitted, 'but without the benefit of wings and a halo, I assure you. I felt bitter, at times, angry and frustrated, utterly useless, wondering what the hell I'd let myself in for playing minder to a man who, frankly, hated my guts even more, then, than he had done before.'

She added, 'By the way, that letter idea of mine didn't work out as planned. Felix came in at the wrong moment, so we had an eyeball to eyeball confrontation ending in the closing of doors between us. Not so much as a kind word from ... Oh,

I'm sorry, Maudie, please forgive me. It's just that I feel so—lost, so lonely and inadequate.'

'Yes, I know, love. Because you're tired out. You won't feel right till you're home. Then you'll have time to go over all that's happened and sort things out in your mind.'

Caroline knew that Maudie was right, and it was good to be with friends for a change. Felix's uncompromising attitude towards her had been hard to live with. Thank God for the 'doll's house', she thought, which had spared her the necessity of sharing space with an uncommunicative stranger.

There had been no lightening of his moodiness even when the contract for his new book had arrived. He had simply flung it down on the kitchen table for her to read, before striding back to his studio. Then had come the feeling that, walking into his office unexpectedly, she would find him making a long distance phonecall to Italy, telling Francesca about his six-figure advance, his churlishness dispelled, face aglow speaking to the woman he loved.

Having said her goodbyes to the Coopers, after breakfast next morning Caroline set forth on the last leg of her journey home. It was a sparkling fresh, clear day.

Lowering the car windows, the breeze that ruffled her hair smelt of sea air and heather, bringing back memories of the October day she had first travelled this way with Peter beside her. The heather had been past its best then, now it was coming into bloom, clothing the hills with vibrant, living colour as far as the eye could see.

Nearing the turning to Robin Hood's Bay, she experienced an intense longing to see Driftwood once more, to stand on the clifftop looking down at the cottage, to watch the waves coming in on the shore as she had done last autumn—a year ago almost to the day.

But nothing in earth or heaven comes as it came before. Her time there was over and done with. The cottage would have been let, time and time again during the summer months, to family parties enjoying the modern amenities provided by Cam McCauley. Children would have built sandcastles near the water's edge, watched over by lithe, bikini-clad young mums and lean, half naked fathers of a new generation of parents.

And so, resisting the temptation to look at Driftwood once more, Caroline drove on towards Scarborough, her beloved bolt-hole, thinking how narrow-minded, how cynical she was becoming in middle-age—an attitude of mind born of tiredness

356

and disappointment, she imagined, which, if allowed to fester, would rob her future of point or purpose, hope or joy. She could not allow that to happen. Somehow, she must create a new hopeful future for herself, built on the burnt out embers of the past.

Driving homeward across the moors, reviewing the facets of her life so far, she realised the hurt involved in parting first with Peter Augustine, then Driftwood, then Tara and finally with the man she had married in the springtime of her life, who had not cared enough about her to even bid her goodbye.

So how to build a future worth the living from the ruins of the past? She could but try ...

The bolt-hole smelt of damp and neglect, she thought, crossing the threshold. Little wonder in view of the time she had spent away from it in London. Entering the flat, she opened the windows to let in the fresh air, before hefting her luggage indoors and switching on the immersion-heater for a hot bath later on in the day.

Meanwhile, she had shopping to do, food to buy, letters to open, Lara Westwood to contact to tell her she was home again.

Home! Thank God, Caroline thought, that she had had the wisdom to purchase this funny little basement flat of hers at a time when she had needed a second home like a hole in the head.

Now it was all she had left to her, plus Margaret Roberts's diaries which, as soon as she felt settled, she would continue to read once more—to discover how the story ended, if at all. Well, so be it. Not every story had a conclusive ending, Caroline thought wistfully, except, perhaps, in romantic novels. In real life, there was no obligatory 'happy ending', Caroline concluded, just the necessity of soldiering on to the best of one's ability towards that 'final chapter'; that pie-in-the-sky notion of love everlasting with the man of one's dreams: a fulfilment denied poor Sarah St Just, for one, she now realised.

Chapter Twenty-Two

In a sense, Caroline was pleased to have been absent from the seaside resort at the height of the summer season when tourists and day trippers jostled along the pavements and crowded the town centre shops and cafés.

Inevitably, September had an end-of-summer air about it when schools reopened, days grew shorter, and 'Final Week' notices appeared on the summer shows' billboards.

Then, blissfully, so far as Caroline was concerned, there would be room to move freely, to savour the natural beauty of the place she had grown to love so much, now that the swallows had departed—a sure sign that summertime was over.

She had seen them gathering for flight on the telegraph wires, for all the world like crotchets and quavers on the staves of a music score, and her heart had gone out to them, such small, tender creatures about to face the unknown, yet imbued with some instinct, beyond the power of human comprehension, to find their place in the sun.

No Indian summer this year, she thought wistfully, not like last. No feeling that summertime would last forever in a seemingly endless procession of hot, sunshiny days beneath breathtakingly blue and cloudless skies.

Even so, she delighted in the benison of occasional rain on her face as she renewed her acquaintance with the gardens leading down to the seashore, bereft now of summer visitors, with gently falling leaves fluttering down from the trees, the scent of autumn trapped in the long grass and the dying wild flowers along the way.

One day, in mid-September, possessed of an overwhelming desire to re-visit Tara, walking through the Valley Gardens, she had come across a sign advertising 'The Valley Hotel', and noticed that the boundary wall of Tara had been partially demolished to allow access to the premises via a curving driveway carved from the garden. Sarah's garden!

Oh God, Caroline thought, shocked by the desecration, all this was her fault. She had allowed it to happen. She was to blame for the wrought-iron gates, the pebbled driveway, the floodlighting cables and fairy-lights which, switched on when darkness fell, would rob Tara of its true significance as a place of mystery, of shades and shadows ...

If only she had possessed the will and wisdom to hold on to it, Caroline wished. Too late now, the damage had been done. She had been so sure, at the time, that the sale of Tara was a sacrifice necessary to her future role as a helpmeet to Felix in his hour of need. She now thought that her sacrifice had been in vain.

'Oh, Sarah,' she whispered, passing the wrought-iron gates on her way to the sea, 'I'm so sorry. Please forgive me!'

She had put Sarah's trunks into store before leaving for London. Sooner or later she would have to decide what to do about the contents. Possibly a private collector would be interested in the dresses, or she might donate them anonymously to a national museum. She could not keep them herself, nor could she find it in her heart to destroy them. What would Sarah have wanted?

That evening, Caroline settled down to read the remainder of Margaret's diaries. Time passed by unnoticed as, turning the pages, held in the grip of the powerfully unfolding narrative, she read on until the early hours of next morning.

At three o'clock, having read the final entry, she closed the last of the diaries and laid it aside with the rest, moved to tears by Margaret's last, painfully written words: 'It is all over now. Commending my spirit to God. I shall go to my eternal resting place in heaven or in hell, according to His Will.'

Next day, a heavy, clinging mist known to Scarborians as a 'sea-fret' enveloped the town like a shroud, the greyness punctuated by the deep, doleful notes of the foghorn on the lighthouse pier sounding a warning to shipping in the area. A scenario matching Caroline's mood of the moment—a general feeling of depression, of malaise, in keeping with the cloud bank of fog engulfing the coastline, reminiscent of the greyness of her time in London.

And perhaps making the best of a bad job was what life was all about, she thought, entering the 'We Aim to Please' agency to visit her bright-eyed, bushy-tailed young friend, Lara Westwood, who still saw life as a shining bubble, radiant with the colours of a rainbow, and rightly so, at her age and with her looks.

'Oh, hi, Mrs Fraser,' Lara said enthusiastically, 'you're just in time for coffee! Long time no see! Would you believe it, I was just about to contact you? I have the letter from Mr Farmer here somewhere. Ah yes, here it is, wanting to know when it will be convenient to remove his mother's belongings from the flat. Apparently he's bought a bigger house to make room for them.'

'Really? Well, that's good news,' Caroline said smilingly, accepting her cup of coffee, beginning to feel much better all of a sudden in the company of a bright young thing who couldn't give a damn about the weather outside her garishly illuminated and over-heated office.

'So when shall I tell him?' Lara enquired. 'What I mean is, when will it be convenient for you to have him shift his ma's gear?'

Giving the matter due thought and consideration, 'Shall we say a week from today?' Caroline suggested, 'to give me time to make arrangements regarding the furniture I have in store, and hire a firm of decorators to freshen up the place a little when Mrs Fraser's belongings have been removed. I'll need to tally one with the other, you see?'

'Yeah, I see right enough. But where will you go to in the meantime? No way can you stay in an empty flat in the process of redecoration. Oh, don't tell me, let me guess! You'll book in for a week or so at the Crown Hotel, or the Royal! No problem! Am I right?'

'No. As a matter of fact, I shall find myself temporary bedsit accommodation,' Caroline replied mischievously. 'You know the kind of place I mean? A curtained off kitchen in one corner of the room, a slot-meter and a Baby Belling cooker the size of a postage stamp; a sagging divan bed, a spring-busted armchair, a formica-topped table and a dodgy electric fire in the other, plus lots of chipped crockery and plastic knives and forks. Well, show me some of your leaflets, why don't you?'

'Know what I like about you, Mrs Fraser?' Lara giggled, 'That crazy sense of humour of yours, that's what! So shall I book you in at the Crown, whenever? I'll receive a bit of commission if I do, if they know the booking came from the agency.'

'Yes, why not?' Caroline acceded thoughtfully, thinking in terms of an invitation extended to the Cooper family, Reg Rossiter and his mother, and Lara Westwood, to spend a weekend at the Crown with her, whilst the decorators were busily engaged in redecoration the bolt-hole. Reg Rossiter would not end up on the shelf if she could help it, Caroline decided.

Finishing her coffee, rising from the arm of the chair on which she had perched, albeit uncomfortably, during the interview, turning at the door of the office, 'By the way, Lara,' she asked casually, 'how do you feel about beards?'

'*Beards?*' Lara stared at her uncomprehendingly. 'You mean face-fungus? Well,

I don't know exactly. To be honest, I've never given the matter a great deal of thought! *Why?*' Startled, 'You're not trying to tell me something awful, are you? Like I should start shaving, perhaps?'

'No, not at all. I meant bearded men in general,' Caroline reassured her, holding her laughter in check. 'You see, there's this very nice man I'd like you to meet—a fellow estate-agent—as kind as they come, unmarried, in need of tender loving care.'

'I see. So what's the snag, apart from the beard?' Lara asked succinctly.

'He has a mother!'

'Oh, is *that* all?' Lara sighed deeply. 'Most blokes do, unfortunately. I've met 'em all, so far, from the fluttery, "Fetch me my smelling salts, darling. Oh, you wouldn't believe what a kind son he is to his mum," type, to the dragon on the drawbridge, not to mention the down-to-earth, fed-up-to-the-back-teeth type who, handing you a bag of his smelly washing, tells you to go right ahead if you think you can handle him better than she ever could. So what type shall I be up against this time?'

'Over-protective, dominant, heart of gold deep down. Easily fettled, I imagine.'

Lara pulled a face. 'Perhaps I should start dating the mother?'

A thought occurred. 'When the time

comes,' Caroline said, 'I think I'll try that new hotel in the Valley.'

'Yeah. Fine. So when am I going to meet the beard with the mother?'

'When your fairy godmother waves her magic wand,' Caroline told her teasingly on her way out of the office.

A reception desk had been placed at the foot of the stairs. Sarah's drawing room, to the left of the staircase, was now the hotel lounge. It was tastefully furnished with deep sofas and armchairs, coffee and side tables, jardinieres of flowers, and spotlit oil paintings.

The dining room opposite contained the usual plethora of small and large tables, well appointed, with crisp white cloths and well polished cutlery. The smaller room beyond was now the hotel bar, softly lit, with discreet background music.

Caroline had pictured it all beforehand. There was a sameness about small, expensive English hotels, in her experience —the inevitable reception desk, residents' lounge, dining room and bar. At least Sarah's home had retained an air of dignity, for which she felt grateful.

She had asked specifically for a room on the first floor, overlooking the garden, the valley cutting, and with a view of the sea beyond. There had been no problem about that. The hotel was not overly busy at this time of the year. And so Caroline found herself in what had once been Sarah's bedroom, the room in which she had died.

But why the much smaller dimensions? Of course, she might have known the room would have been partitioned to accommodate an en-suite bathroom. No getting away from modernisation these days, apparently, she thought wistfully.

Today was Friday. Mrs Farmer's furniture had been removed from the flat, and the decorators were now in charge. She had hired a reliable firm, handed the keys to the foreman, and explained precisely what she wanted done—the walls stripped of paper and emulsion-painted in plain, pale uncluttered shades of turquoise, tangerine and barley—to create an illusion of space. And yet she had been surprised to discover, once Mrs Farmer's heavyweight furniture had been stowed away in the removal van, how much space there really was. Far more than she had imagined there would be.

Tomorrow, Saturday, her weekend guests —the Cooper family, Reg and his mother, and Lara Westwood—would arrive in time for lunch. Seven people in all, for whom she had booked the appropriate number of rooms—the other master bedroom across the landing for Maudie and Sam, a twin-bedded room for Jake and Zach, separate rooms on the upper floor for Mrs Rossiter, Reg and Lara.

Looking out of her bedroom window, remembering poor Sarah St Just whose lifeless body had once lain close to where she was now standing, all this was mine once, Caroline thought, and I let go of it? Why? Why had she done that? But, of course, she knew why: it had to do with an overwhelming sense of duty in the cause of the living, not the dead.

Then, joyfully she recalled that the living would arrive in full force tomorrow; that it was up to her to give them a weekend to remember—small payment for all the happiness they had given to her. Only one person, the most important of all, Peter Augustine would be missing from this weekend occasion, and one other besides—Cameron McCauley.

Cam! But why bother to think of him at all in the context of a happy weekend spent among friends? She scarcely knew why, except that she felt intensely sorry for the man, despite, or possibly because of his reunion with Gloria. But who was she to judge? Latent fatherhood must have awarded him a great deal of physical satisfaction. The pity was that they had parted company in the early days of their marital relationship, with so much unnecessary pain involved in the break up of their marriage. Would they re-marry, in time? More than likely, Caroline surmised. And yet ...

Somehow she could not bring herself to believe that Cam would ever be entirely happy with Gloria. Knowing him, his uncertain temperament, forcefulness, egoism and innate rudeness, linked to his sharp intelligence, she could not imagine him as a placid father-figure playing second fiddle to a scrap of a girl, however beautiful and desirable, with whom he had nothing in common—apart from sexual attraction.

But of course she was wrong, as usual, she thought wryly. In the final analysis, sexual attraction was, after all, the be-all and end-all of the human race, without which mankind would cease to exist. What price intelligence then, when all that really mattered was, not brain power but sexual intercourse between a man and his mate?

In any case, why worry about the future welfare of a man whom she heartily detested?

Later, having dressed, for dinner, she went downstairs to choose her evening meal from a menu in which chips were referred to as *'pommes frites'*, chicken as *'poulet'*, fish as *'poisson'* and cheese as *'fromage'*.

'Look,' she told the hovering waiter succinctly, 'all I want is grilled plaice, a side salad, a bread roll with *'du beurre'*, and a glass of mineral water. Okay?'

They exchanged glances. The waiter smiled. 'Don't blame me,' he said, sotto voce, 'I only work here, an' the Chef comes from Bradford! Fair enough?'

Scribbling on his order pad, 'So what you want is a fillet of plaice, no chips, a bread roll with butter, and a glass of Ballygowan? How about dessert? There's *'tarte tatin'* avec custard, or crepes Suzettes, flambé. In other words, flaming pancakes! Frankly, I'd give 'em a miss if I was you!'

Smiling, a man after her own heart, she suspected, praying inwardly that her weekend guests would not be offput by the 'French' menus.

She need not have worried unduly. To her surprise and delight, Sam Cooper, who had spent some time in France during the Second World War, did the ordering, albeit in a Yorkshire accent, and the entire party tucked into excellently cooked portions of steak and kidney pie, mashed potatoes, gravy, and a mouthwatering selection of freshly cooked carrots, cauliflower and courgettes.

Sitting next to Reg at the dining table, having reached the conclusion that she quite liked his neatly trimmed beard and moustache, Lara decided that it might be well worth her while to ingratiate herself with his mother. And so, leaning forward in her seat, she said winsomely to Mrs Rossiter, 'This pastry's a bit on the tough side, isn't it? What's wrong with it, do you suppose?'

'Ha, that's easy,' Mrs Rossiter replied airily, falling into the flattery trap as easily as a fly falls into a spider's web, 'they've skimped on the fat, used the wrong kind of flour, and the oven wasn't hot enough to begin with! Take my word for it! After all, *I* should know! Ask my son, if you don't believe me!'

'I'm sorry, but which one *is* your son?' Lara asked mildly, glancing around the table, pretending not to know.

'Why, the one sitting next to you, of course,' Mrs Rossiter said explosively, piqued that her son had been overlooked by so charming a girl. What was wrong with the silly ninny anyway? Looking for all the world like a dying duck in a thunderstorm! He'd never find himself a girlfriend, a potential wife, at the rate he was going. Besides which, truth to tell, she was sick and tired of looking after him; sick and tired of snide remarks from her friends and neighbours, and all because Reg kept himself to himself and was kind to his mother!

'Did I overdo it just a little?' Lara asked Reg later on after dinner, when the pair of them were walking round the garden together by moonlight.

'Overdo what?' Reg frowned.

'Chatting up your mother. I wanted to make a good impression on her.'

Reg laughed, 'You did make a good impression. Ma said you had your head screwed on right. As a matter of fact, she's going to give you her recipe for flaky pastry.'

Cracked it at last, Lara thought happily. Mrs Fraser was right about Reg—he *was* nice, smartly dressed, his beard well under control. She'd been worried initially that he might be growing on his face what he couldn't grow on his head, but no, he had a good head of hair, great teeth, a kind of shyness about him which she found refreshing in view of the brash types she'd been lumbered with recently.

Plucking up his courage, Reg said, 'I was just wondering ... That is, would you care to have dinner with me one evening next week?'

'Hmmm, well yes, I think that could be arranged,' Lara replied demurely. 'How about the Crown Hotel, Tuesday? Seven sharp!'

Awaking suddenly in the early hours of the morning, lying still in bed, listening intently, Caroline heard the soft closing of the door, the click of a key turning in the lock, the whisper of skirts on the carpets.

The curtains were undrawn, the room lit by a trace of moonlight, no longer bright, as though the moon had slipped behind a cloud. Holding her breath, it seemed to her that someone was slowly crossing the room towards the window. Or was the sound she heard nothing more than a breeze blowing in from the sea? Had she really heard, or imagined she'd heard the closing of the door, the click of a key? Then suddenly, unmistakably, she caught the scent of a half-familiar perfume, subtle yet strangely potent and lingering, a musky distillation of roses and verbena.

Straining her eyes into the semi-darkness, she thought she saw the faint outline of a woman standing near the window, looking out at the garden—a momentary illusion. When the moon emerged briefly from behind the clouds and shone through the glass, the outline had disappeared, if it had ever existed. And yet the scent of roses and verbena still lingered in the air about her.

Switching on the bedside lamp, getting up, slipping into her dressing gown, Caroline went across to the window and looked out. The fragrance was fading now. Soon it would be gone. If only she could remember why it had seemed so familiar to her.

Suddenly she knew why. Knew that her imagination had not been playing tricks after all. It was Sarah St Just who had entered the room, turned the key in the lock, whose skirts had whispered across the carpet towards the window, whose outline she had discerned standing on the spot where she had died a long, long time ago.

As for the perfume—Caroline remembered—opening Sarah's trunk that day in the hall, when the workmen had brought it down from the attic, lifting out the garments one by one, how amazed and touched she had been by their fragrance—an amalgam of roses and verbena, a haunting reminder of the beautiful woman who had once worn those dressses ...

The weekend had been a great success. Following a full English breakfast on Sunday morning, Caroline had suggested a visit to Castle Howard for herself, Maudie and Sam and Mrs Rossiter, leaving the younger folk, Zach, Jake, Reg and Lara, to their own devices, realising as she did that a visit to a stately home might not be their idea of a fun day out.

Jake and Zach, she guessed accurately, would be far happier finding themselves a nice little pub on the sea-front for a few beers, a game of darts or bar-billiards, or chatting up a couple of good-looking lasses than a guided tour of the rooms and picture galleries of a mansion, however magnificent, which would surely bore them stiff.

As for Reg and Lara, who appeared to have taken to each other in a big way, they would most probably walk hand in hand through the Spa gardens, starry-eyed, saying all the vitally important things that young folk, on the verge of falling love, have said to each other since time immemorial.

At six-thirty that evening, they had all joined company for a slap-up dinner, after which they had bade fond and lingering farewells to one another.

'Eh, Caroline love, it's been great, just great, a real treat,' Maudie said tearfully. 'You've done us proud, and I've enjoyed every minute!'

So, apparently, had everyone else, in-cluding Mrs Rossiter. A triumph indeed, Caroline thought, as rear lights dwindled into the dusk, and she was left alone to spend a final night beneath the roof of the Valley Hotel, this time without incident.

Up early next morning, she breakfasted, settled her bill, and returned to the bolt-hole to discover the decorators in the process of packing their gear into their van.

'Well, I hope you'll be pleased with it,' the foreman said, returning her keys. 'Frankly, I had my doubts about the colours you chose, at first, but I've changed my mind now. They look lovely. Just right, somehow.'

'Thank you, I'm so glad you approve,' Caroline said mistily, wandering from room to room, amazed at the transformation, the restfulness and feeling of space her quiet colour-schemes had created.

Now all she had to do was await the arrival of the carpet and curtain fitters she had engaged to complement the wall-colourings she had chosen with so much care; later, the arrival of her long-stored furniture to complete her home—her beloved bolt-hole.

She could picture it all in her mind's eye, the soft turquoise walls of the sitting room complemented by a fitted carpet, and lined velvet curtains in a matching but much deeper shade of green.

And yet, deep down, she knew there was

something missing from her life. Possibly because of the time of year, with the first anniversary of Peter Augustine's death looming up on the horizon?

Chapter Twenty-Three

From where she was standing, the cottage looked like a miniature Noah's Ark washed up by the tide and stranded on a ledge of rock out of reach of the tide.

Everything looked the same as it had done before. The beach was empty, the sun was shining, the sea lapping the shore: seabirds wheeling and crying overhead, yet nothing was the same, nor ever could be again. The past year had altered her life beyond recognition. She was a far different woman from the one who had walked down the cliff-path last October, numb with grief over the death of Peter Augustine, exactly a year ago today.

This was a pilgrimage of remembrance. Nothing could have kept her away from Driftwood today of all days.

Carrying the flowers she had brought with her, she walked slowly down the path to the cove, remembering the day she had come this way to find Peter alone on the beach; the way he had looked up and smiled at her, his hands outstretched in greeting as he hurried forward to meet her.

378

She had at least the memory of their love to sustain her. Given more time, would they have married one day? she wondered. Impossible to say. Fate had decided the outcome, leaving her no choice, no further say in the matter.

Nothing had been solved or settled, Caroline thought, apart from the divorce, which would happen as she had hoped it might, quietly and without fuss, with a modicum of dignity, early next month, when she would be free—to do what exactly? What price life without love, some hope for the future, however distant?

And yet she was luckier than most women of her age, she reminded herself sharply, in having a place to call home, financial security and friendship. But were these things enough to fill the empty corners of her life, without love?

Poor Sarah St Just had been pretty much in the same boat, she thought compassionately, awaiting the arrival of a lover who would never come again, drifting slowly into the loneliness of old age, living in a fantasy world which had no bearing on reality. Forever watching and waiting by her bedroom window to witness the arrival of her prince and his retinue; issuing orders to servants who had left her long ago, blissfully unaware that she and Margaret Roberts were alone in the house, that it was Margaret who cooked the food they ate, laid the fires and polished the dining room silver in readiness for a sumptuous dinner party that would never take place except in the imagination of an old woman in the early stages of senile dementia.

Walking along the beach to the break-water, standing there alone, Caroline cast into the sea, one by one, the flowers she had brought with her—three red roses in memory of Peter Augustine, Sarah St Just and Margaret Roberts—the Woman in White. Caroline knew now that it was Margaret's spirit, not Sarah's that haunted Driftwood. Poor Margaret who, unable to bear to go on living without her lifelong friend, her beloved Sally, having kept her promise to destroy Sarah's diaries, unread, had walked into the sea uncaring of her own fate, the tide bubbling about her, until succumbing to the force of that tide, her lifeless body had been swept out to sea, beyond all earthly cares. But her spirit would be in need of absolution, of forgiveness for that final act which she had feared would separate her forever from the love of God, hence the final sentence in her diary: 'It is all over now. Commending my spirit to God, I shall go to my eternal resting place in heaven or in hell, according to His Will'.

It would be a cruel God indeed, Caroline

thought, watching the roses drifting away on the tide, who turned His face against a woman whose entire life had been dedicated to the service of a friend. After all, 'Greater love hath no man than this ...'

Turning away from the sea, she saw coming down the cliff-path towards her, a man with red hair. Cam McCauley. Oh no, she thought, not McCauley. She dreaded a confrontation, harsh words between them, when what she most needed was gentleness and understanding.

On the defensive, she said coolly, 'No need to tell me—I'm trespassing on private property! Not to worry, I'm just leaving.'

He looked at her intently. 'It doesn't matter. I was half expecting you, hoping you'd come. That's why I'm here. I have something to show you.'

'I—don't understand.'

'You soon will. Come with me!'

'Where to?'

'Driftwood, of course. Where else?' He smiled briefly, 'What a woman for argument. Don't you ever take anything at face value?'

'The last time we met, you turned your back on me,' she reminded him, 'in the bar of the Mallyan Spout Hotel, remember?'

'Oh yes. I was feeling a little fraught that day. Well, are you coming or not?'

Turning away, he walked across the beach towards the path to the verandah, Caroline following in his wake, mistrustful of his motives, resentful of his air of authority, his ability to put her back up as he had done the first time they met and on countless occasions since then. Yet she was curious to know what he wanted her to see that was so important, and why he had been 'half expecting' her. Unless he had remembered that today was the anniversary of Peter's death.

Mounting the steps of the verandah, she noticed that the front door was flanked with metal 'flower containers', which she now recognised as charcoal burners of the kind that had graced London Bridge when the Danish Princess, Alexandra, had made her triumphal entry into the City as the future wife of Edward, Prince of Wales, in the year 1863.

'In case you're wondering, and I can see that you are,' Cam said off-handedly, following her gaze, 'I picked up the second burner from a scrap-metal yard near Whitby. The man hadn't a clue what it was, and I wasn't about to enlighten him. I simply haggled him down in price from ten quid to five, called him a robber, stowed it away in the back of my car, and got the hell out of there as quickly as possible. Apparently it came from—'

'No need to tell me,' Caroline inter-rupted, 'I know exactly where it came from—Sarah St Just's town house in Scarborough. *My* house, before I was fool enough to part with it. It was in the centre of a pond in the garden the last time I saw it. That garden's gone now, so has the pond. The new owners brought in bulldozers to make a driveway.' She added bitterly, 'Every hotel should have one, plus floodlighting and plenty of parking space for the summer visitors, don't you agree?'

'*Your* house? I had no idea,' Cam said, frowning. 'So why did you part with it if it meant so much to you?'

'Let's just say that my capital investment was needed elsewhere at the time, and leave it at that, shall we?' She continued edgily, 'Well, now you've suitably impressed me with your bartering skills, I'll be on my way! Not that I needed reminding of your business acumen. You've made that abundantly clear to me all along!'

'You never let up, do you?' Cam said levelly. 'I didn't bring you here to look at a charcoal burner, but—*this!*'

He flung open the door of Driftwood and stood aside to allow her to enter the house, watching her intently as she crossed the threshold. It had all been worthwhile, he thought with a deep, inner feeling of relief, to witness the expression of disbelief, of joy on her face as she saw ...

Cam had worked all summer long to restore Driftwood to its former glory.

First of all, he had torn up the fibrous matting from the floors, then, patiently, referring to books on Edwardian decoration, he had stripped and redecorated the walls, preparing scratch meals for himself in the kitchen, sleeping on a camp-bed in whichever room had seemed appropriate to him at the time.

Standing in the hall, gazing at the staircase now richly carpeted in a deep shade of blue, the walls hung with gilt-framed oil-paintings, and the half-moon hall table in situ at the foot of the stairs, 'This is—magnificent, unbelievable,' Caroline said, 'but I ...'

She had been about to say that this entrance hall, the furnishings, were more in keeping with a private home than a holiday cottage, but decided not to. This, after all, was Cam's property, as he had often reminded her in the past, and if he was prepared to risk having the carpet ruined with sand and salt water, the surface of the table scratched, that was his business, not hers.

Cam said, 'Why not take a look round? I'll be in the kitchen, making coffee. You will join me in a cup, I take it, when you've finished your tour of inspection?'

Every item of Sarah's furniture had been returned to its original setting. The drawing room fireplace had not been re-boarded, the overmantle remained in place. There was no sign of the 'green-faced woman', the chintz curtains or the television.

Crossing the hall to the dining room, Caroline saw that Sarah's elegant table and chairs, the long, rosewood sideboard, silver candelabrum and cut-glass decanters had replaced the cheap and cheerful scratch-resistant furniture she had loathed so much.

Upstairs, a similar pattern had been repeated. Gone were the bunk-beds and mobiles in the children's room; all it now contained was a camp-bed and a sleeping-bag, a stool with an alarm clock, torch and a radio. The main bedrooms, however, bore a full complement of wardrobes, dressing tables and tall-boys of Victorian design, neatly tailored to occupy the much smaller space of a summer residence, and there were brass bedsteads, so far unmade.

The turret room remained much the same as she remembered it. Deeply moved, she recalled the night she and Peter had made love there on his last night; the way he had looked up at her and smiled the next morning when she had given him the painting of Whitby Abbey, his words, 'I'll treasure it all the days of my life'.

And then she saw that Sarah's carved oak chest had been returned to its bedside position, and remembered the day Cam had summarily ordered its removal, to break the lock and discover the contents. Slowly, thankfully, dawned the awareness that he had not done so. The lock had not been broken. The chest, once the repository of Sarah's secret diaries, remained intact.

Caroline knew now that Margaret Roberts' main purpose in coming to Driftwood after Sarah's death had been to burn the contents of that chest, which she had afterwards filled with books of a less sensational nature and then re-locked, before fulfilling the second purpose of what she had regarded as a homecoming, her final visit to her beloved cottage by the sea.

Everything about Margaret Roberts, gleaned from her journals, convinced Caroline that a woman of her calibre would have faced death bravely, when she had destroyed her friend's diaries, with no regrets, save one—that the manner of her dying might forever distance her from the love of God.

Cam was in the kitchen when Caroline went downstairs. 'Well, what do you make of it?' he asked in that casual way of his. 'Do you approve of all my hard work?'

'Yes, of course, how could I do otherwise? The thing that puzzles me is—*why?* Why have you done all this? For what possible reason?'

He handed her a mug of coffee and she sat down at the table to drink it. Cam sat down opposite. 'Let's just say that I had time on my hands and felt like doing something constructive for a change.'

'Time on your hands? Surely not—as the father of a brand new baby, I find that hard to believe.'

'What? That I fathered a child at my age?' He laughed, 'Thanks for the compliment.'

'I didn't mean that at all, and you know it! Why must you twist everything I say? Are you ashamed of fatherhood, is that it?'

'A question I can't answer, I'm afraid, since I haven't had the doubtful privilege of becoming a father so far.'

'So you're not the father of Gloria's baby?'

'The father, to the best of my knowledge and belief, is a soldier presently serving his Queen and Country in Northern Ireland.

'Let me explain, if I may. When Gloria turned up at Gull Cottage last Christmas, she did so as a last resort. Her husband had found out about the affair and told her to clear out, or words to that effect.

'What one might call a timely intervention, wouldn't you say? I might well have succumbed to the effects of the booze and the sleeping pills combined if she hadn't turned up when she did.'

He was speaking more seriously now. 'I was at rock bottom at the time, knowing what a rotten mess I'd made of my life, blaming myself for the death of Peter Augustine, regretting not having said goodbye to him, and lots of other things besides.

'To cut a long story short, taking a long hard look at my life that Christmas Eve, I reached the conclusion I'd be better off dead. Who gave a damn about me anyway?

'Next thing I knew I was in hospital, having horrible things done to me, with everyone feeling sorry for me, being nice to me because I'd been a "naughty" boy—at least that's the impression I had.'

He paused. 'Then you came to the hospital, remember? Not to whisper soft words of comfort to a failed suicide, oh no, not you! Quite the reverse—to give me a lecture on selfishness, as I recall. What's more, it worked.

'Your plain speaking did me more good than all the sympathy in the world could have done. And so, when I realised the fix Gloria was in, it seemed the decent, the only thing to do to stand by her, to act as her minder until the baby was born. It seemed a reason for living, and I badly needed a reason for living right then.'

His voice roughened suddenly, 'Can you understand, Caroline, that this was something I had to do—that and restoring Driftwood to its former glory—to make peace with myself and my conscience?'

'Oh yes,' she said quietly, seeing a side of Cam McCauley she had never known existed before this moment. 'So what are you going to do now? Live here at Driftwood? If so, what about Gull Cottage? You can't be in two places at once.'

'Gloria is welcome to stay at Gull Cottage until her boyfriend comes back from Ireland,' Cam said. 'The poor girl has landed herself in a bit of a jam one way and another.'

'She's very attractive,' Caroline remarked.

'Yes, she is, and that's been her downfall so far.'

'Are you still in love with her?'

'No, not any longer. I'm beginning to doubt that I ever was. There's a world of difference between love and physical attraction, I've discovered.'

He paused, then, 'I've often wondered

389

about your marriage. You told me about it, remember, the day you came to Gull Cottage? I behaved abominably that day, I'm afraid.'

'It doesn't matter now,' Caroline said, 'I behaved pretty badly myself, as I recall. Strange, isn't it? We seem to have been at loggerheads from the beginning—until now.' She smiled. 'As for my marriage, it's all over bar the shouting.'

'Is he still with the artist you mentioned?'

'Not as far as I know, but I think he soon will be now he's back on his feet. Felix and Francesca thrive on success, the good things of life. Things fell apart between them when Felix hit a rough patch in his career. He was badly in need of help at that time, much as Gloria is right now.'

'So you stepped into the breach?' Cam suggested quietly.

'Something like that. But you haven't told me about Driftwood. Are you planning to live here in future?'

'Some of the time, not all. You see, I've an idea in mind to offer it as a holiday home for what used to be known as "distressed gentlewomen" in need of a change of venue and a bit of tender loving care, during the summer months.' He grinned awkwardly, 'I'll be signing the pledge and holding prayer-meetings next, if you don't watch out!'

His diffidence and self-deprecation were born of shyness, Caroline realised. 'It sounds like a marvellous idea,' she said. 'Tell me more.'

'I haven't gone into it in any detail. Much would depend on finding the right person to take charge of them, cook for them and so on.'

'The way Margaret Roberts looked after Sarah St Just,' Caroline said tenderly. 'Yes, I think I'd like that.'

'You?' Cam looked dumbstruck.

'Yes, why not? Have you an application form handy?' She laughed as she had not done for some time past, warmed by the feeling that the barrier of mistrust between herself and Cam no longer existed. 'I meant what I said. I need to feel useful, to do something for others, not just myself, and you can't imagine how much it would mean to me to be a part of Driftwood once more.'

'I think I can,' Cam said quietly. He paused. 'What would you say if I told you that all this, the work I've done here, had a far deeper motive than a conscience-salving exercise on my own behalf, however necessary that may have been?

'The plain truth is, I did it for you, because I knew how much Driftwood meant to you. It was always at the back

391

of my mind that you might come back here one day—especially today, the anniversary of Peter's death—and I wanted it all ready and waiting for you, just as you had always visualised it, a house restored to its former glory, a fitting background for the spirit of Sarah St Just.'

'You really did all this for me?' Caroline looked at him as if she had never seen him before, noticing the colour of his eyes, the warmth of his expression now that he had stopped being angry. She could not believe that she had once thought of him as an ugly man, an insensitive human being, greedy for money, bombastic and overbearing. And yet he had been all those things in the past, to her way of thinking.

The trouble was, she had not taken the trouble to discover what lay behind the grim façade he presented to the world in general, and her uncompromising attitude towards him at their first meeting had stiffened their resistance to one another, she knew that now.

He said, 'What better reason could I have had? I have you to thank for making me realise how wrong I'd been in so many ways. You stood up to me, fought me every inch of the way. I gave Reg Rossiter hell when he told me he'd given you permission to raid Sam Cooper's repository. I had you figured as a fussy, hysterical woman demanding special attention, but I was wrong. For the first time, I came up against a clear-sighted, straight thinking lady who knew exactly what she wanted and told me so in no uncertain terms.'

'Straight thinking?' Caroline pulled a face. 'Scarcely that. I was angry. You'd been rude to Peter, and I resented that.'

'You cared about him even then. I could tell. I was jealous of your relationship from the beginning, and did all in my power to come between you, said terrible things to both of you. What I'll have to live with for the rest of my days is not being there to say goodbye to him.'

'Please don't, Cam. What's done is done. For what it's worth, Peter and I talked about you on our way to Heathrow. He still regarded you as a kind of knight in shining armour. He said that meaningless words are often spoken in anger.' She added gently, 'Peter was one of those rare human beings who see no fault in the people they love—and he loved you, Cam. He died loving you. You must believe that and try to forgive yourself.'

'The thing is, can *you* forgive me, Caroline?' Cam rose to his feet, pushing aside his chair, spilling the remainder of his coffee, unaware that he had done so, moving towards her, holding out his hands to her, drawing her up to face him. 'Please say that you forgive me!'

'Of course I do.' Could this sudden warmth of feeling towards Cam be construed as love? Caroline wondered. If not, why the urge to feel his arms around her, to be held by him? But all Cam had asked of her was forgiveness. Nothing more. At least she had his friendship, a glimmer of hope for the future if his plans for Driftwood came to fruition and she could become a part of that dream.

Cam said, 'When Gloria's affairs are settled, soon, I hope, I'm going to Jamaica to see Peter's parents, make sure they're all right. They're fine people. It's the least I can do.'

'Yes, that's a wonderful idea.' Gathering together her belongings when Cam had released her hands, turning towards the door, 'How long will you be gone?'

'Difficult to say. A month, maybe two.'

As long as that? she thought bleakly. Stepping onto the verandah, she said cheerfully, hiding her feelings, 'Have you thought? Your "distressed gentlewomen" could sit out here when the weather's warm!'

Cam smiled, 'You mean *our* distressed gentlewomen, don't you? And why have I the feeling that the gentlewoman I'm looking at right now is also a little distressed?'

'Who? Me? Whatever gave you that idea?'

Drawing her into his arms, 'It has been known to happen to people in love; they can't bear to be separated for even a day, an hour, a minute. You're coming with me, my love. I certainly couldn't bear the separation, even if you could.'

Lying in bed late that night, listening to the shipping forecast, Caroline harboured the strange inner feeling that Margaret and Sarah were at peace now, absolved by the prayers she had said for them as the red roses floated away on the tide ebbing from the beach at Driftwood.

Then, smiling, ready for sleep, she thought of the man she had come to love lying in his camp bed at Driftwood, listening to his radio, sharing her pleasure in the forecast, and of all the seas they would sail across together in their journey through life; of homecoming at the end of the journey.

The publisher hopes that this book has given you enjoyable reading. Large Print Books are especially designed to be as easy to see and hold as possible. If you wish a complete list of our books please ask your local library or write directly to: Magna Large Print Books, Long Preston, North Yorkshire, BD23 4ND, England.

This Large Print Book for the Partially sighted, who cannot read normal print, is published under the auspices of

THE ULVERSCROFT FOUNDATION

THE ULVERSCROFT FOUNDATION

. . . we hope that you have enjoyed this Large Print Book. Please think for a moment about those people who have worse eyesight problems than you . . . and are unable to even read or enjoy Large Print, without great difficulty.

You can help them by sending a donation, large or small to:

**The Ulverscroft Foundation,
1, The Green, Bradgate Road,
Anstey, Leicestershire, LE7 7FU,
England.**
or request a copy of our brochure for more details.

The Foundation will use all your help to assist those people who are handicapped by various sight problems and need special attention.

Thank you very much for your help.